Nervous Water

Also by William G. Tapply

NERVOUS WATER

William G. Tapply

St. Martin's Minotaur

New York

www.minotaurbooks.com

Library of Congress Cataloging-in-Publication Data

Tapply, William G.
  Nervous water : a Brady Coyne novel / by William G. Tapply.
    p. cm.
  ISBN 0-312-33744-2
  EAN 978-0-312-33744-5
  1. Coyne, Brady (Fictitious character)—Fiction.　2. Murder victims'
families—Fiction.　3. Conflict of generations—Fiction.　4. Fathers and
daughters—Fiction.　5. Missing persons—Fiction.　6. Terminally ill—
Fiction.　7. Boston (Mass.)—Fiction.　I. Title.
PS3570.A568N47 2005
813'.54—dc22   2005046086

First Edition: September 2005

In memory
Al Blanchard

Author's Note

My wife, Vicki Stiefel, and my editor, Keith Kahla, gave me a lot of thoughtful and needed criticism on various versions of this story. I always listen to what Vicki and Keith say. Sometimes they know what I'm trying to do better than I do.

Anyone who happens to know that my mother comes from a Maine family might suspect that I've modeled some of the characters and events in this novel on my own relatives and their lives.

I did not. I made it all up.

This much is true: When I was a kid, my father and I sometimes went out with my Uncle Woober on his lobster boat. We helped him haul his pots and rebait them with smelly fishheads, and after we were done, if the stripers were in the river, we went fishing. Those were happy times.

"When you wake up in the morning, Pooh," said Piglet, "what's the first thing you say to yourself?"

"What's for breakfast?" said Pooh. "What do *you* say, Piglet?"

"I say, I wonder what's going to happen exciting *today*?" said Piglet.

Pooh nodded thoughtfully. "It's the same thing," he said.

—A. A. MILNE, *The House at Pooh Corner*

NERVOUS WATER

PROLOGUE

When I was a kid, we used to drive from our home in suburban Boston to Moulton in southern Maine once or twice every summer, my mother and my father and I, to spend the weekend with Gram Crandall, my mother's mother.

The best part of those visits, as far as I was concerned, was going out on the Piscataqua River in my uncle's lobster boat with my old man. It was one of the few things my father and I did together when I was a kid. We helped Uncle Moze tend his string of lobster pots, and after that, we went fishing. We watched the horizon for clouds of diving birds, which would surely signify a gang of big striped bass chasing and slashing at bait. We scanned the bays and coves where wakes or swirls or what Uncle Moze called "nervous water"—the subtle, barely perceptible trembling agitation of the flat water—would betray a cruising school of predatory fish just beneath the surface. I yearned to spot a swirl or a patch of nervous water before Uncle Moze did, but it never happened.

My old man left the looking up to me and Uncle Moze. He just went fishing. He'd just grab a rod and troll a plug off the stern. Naturally, I yearned to catch one of those big fish myself, but my old man thought I was too little to hold a rod.

Uncle Moze would say, "Why'n't you let Brady catch a fish?" but my father would just mutter, "Stripers are men's fish."

I had to admit, he had a point. Those striped bass were almost as big as I was. They engulfed the plugs behind the boat in a swirl the size of a bait tub. They made my old man's rod buck and bend, and they zinged line off the reel, and he whooped and hollered and cursed and groaned as he tried to bring them in.

It was about the only time in my childhood that I can remember being pretty sure that my father was having fun.

The summer I turned eleven, Aunt Mary, the youngest of my mother's five siblings, was at Gram's house when we got there. This was odd, since we'd gone to Mary's wedding the previous April, and she had presumably moved into a trailer with her new husband, a pipe fitter from Kittery named Norman Dillman.

Aunt Mary was sixteen that summer. She had curly blondish hair and blue eyes and a chubby face. She was only five years older than me, and she'd always treated me more like a cousin than a nephew. When she was still living with Gram, we used to play gin rummy and listen to rock and roll on the kitchen radio.

On this July morning, Aunt Mary was sitting in a rocking chair on Gram's sunporch, just staring out the window. It was nearly noontime, but she was wearing a pink terry cloth bathrobe and fluffy pink slippers. Her arm was in a sling, and her face was kind of yellowish and puffy, and she was twisting a handkerchief in her hands, which were resting in her lap. Or, I should say, *on* her lap. It looked like she was holding a basketball under that pink bathrobe.

I said "Hi" to her, but she didn't even look at me.

2

A minute later my mother and father came out to the sunporch. My mother touched my shoulder and said, "Brady, sweetie, we want to talk with Aunt Mary for a minute, okay?" which meant she wanted me to leave the room.

I went into the living room and turned on Gram's TV, but I could hear the murmur of voices, my mother's and father's and Aunt Mary's, coming from the sunporch.

My mother said: "Norman did that to you?"

"Ayuh."

"And he kicked you out?"

Aunt Mary snuffled. "He was pretty drunk."

"When was this?"

"I dunno. Four, five weeks ago, I guess."

"You're not thinking about going back to him, are you?"

"He's my husban'," said Aunt Mary. "What'm I spose to do?"

I heard my mother blow out a breath. "You talked to him since then?"

"Uh-uh. Not since then. Moze and Jake went over a couple times, but Norman wasn't home."

The only thing my old man said was: "You better get yourself a lawyer."

About then Gram called from the kitchen, said she had corn chowder with pilot crackers for lunch, so I didn't hear any more about Aunt Mary.

I was just finishing up my second bowl of chowder when Uncle Moze came stomping into the house. He was a tall, heronlike man about my father's age. He had a face like a hatchet, with dark stubble on his cheeks and chin and creases at the corners of his squinty blue eyes. He was wearing black rubber hip boots folded down at his knees, blue jeans, a blue work shirt rolled up over his elbows, and a long-billed fisherman's cap. He said, "Hey, sonnyboy," and punched me on the shoulder. He had a half-smoked cigarette stuck in the corner of his mouth. "Gonna help me haul my pots?" Uncle Moze's voice sounded like rocks rubbing together.

"You bet," I said.

"Stripers're in the river," he said, "and the tide should be about right. Where's your old man?"

I jerked my head in the direction of the sunporch.

I went outside and leaned against Uncle Moze's pickup truck so he wouldn't forget to bring me along, and after a while he and my father came out. They were muttering to each other, and I heard Uncle Moze saying, ". . . always was a useless son-ofabitch." Then he looked up and saw me and said, "Git your ass in back, sonnyboy."

So I hoisted myself up into the bed of his truck and found a place to sit amid the tub of lobster bait, the stubby rods rigged with trolling plugs, the stack of mossy old wooden lobster pots with strands of dried seaweed clinging to them, the big coils of thick rope, and the cooler filled with Coke and Narragansett beer. Uncle Moze grabbed two beers, tossed me a can of Coke, and he and my old man climbed in front.

When we got to the cove where Uncle Moze kept his lobster boat, *Miss Lil*, moored, we lugged the stuff from the truck to his dinghy, dragged it over the mud to the water, piled in, and rowed out to the boat, and pretty soon the sturdy diesel engine was thrumming and we were chugging out into the river. Uncle Moze's lobster boat was broad-beamed and chunky and solid. *Miss Lil* didn't go very fast, but you had the feeling she could plow straight through a hurricane without tipping over Uncle Moze's beer bottle.

After a few minutes we came to the wide bay in the Piscataqua River where Uncle Moze set out his pots, and for the next couple of hours we were busy hauling them in, culling the shorts and the one-claws from the keepers, rebaiting them, and pushing them

4

back into the water. We ended up with one empty bait tub and two tubs full of seaweed and lobsters.

Then my old man picked up one of the rods, unhooked the plug from the first guide, dropped it over the side, and let it free-spool back until it was about a hundred feet behind the boat. Uncle Moze cut back the engine until we were barely moving. "Keep an eye out for nervous water, sonnyboy," he said to me, squinting against the smoke from his unfiltered Camel.

Maybe ten minutes later, while I was staring at the calm water near shore hoping to spot a wake or a swirl, my father grunted. I looked back in time to see the big hole in the water where the plug had been. Uncle Moze threw the engine into neutral, and my old man heaved up on the rod, then lowered it, cranked the reel, lifted again, and after a while the big striper came silvering alongside. Uncle Moze reached down with the gaff and levered the sleek fish into the boat. It was close to four feet long.

Uncle Moze and my father were grinning.

Then, almost as fast as my father could reel them in, there were four more of those three- and four-foot striped bass flop-ping in the bottom of the boat. Big fish were boiling and sloshing all over the river, and the air was alive with squawking, diving gulls and terns. It was the best fishing I'd ever witnessed, and I yearned to participate in it.

I guess Uncle Moze read my mind, because he looked at my father and said, "Why'n't we let Brady give it a shot?"

My old man narrowed his eyes at me, then shrugged. "You better not let one of those leviathans catapult you overboard," he said. My father was the kind of man who used words like "leviathan" and "catapult" in everyday conversation. "Your mother would murder me."

I grinned and made a muscle for him, then picked up a rod and unhooked the red-and-white plug, and I was just about to drop it off the stern when Uncle Moze muttered, "Now what the hell."

I looked up. Another lobster boat had cut across our wake and was coming up beside us. The guy at the wheel was waving his arms and yelling, but over the drone of the engines I couldn't hear what he was saying.

Uncle Moze said, "Keep that plug in the boat for a minute there, sonnyboy." He put the engine in neutral and the other boat eased alongside. My father reached out and grabbed onto it.

A man who appeared to be quite a bit older than my father and Uncle Moze was at the wheel of the other boat. He wore a baseball cap and yellow rubber overalls.

Uncle Moze said, "What the hell, Lyle? We was into some stripers."

"Got us a floater," said Lyle. "You ain't got a radio, do you?"

Uncle Moze shook his head.

"Me neither," said Lyle. He took off his cap, swiped the back of his wrist over his bald head, then twisted the cap back on. "I'm gonna go git the coast guard. You better head over there and stay with the goddamn body."

"Well, shit and be damned," said Uncle Moze. "They was bitin' awful good."

Lyle went up on tiptoes and looked into our boat where our five giant striped bass were laid out side by side like big slabs of cordwood. He whistled. "Damn," he said. "Well, it cain't be helped." He pointed off toward the shore. "He's over by them reeds. I tied a buoy onto him. Tide's gonna start runnin' pretty soon. You better git over there and keep an eye on him so's he don't git washed away."

Lyle put his engine into gear, gave us a wave, and headed across the river to the New Hampshire side, where the coast guard station was. Uncle Moze steered us to the shoreline where Lyle had pointed.

He slowed down as we approached the reedy area, and then my old man said, "Jesus H. Christ," and then I saw it. I'm not sure I would've known it was a man's body if Lyle hadn't said it was. He was floating on his belly with his face in the water and his arms and legs stretched out just under the surface, so that only his back was out of water. He looked like a big white basking turtle. He was wearing a sleeveless undershirt and khaki-colored pants, and the skin on his neck and face and arms was shiny and swollen and white as lard. A crab had latched onto the side of his face, and a rope of seaweed was hooked around one of his legs. Lyle's buoy was looped around the other leg.

My father leaned close to Uncle Moze and mumbled something.

"Ayuh," Uncle Moze said. "That there's fuckin' Norman, all right." He glanced over his shoulder at me. I suppose I was staring at the body. I probably looked like I might puke. "That's right, sonnyboy," he said. "Norman fuckin' Dillman. Mary's new husband, the sonofabitch who punched her face and busted her arm. Your goddamn uncle."

We idled there beside Uncle Norman's body for a few minutes, and then Uncle Moze said to my father, "Tide's gonna take him out. Grab the boat hook."

My old man picked up the long-handled hook they used for snagging the lines attached to the lobster buoys, reached out, and tried to catch it around Uncle Norman's swollen leg. The curved point sank right in, and I could see little pieces of flesh puff off and form a greenish white cloud in the water.

"Avert your eyes," my old man said to me over his shoulder.

Not likely. No way. It wasn't every day you got to see a dead body.

We drifted on the outgoing tide, my old man hanging on to the boat hook stuck in Uncle Norman's leg, for nearly an hour before a coast guard boat came speeding across the river and pulled alongside us. Uncle Moze seemed to know the coast guard men, and they talked for a while. Then my father pulled the boat hook out of Uncle Norman's leg, and Uncle Moze started up the engine, and we pulled away.

I watched as they looped ropes around Uncle Norman's bloated body and pulled it over the transom of the coast guard boat.

By then the tide was ebbing hard and the birds had disappeared. We trolled around the bay for a while—my old man let me hold one of the rods for the first time in my life—but the fish had moved on. So Uncle Moze headed in, and we moored his boat, loaded the lobsters and stripers into his dinghy, and rowed to shore.

I got a lot of attention when I told my friends back home about finding Uncle Norman's body in the Piscataqua River. In my version of the story, I was the one who spotted the floater, and it was I who rammed the boat hook through his leg and held on until the coast guard arrived. The girls, especially, loved hearing my story.

Later my old man told me that when the coast guard brought Uncle Norman's body onto their boat, they saw what appeared to be a bullet hole in his forehead.

ONE

The end of a muggy Thursday afternoon in early July. Thunder grumbled from the direction of the western suburbs, and the air hung still and heavy and moist over the city.

I'd shucked off my courtroom pinstripe, slipped into a pair of cutoffs and a T-shirt, and made myself a tall gin and tonic, and I was sitting in one of the Adirondack chairs in the walled-in patio behind our town house on Mount Vernon Street reading the *Globe* sports section and waiting for Evie to come home.

Henry David Thoreau, our middle-aged Brittany spaniel, lay under the picnic table with his chin on his paws eyeing a pair of evening grosbeaks, which were jabbing at sunflower seeds on one of the hanging birdfeeders.

I'd finished my drink and was pondering a refill when I heard the kitchen phone ring. I figured it was Evie. She was a little late.

When I stood up, the grosbeaks burst away in a bright flash of yellow and black.

"Sorry about that," I said to Henry, who'd lifted his head and was frowning at me. Brittanies are bird dogs. Their genes carry the powerful instinct to point grouse and woodcock and quail for the hunter. Poor Henry, the city dog, had to be satisfied with grosbeaks and finches and titmice.

When I answered the phone, a gravelly voice said, "Hey, sonnyboy."

Only one person ever called me "sonnyboy." I hadn't heard that voice for over thirty years. But I recognized it instantly.

"Moses Crandall," I said. "Jesus Christ. What's up, Uncle Moze?"

"Just wonderin' how you'd feel about helping me haul my pots." I heard him take a wet drag on a cigarette. "Maybe go fishin' afterwards. Stripers're in the river. Gittin' some blues, too. They ain't gonna hang around much longer."

"Is everything all right?" I said.

"Why the hell wouldn't it be?"

"Well, okay, good," I said. "When did you have in mind?"

"Saturday okay with you?" he said. "Git here around noon, we'll catch the turn of the tide."

"I'll be there," I said. "Your boat still moored in the same place?"

"Same river, same mooring, same boat," he said. "Mostly the same string of pots. Nothin' much changes, sonnyboy. We just keep gittin' older. See you then."

I was back out in the Adirondack chair when Evie came out through the back door a half hour later. She bent down, hooked her forearm around the back of my neck, and gave me a long juicy kiss on the mouth.

She'd snagged a bottle of beer from the refrigerator on her way through the kitchen. She flopped down in the chair beside me, pried off her high heels, propped her feet up on the table's bench seat, hiked her skirt up to the tops of her thighs, and pressed the bottle against her cheek. "Hot one, huh?" she said.

"It's not so much the heat—"

"Yeah, yeah," she said, "it's the damn humidity," completing the hoary New England cliché.

"Thunderstorm brewing," I said. "You can smell it."

She looked up at the sky, where dark clouds were roiling. "No doubt," she said. "I love thunderstorms."

"Tough day?"

"Budget crap." She waved the subject of budget crap away with the back of her hand. Evie was an administrator at Beth Israel Hospital. She worked a lot harder than I did. "How 'bout you?"

"I had the MacPherson suit today. We settled in the lobby a half hour before the hearing."

"That's good, huh?"

"This time it was." I took a sip of gin and tonic. The grosbeaks had not returned, but a couple of chickadees were flitting back and forth between the lilac bush and the feeder with sunflower seeds in their beaks, and three or four goldfinches were perched on the thistle-seed feeder.

Henry had taken up a position beside Evie's chair and was pretending to ignore the birds. Evie's arm dangled down and she was scratching the top of his head. She was slouched in the chair with her eyes closed.

"Looks like I'll be heading up to Maine on Saturday," I said.

"What's up?"

"I got a call from my uncle. Uncle Moze. Moses Crandall. My mother's brother. Lives in Moulton, just over the New Hampshire border. He wants me to go out on his boat with him, help him tend his lobster pots. Maybe we'll try to catch a striper."

"Sounds like fun." Evie took a sip of beer and looked at me over the bottle. "I don't remember you ever mentioning your uncle Moses."

"I haven't seen him for over thirty years. When I was a kid Uncle Moze used to take me out on his lobster boat. He was my favorite uncle."

11

She looked up at the sky. The dark clouds were thickening, and the air had become noticeably cooler. "I think you're right about the thunderstorm."

I smiled. "Of course I'm right."

After a few minutes of comfortable silence, Evie said, "So why now?"

"Hmm?"

"Why after—what, thirty-odd years?—why is it today that your uncle invites you to go lobster fishing?"

"That," I said, "is the question. Did I ever tell you about when I was a kid and we found my Uncle Norman's body floating in the river?"

"You never talk about your childhood, Brady."

"Well, what do you want to know?"

"Everything."

My mother grew up in the village of Moulton on the estuary of the Piscataqua River in southernmost Maine. Her name was Hope. Jacob and Moses were her older brothers. Uncle Jake and Uncle Moze.

My mother had three sisters. Faith, Charity, and Mary. Mary was the baby of the family. My grandparents apparently ran out of virtues by the time they got to Mary, so they named her after a virgin, which turned out to be pretty ironic.

Gram Crandall had white hair and a large bosom and smelled like violets. She is, in my memory, a kind of mythic presence, sweet and gentle and beloved by everybody. I associate her primarily with the aroma of corn chowder and warm apple pie and boiled new red potatoes doused in butter and sprinkled with parsley.

My grandfather worked for the paper company running pulp on the Kennebec River. He died in some kind of accident when I was four or five. I have no memory of him.

My mother was the only one in the Crandall family who actually left home. Her sisters married local boys and settled right there in Moulton. Her brothers chased the local version of the American Dream, which was owning their own lobster boats.

My mother was the rebel. She went to college in Massachusetts, taught seventh-grade English, and married Alan Coyne, who was a lawyer with a big firm on State Street.

All of that made my family members objects of awe and suspicion among my aunts and uncles and cousins and their neighbors in Moulton, Maine, and probably accounted for the fact that we didn't visit Gram Crandall more often.

Except for Mary and Moses—Uncle Moze—I didn't know my aunts and uncles very well. Faith and Charity were younger, more nervous, less loving versions of my grandmother. Uncle Jake pretty much ignored me whenever he was around.

Uncle Moze was my favorite. He was strong and independent and profane, the closest thing to a New England cowboy that you'd meet in those times thirty-odd years ago. He was the only uncle who paid any attention to me, actually. He seemed to enjoy having me on his boat, maybe because he didn't have kids of his own. Uncle Moze gave the impression of being taciturn, but when he was in the mood, he loved to tell long, ironic stories. They involved colorful Maine characters he'd presumably known—poachers and drunks and adulterers, mostly—and it flattered me that he didn't censor his stories because I happened to be there.

To me, going lobstering with Uncle Moze was another kind of fishing. We chugged around the broad tidal river spewing diesel fumes, and he and my old man snagged the buoys with the boat hook, looped the thick line around the power winch, and hauled up the pots.

I liked anticipating what we might find inside the big wooden lobster pots. It wasn't that different from seeing my bobber start to jiggle on my neighborhood millpond back in Massachusetts and wondering what kind of fish might've eaten my worm. I was seriously hooked on fishing of all kinds when I was a kid.

In those days, lobsters were abundant, and Uncle Moze's pots generally came up crawling with them. He wore rubber gloves that came up to his elbows, and he groped around inside the pot, came out grasping a lobster around its middle, and quickly measured it with his steel lobster ruler. He threw the shorts overboard. The keepers went into tubs filled with seaweed—those with both claws, which Uncle Moze sold to a wholesaler in Kittery, in one tub, and the unsalable ones with a missing or deformed claw, which he kept for himself or gave to Gram, in the other.

My job was rebaiting the pots. For bait Uncle Moze used pollock and haddock minus their fillets but with the heads still attached that he got cheap from the wholesaler he sold his lobsters to. I liked digging my hands around in the tub of smelly fish skeletons and stabbing them through their eye sockets onto the metal hooks inside the wooden pots. I liked how I smelled fishy for several days afterward.

Most of all, I liked the fact that Uncle Moze, unlike my old man, made me feel useful.

That's why he was my favorite uncle.

Two months after we found Uncle Norman floating in the Piscataqua River, Aunt Mary gave birth to a girl. She turned the baby over to Uncle Moze and his wife, a quiet little woman named Lillian who, my mother once told me, couldn't have children. It was Lillian and Moze, not Aunt Mary, her actual mother, who named the baby Cassandra.

Aunt Mary lived with my grandmother until the following spring, when she hooked up with a boy from Portland who'd just been drafted by the Detroit Tigers. She followed him to someplace in Iowa where he'd been assigned to a minor-league team, and that was the last I heard of Aunt Mary.

Cassandra, her baby, stayed in Moulton, Maine, with Uncle Moze and Aunt Lillian.

My grandmother moved to Florida a year or two later, and after that my family stopped going to Moulton, and I pretty much lost track of the Crandall side of my family.

They never did figure out who plugged Uncle Norman in the forehead. They questioned a lot of people, but nobody had seen anything or had much to say. Forensics, such as they were, weren't much help. His body had been in the water for quite a while.

Or maybe they just didn't try very hard. Nobody had much tolerance for a beer-bellied drunk who'd break his pregnant wife's arm and punch her face and kick her out of their trailer.

Anyway, it turned out that Norman Dillman had plenty of enemies. He'd been transporting more than lobsters and fish on the boat he kept moored over in Kittery, and he owed a lot of money to some shady people in Boston.

The consensus in the Crandall family was that all in all, things hadn't turned out so bad.

Two

I left for Moulton at ten on Saturday morning, allowing myself two hours to drive from my town house on Beacon Hill to the cove near the estuary of the Piscataqua River where Uncle Moze kept his lobster boat moored. I figured it would be less than a two-hour drive, pretty much a straight shot up Route 95 to the first Maine exit, but I allowed myself some time to get lost in Moulton. The old landmarks were burned into my brain, even after all those years, but I assumed they'd mostly be gone, replaced by new landmarks to deceive me.

There were plenty of new, deceptive landmarks. Since I'd been there thirty years ago, Moulton had become a suburb almost indistinguishable from the suburbs around the 128 belt west of Boston, except somewhat less posh. Where in my memory there were orchards and pastures and fields and vacant lots and dusty roads, there were now condominium complexes with names like Royal Ridge Estates and residential cul-de-sacs with tightly packed rows of identical McMansions. The main roads were lined with Ford dealerships and Chinese restaurants and tanning parlors and supermarkets.

But the old roads that I remembered from the backseat of my old man's car were still there, and I didn't get lost. I pulled into the gravel parking area beside a seafood restaurant that hadn't been there the last time I went lobstering with Uncle Moze. I was almost half an hour early.

Now there was a small marina in the cove where Uncle Moze parked his boat. A dozen boats—mostly Boston Whalers and speedboats, with a couple of blocky working boats—were lined up along the floating docks. There was a gas pump and a small shed for the attendant.

There were a dozen or so vehicles in the parking area, many of them sporting boat trailers. At the far end I spotted a black pickup truck. A man was leaning against the front bumper smoking and looking at the water.

I drove over, pulled up beside the truck, and got out.

Uncle Moze turned and looked at me with narrowed eyes. Aside from the fact that his beard stubble had turned steely gray and the creases on his sun-baked face had deepened, he looked the same. He wore black hip boots turned down at his knees, blue jeans, a blue denim shirt, and a long-billed fisherman's cap, just as I remembered. A half-smoked unfiltered cigarette dangled from the corner of his mouth.

It couldn't have been the same truck, but it looked the same, too.

"Uncle Moze," I said. "It's me. Brady."

He grinned and stuck out his hand. "Sonnyboy," he said. "You're early. Don't think I would've recognized you."

I gripped his hand. It felt like cracked leather. "You haven't changed."

"Oh," he said, "I've changed plenty." He pointed out to the boats, and I spotted the one with *Miss Lil* painted on her transom. "I got her all loaded up. Might as well get to it."

We walked out onto the dock and climbed aboard the boat. It was, as I remembered it always had been, clean and tidy. The lines were coiled, the tubs stacked, the deck spotless, the brass polished. Uncle Moze always kept *Miss Lil* shipshape.

He got the engine going, and I untied the lines from the cleats on the dock, and then we were chugging out of the little harbor. Uncle Moze steered through a maze of buoys, scanning the horizon, squinting against the glare of the midday July sun on the water, dragging on his cigarette. Way off to our left arched the Route 95 bridge, spanning the river that separated New Hampshire from Maine.

The salty air was rich and evocative. It smelled of wet mud and rotting seaweed and dead fish and diesel fumes, and it transported me. I was eleven years old again, riding on Uncle Moze's lobster boat with my old man, looking for clouds of diving birds and the swirls of giant striped bass.

I wanted to ask him about his health, and what he'd been up to for the past three decades, and his family—which was also my family. I remembered that his wife, my aunt Lillian, had died back when I was a teenager, and that he'd raised Cassandra, my cousin, Aunt Mary's baby, pretty much on his own.

I wanted to ask him why, after more than thirty years of silence, he had suddenly decided that he and I needed to get reacquainted. But there was very little idle chitchat with Uncle Moze when he was out on his boat tending his lobster pots. Never had been. Lobstering was serious work and he gave it his full attention.

So we worked in silence. He steered us from buoy to buoy, and I snagged the lines with the boat hook and looped them over the power winch the way my old man used to do, and Uncle Moze hauled up the old wooden pots, balanced them on the flat place on the gunwale, opened their trapdoors, and plucked out the lobsters. Two-clawed keepers went in one tub, single claws in the other, shorts and crabs over the side.

Uncle Moze's only apparent concession to the passage of thirty years was his choice of bait. Now he used salted herring instead of ripe fish skeletons. I jabbed two herrings through their eye sockets onto each bait hook and latched the trapdoor before he pushed the pot over the side.

"You ain't forgotten how it's done, I see," he said at one point. It sounded like a compliment, and it occurred to me that he might've arranged this outing as some kind of test. If it was, it felt important to me that I pass.

"Any money in lobstering these days?" I said. I hoped to spark a conversation, see where it might go. Uncle Moze wanted something from me. Most people, when they want something from a relative, however distant, it's money.

"Never was any money in it," he said. "I got a couple restaurants buy direct from me, take whatever I got, pay a little better than the wholesaler. Still, when the lobsters're crawlin' good, they don't give much per pound. When I ain't got many to sell, that's when they pay good. Either way, by the time I'm done buying bait and fuel, scraping *Miss Lil*'s hull, paying for her mooring, gittin' her engine overhauled, replacing the old lines every year, repairing my pots and buoys, all that"—he waved his hand at all his expenses—"I guess I might come close to breaking even, if you don't give me nothin' for my hours, with the one-claws for me and my friends as profit." He flicked his cigarette butt over the side. "If I did it for money, sonnyboy, I wouldn't do it at all."

"It's hard work," I said.

"For an old geezer, you mean." He cocked his head and squinted at me.

I smiled. "I guess that's what I meant."

"I been doin' it for more'n fifty years," he said. "Just haven't gotten around to quittin' yet. Wouldn't know what to do with myself, anyway." And then he frowned and shook his head, as if he'd revealed too much.

After we finished hauling and rebaiting Uncle Moze's string of lobster pots, we trolled plugs around the bay and up and down the river for a couple of hours. We saw no clouds of seabirds, no wakes or swirls, no nervous water, and we didn't get a strike.

After a while, Uncle Moze said, "Well, the tide's turned. If we was going to catch anything, we would've already. Might as well head in. You'll come back to the house for a beer."

He didn't make it a question, so I didn't give him an answer. I figured he'd tell me what was on his mind when he was ready.

Uncle Moze's house looked the way I remembered it, except it appeared to have shrunk. It was about the size and shape of a double-wide trailer at the end of a long dirt driveway. A couple of wooden rowboats lay upside down on sawhorses in the side yard, and lobster pots, buoys, and oars spilled out of an open shed with flaking red paint. A pair of enormous maple trees flanked the house, and the lawn grew scruffy and sparse—not really a lawn, just tufts of grass and weeds pushing up through the hard-packed sandy soil.

The house featured window boxes with nothing growing in them, and dirty white paint, and a screen door with a rip in it, and a pair of big propane tanks beside the door. The rhododendrons and yews against the foundation were leggy and sprawling.

It was dark and cool inside, and stuffed with old furniture that, except for an enormous console television set, might've been the same furniture I had sat on thirty years ago. I'd only been inside a few times, and what I mainly remembered was the smell of Lysol and Aunt Lillian shuffling silently around in her housedress and slippers and pin curlers, fetching beers for Uncle Moze and my old man and an Orange Crush for me.

Aunt Lillian, I remembered, was a compulsive cleaner. Even when I was sitting in the living room watching the ball game with Uncle Moze and my old man, she would be gliding around with a rag in her hand, wiping off the coffee table, straightening out the piles of magazines, adjusting the Venetian blinds.

Uncle Moze apparently expended all his clean-and-neat energies on his boat. Now newspapers were scattered on the sofa and floor, and a soup bowl, a pizza box, and a couple of mugs sat on the dust-covered coffee table. Thin white curtains covered the windows, leaving the inside dim and shadowy. The place smelled faintly of propane.

He asked me if I wanted a beer, and I said I did. He went into the kitchen and left me in the living room.

A collection of framed photographs stood on the top of the TV. Aside from a studio-type hand-colored wedding portrait— Uncle Moze looking about the same, except for the crew cut and uncreased face and white dinner jacket and red bow tie, and Aunt Lillian looking bewildered in her white wedding dress—all the other photos showed a dark-eyed girl at varying ages.

Cassandra. My cousin Cassie, Aunt Mary's baby, whom I hadn't seen since she was a toddler and I was a young adolescent. The photos atop Uncle Moze's TV chronicled the first eighteen years or so of Cassie's life. . . .

Cassie as a toothless infant in Uncle Moze's arms, her big dark eyes peeking over his shoulder gazing straight and calm into the camera's lens.

Cassie as a chubby-legged little girl, barely past the toddler stage—the way I remembered her, the way I had seen her last— wearing shorts and a T-shirt with a yellow smiley face on it, squinting into the sun.

Cassie in a little plaid skirt and a white blouse, with a square lunchbox in her hand. Her knees were knobby and her arms were skinny. Her black hair was short and curly. Her dark eyes were fearless.

Cassie at eleven or twelve, at the wheel of Uncle Moze's lobster boat, tiptoeing up so she could peer squinty-eyed at the sea, suddenly tall and lanky and almost womanly, wearing blue jeans, a blue denim shirt, a long-billed fisherman's cap, and hip boots turned down at the knees, an exact replica of Moze's standard lobstering outfit.

Then Cassie a few years later, a teenager now, this photo a professional head-and-shoulders shot. A yearbook portrait, probably. Black hair with bleached-in blond streaks, long now, not so curly, and pulled back in a loose ponytail. Dangly silver earrings, pale lipstick, made-up eyes staring directly into the camera lens, not smiling. That same defiant fuck-you look, only now it was in the eyes of a strikingly pretty woman, not a girl.

Cassie in cap and gown raising a rolled-up diploma in her fist like a weapon—

"You probably don't remember Cassie."

I turned around. Uncle Moze was holding a can of Budweiser out to me.

I took the beer and pointed to the photo of Cassie wearing the smiley-face T-shirt. "This is how I remember her."

"Long time ago, sonnyboy."

I nodded.

"Your mother stopped coming up here after your grandma went to Florida," he said. "You lost track of your family. We lost track of you."

I nodded. "It wasn't my choice. I loved going out on your boat. I always believed my mother wasn't very proud of her origins."

"Moulton, Maine? Old man a logger who got drunk and drowned in the Kennebec?" He smiled. "Your mother couldn't wait to get away from here. Hard to blame her, I s'pose. Hope Crandall was always smarter than everybody else. Lots of folks—including some of her brothers and sisters—figured she liked to bring your old man up here now and then in his big Cadillac just to make sure us poor dumb Mainers wouldn't forget how she'd snagged herself a rich Boston lawyer." He shook his head. "Jealousy, that's what that was. Hope wasn't like that. She loved your grandma. That's why she come up here. She once told me, she

23

said she wished to hell Alan—your old man—she wished he'd git himself a less show-offy vehicle."

"I'm glad to know that," I said.

Moze smiled, sat on the sofa, and lit a cigarette. I took the overstuffed chair opposite him.

He leaned toward me with his forearms on his thighs. "So you're a lawyer like your old man, huh?"

"Not like him," I said. "He was a partner in a big firm, did corporate work, made piles of money. Defended big businesses against lawsuits, found loopholes, created tax write-offs, hid profits. Screwed people for a living is what my old man did. Me, I've got my own one-man office. Just me and my secretary. Small practice, mostly family law. My clients are people who need help." I shook my head. "Nothing at all like my old man."

Uncle Moze nodded. "Doin' okay, though?"

I smiled. "Doin' fine."

So. He wanted money.

He looked up at the ceiling. "I don't know how this works, sonnyboy."

I reached over and touched his leg. "Uncle Moze, is there something I can do for you? You need some help?"

He swiveled his head around and glared at me. "You think this is about money?"

I shrugged.

He blew out a quick, angry breath. "I don't need that kind of help."

"Do you need a lawyer?"

He shook his head. "I know some lawyers."

"Any you can trust?"

He laughed quickly. "Probably not."

"Well," I said, "I do happen to be a lawyer, but I'm also your nephew. That means something to me."

"Me, too." He blew out a long breath. "Don't know what you recall about Cassie."

"I remember she was Aunt Mary's baby," I said. "I remember you and Aunt Lillian took care of her. After that . . ." I waved my hand in the air.

"Mary had that sickness after Cassie was born." Uncle Moze tapped his temple with his forefinger.

"Postpartum depression?"

He shrugged. "Maybe. Or maybe she was just young and scared. Whatever, she wanted nothing to do with the baby. Didn't even bother givin' her a name. We did that. Me and Lillian." He smiled. "Cassandra. Can't even recollect how we come up with Cassandra, but it seemed to fit. Cassie Crandall. Lillian used to say it sounded like a movie star. It was just what we decided to call her 'til Mary got back on her feet. I dunno. I s'pose you can understand it. That no-good husband of hers, fuckin' Norman Dillman, beatin' her up, kickin' her out of the house, then gittin' himself killed, Mary barely sixteen, knocked up, just a baby herself . . ."

"I remember the day we found Norman's body," I said.

"Ayup," he said. "Murdered. Shot in the head and dumped in the river."

"And they never found who did it?"

He shook his head. "They asked around. Even had some feds involved for a while, on account of his body was found in the river and it involved two states. But nothin' come of it. Far as I know, they never even come up with a suspect."

"It's a genuine unsolved mystery, then," I said.

Moze shrugged. "Norman was a pig. Got what he deserved. Everybody said so."

I smiled. "So what happened after that?"

"Well," he said, "after Mary gave birth, she just stayed in bed, didn't want to even look at the child. Your grandmother was

25

gettin' along in years by then, and she had her hands full with Mary, so Lillian and me, we said we'd take care of the baby. Lillian couldn't have kids, you know. Best thing ever happened to Lil, it turned out, having that little baby in the house. It made her happy, and that made me happy, because your aunt Lillian never was a very happy woman. We thought it was going to be just for maybe a month or two, 'til Mary felt better. But when Mary got back on her feet, she showed no interest in Cassie. Then the next spring Mary run off with that baseball player, never said good-bye, not even to our mother, never come around to see Cassie, and we was, well, that was fine by us. It had got to the point that Lil was all depressed, thinking we'd have to give Cassie back. By then we was loving her, thinking of her as our own. Folks around here, pretty soon they seemed to forget she was Mary's, or if they remembered they didn't say nothin' about it." He smiled. "Everybody in Moulton has got something in their family they'd just as soon nobody else remembers. We're all pretty forgetful for each other."

"So you adopted her?" I said.

He shook his head. "That would've involved Mary, required her to sign papers and whatnot, and by then she was gone, and we figured it was best to just leave well enough alone. Lillian was terrified that if we raised the subject, Mary would say no, decide she wanted to take Cassie back. My sister Mary could be like that. Perverse. She'd do things she didn't really want to do just to see if she could piss you off."

"I guess I didn't know Aunt Mary very well," I said. "In my mind, she was a kid not much older than me."

"Younger than you in some ways. Always pretty innocent." He smiled. "Well, kinda dumb, actually." He shrugged. "So anyway, we just went on, Lillian and me, one day after the other, thinkin' of Cassie as our own, and pretty soon we come to believe it. Soon as she learned to talk, I was Daddy and Lillian was

Mommy." He blinked a couple of times, then smiled quickly and took a sip from his beer can. "Then Lillian got the cancer. Spent the last two years of her life right in there"—he jerked his thumb over his shoulder in the direction of the bedroom—"with the shades drawn, just watchin' television all day and night. Every day, as soon as Cassie got home from school, she'd go stand in the doorway lookin' in. She'd stand there for a half hour or more sometimes, just waiting, and Lillian would never even look at her." He shrugged. "After a while, Lillian died. Cassie was nine that year."

"So you raised her by yourself?"

"From the time Lillian first got sick, really, it was just Cassie and me." He smiled. "That little girl could row a dinghy, steer the boat, bait the pots, stick her hand in, grab a lobster, measure it, and toss it into the tub without lookin'. She was as good at lobsterin' as me. Loved to go trolling for mackerel. Good at that, too. She had the feel for fish." He shook his head. "She was a lot like you, sonnyboy. Good at things. Quiet, the way you were, but you knew there was always something goin' on in her head. Smart as a whip, she was. Don't know where she got that. Mary wasn't much in the brains department, God knows, and fuckin' Norman was dumber'n a pickled hake." He jerked a Camel from the pack in his shirt pocket, tapped its end on the face of his wristwatch, lit it with a match, and squinted at me through the smoke.

"Uncle Moze," I said, "when you called the other day I asked if everything was all right. You didn't say it wasn't, but you didn't say it was, either, exactly. This is nice, what we did today, going out on the boat, getting reacquainted, and I hope it means we can do it some more. But something's going on, isn't it? Everything *isn't* all right. So maybe there's something I can do for you?" I made it a question.

He shook his head. "After all these years, I can't—"

27

"Is it Cassie?"

He peered at me for a minute, then nodded.

"What?" I said.

"I feel bad. This ain't your concern, and it ain't fair to dump it on you. I shouldn't've called you. Regretted it soon as I done it."

"You called me because you had a problem," I said, "and I came up here because I figured you had a problem. If there's anything I can do, I want to do it."

"Well, okay," he said. He took a deep breath and let it out slowly. "I'm sorry to be so damn long-winded about it, but I don't know any other way to explain it to you." He took a quick drag on his cigarette, then stubbed it out in a clamshell ashtray on the coffee table. "Cassie finished first in her class. Not that that's much of an accomplishment for Moulton High School, you know, but it was enough to get her a nice scholarship to the university up to Orono. I missed her something terrible that first year, but she called me once a week, regular as the tides, every Sunday evening it was, told me about her classes and her new friends and how she was on the track team, all happy and enthusiastic, and when she come home that summer she was still the same old Cassie. As far as I could see, college didn't change her at all except make her even smarter."

Moze paused, gazed out the window, took a sip of beer. "But then something did change, because halfway through her sophomore year she up and quit school. I didn't even know she done it until she called me, said she was in San Francisco livin' with some friends, had a job as a waitress, was thinking about going to school out there." He stopped and looked at me. "Hell, you don't want her damn life story, and this is sounding like poor old Moze, and that ain't my intention."

"Take your time," I said.

He lit another cigarette and blew a plume of smoke up at the ceiling. "Next several years, Cassie knocked around. San

Francisco, then someplace in Colorado, then Key West, back to Frisco, D.C. for a while. She always kept in touch, though, no matter where she was, every Sunday evening, and whenever she was on the East Coast we'd get together. She turned out to be an awful pretty woman. Dressed nice, talked proper. She always was smart. Had a lot of different jobs, I guess, doing I don't know what. She never said much about what she did. I had the feeling she didn't think a dumb old lobsterman would understand. But she seemed to have plenty of money. Every year or two she'd be living somewhere new. Never got married, but a couple years ago she took up with a feller down there in your neck of the woods, ended up moving in with him, told me she thought she might marry him." He hesitated, then laughed softly. "Grannie, she called him. Don't know where that came from. Anyway, she still called me every Sunday evening, and maybe once every couple months we'd get together, meet in Portsmouth, have dinner, get caught up. I never met this man, Grannie, but I liked him from the way Cassie talked about him. He was teaching English at some college in Boston. She said he treated her good. I kept telling her, one day you ought to bring your Grannie along so I could meet him. She'd say, sure, we'll do that sometime." He stopped, looked out the window, and blinked several times.

"Uncle Moze—"

"No, sorry." He coughed into his fist. "Anyway, next thing I know she tells me she's going to get married. But no, it ain't that Grannie who I never got to meet. It's some dentist twenty-five years older'n her, she says, with grown-up kids, whose wife died a few years before, lives in Madison, there, outside of Boston, who she never even mentioned to me before. I know what I should've said. I should've told her, 'That's great, honey, congrat-ulations, you found a man you love, who loves you.' But instead, what comes out of my mouth? I say, 'What the hell, Cassie? You're going to marry some horny widower old enough to be your father? A goddamn dentist with grown kids? What's wrong with that nice English teacher, that Grannie feller? Ain't he rich enough for you?'" He shrugged. "She hung up on me. Don't blame her. You want another beer?"

I nodded. "Sure."

Moze groaned, pushed himself to his feet, picked up our empty beer cans, and shambled into the kitchen. For the first time all day he looked his age, which I figured was about seventy-five.

He was back a minute later. "Here you go, sonnyboy." He handed me another Budweiser and sat on the sofa. "Where the hell was I?"

"The goddamn dentist," I said "Cassie hanging up on you."

"Right." He smiled quickly. "That was a year and a half ago, Brady. It was in the winter, I remember." He took a slug of beer. "I ain't heard a word from her since."

"A year and a half?"

"Ayup."

"Just like that? No warning? No explanation?"

"Just like that." He shook his head. "I should never've spoken my mind about her marrying the damned dentist. Made her mad. S'pose I can understand that. And it appears she just kept on being mad. Cassie always was a damned pigheaded woman."

"It runs in the family," I said.

He smiled.

"You tried calling her, didn't you?"

He nodded. "Oh, hell yes. Not at first. Like you say, I can be pigheaded, too. At first I was mad that she didn't call. It's okay to be upset for a little while. But hell. This is her old daddy. You ain't supposed to hold grudges with your daddy. So I figured I'd just wait her out. But after a while I stopped being stubborn. I wanted to hear her voice. So I called her. I had the number of her cellular. Left her a message, but she didn't get

30

back to me. I did that a few times, leaving messages. She never answered. I figured, when her phone rang, she could tell it was me and was still being stubborn. So I stopped trying for a while. Figured I could be as stubborn as her." He shook his head. "I couldn't, though. Nobody's as stubborn as Cassie. So I started calling again. Tried to keep my messages light, you know, even though my heart was thumpin' in my chest, just prayin' I'd say the right thing and she'd call me back. 'Hi, honey,' I'd say. 'How you doin'? I know you're probably pretty busy and all, but maybe you could give your old daddy a call if you get a chance, okay?'" He shrugged. "She ain't done it yet." He shrugged. "A year and a half."

"That's pretty rough," I said. I was thinking of my own two boys, Billy and Joey, and how crazy it would make me if they refused to talk to me.

Moze stared down at the floor. "A year and a half, Brady," he said softly. "That's a long time for an old man." He sighed. "Okay, so anyway, I tried calling her again the other night—the night before I called you—and I was going to just spill it all out, the hell with keeping it light. I was going to tell her I hoped to hell she was okay, and if I'd done something or said something to upset her, make her mad, I was sorry, but that was a long time ago and it was time to make things right again between us. I was going to ask her please to call me back, tell her I missed her something fierce, but then this recorded voice comes on, tells me her mailbox is full, so I can't even tell her what I want to tell her."

"That was the first time her mailbox was full?"

He nodded.

"When was the last time you tried her that you were able to leave a message?"

He shut his eyes for a moment. "Three weeks, maybe a month ago."

31

"And you find it worrisome."

"I guess I do," he said. "I sure do miss her, but mainly, I just want to know she's all right."

"You want me to find out what's going on, is that it?"

"It ain't fair to ask you."

"Uncle Moze," I said, "I'm a lawyer. I'm pretty good at finding things out. And besides, I live pretty close to Madison. That's what you were thinking, right?"

"I guess I was."

I looked at him. "So why now?"

"Huh?"

"It's been a year and a half since you talked with Cassie, you said. Why did you wait 'til now to talk to me? Is it because her voice-mail box was full?"

He shrugged. "I s'pose. I can't even leave her a message. It makes me think something's happened to her. Makes me miss her even more. I need to talk with her, Brady. In the worst way. It's eatin' me up. I feel like I've got to clear the air. Make things right with her. Apologize for anything I might've said. I want us to be in touch again, talk on Sunday nights, maybe get together once in a while, meet her husband, have dinner or something, you know? I can't hardly stand being on the outs with her like this."

"Have you tried calling the dentist's house?"

He nodded. "I finally did. I didn't want to. Didn't feel like talking to that dentist if I didn't have to. But when I found Cassie's voice-mail box full, I did it. I called his house. This was the day I called you. It's what decided me to give you a call."

"What happened?"

"The dentist answered the phone," he said. "I was hoping it would be Cassie, but it was him. Hurley. Richard Hurley's his name. I said I wanted to talk to Cassie. He said she wasn't there. I asked where she was, did he expect her back soon, I could call again. He says, 'You better tell me who's calling.' So I take a deep breath and I say, 'This is Moses Crandall, sir. I'm Cassie's father.' And with that, he says to me, 'Listen, whoever the hell you are. I don't know what you're after, but you better leave us alone and not call here again or I'll call the police.'" Moze looked up at me. "Then before I could say anything else, the sonofabitch hung up on me." He looked at me. "What do you make out of that?"

"Not a very friendly fellow."

Moze nodded. "Nope."

"Were those his exact words, Uncle Moze?"

"Damn close to it."

"It sounds almost like . . . like he didn't believe you."

Moze nodded.

"Like he thought you were lying about who you were."

He shrugged. "I don't like him much."

I smiled. "Did you try calling again?"

He shook his head. "I s'pose I should, but I really don't want to talk to that man again."

"I'll do it," I said. "I'll see if I can talk to Cassie. Okay?"

He nodded. "I was hoping you'd say that."

"I'll try to figure out what's going on."

He smiled. "Just tell her her old man misses her something fierce. Whatever's going on, don't matter to me. I just want to connect with my little girl again."

"Do you have a recent picture of her?"

"Huh? What for?"

I shrugged. "So if I see her, I'll know it's her."

He shrugged. "Sure. Hang on."

He got up and left the room.

He was back a few minutes later. He handed me a four-by-six color snapshot. It showed Moze and a strikingly pretty dark-haired woman sitting side by side on what appeared to be a park bench. "Me and Cassie," he said. "About three years ago. We were having dinner in Portsmouth. Cassie had a camera with her, asked a lady to take our picture. She mailed it to me a couple weeks later. I'd like to have it back."

"I'll take good care of it," I said.

THREE

It was a little after six that Saturday evening when I got home from my visit with Uncle Moze. I left my car in its reserved space in the parking garage on Charles Street, walked the six blocks to Mount Vernon Street, climbed the hill, went in the front door, and called, "I'm home, kids." When Evie didn't answer and Henry didn't come bounding out to greet me, I snagged two bottles of Sam Adams from the refrigerator, picked up the cordless telephone, and headed for the garden.

When I opened the back door, I saw Evie on her hands and knees with her butt sticking up in the air, pulling weeds from the garden. She was wearing sneakers and overalls with, as far as I could tell, nothing underneath. Even in those baggy overalls, you could see that she had a perfect butt.

Henry was snoozing under the table. When I stepped through the doorway, he raised his head, yawned, and started to scramble to his feet, but I pointed at him and held up my hand, and he lay back down.

Evie continued weeding. She hadn't heard me. So I put the beer bottles on the table, tiptoed up behind her, bent down, and

35

stroked my hand over her ass and down between her legs. I expected her to jump, but her only reaction was to stick her butt up higher and push back against my hand.

She remained there on her hands and knees and murmured, "Umm. Whoever you are, don't stop."

I knelt beside her, leaned over, and nuzzled the back of her neck. "It's me again," I whispered. "Your friendly UPS deliveryman."

Without turning, she reached behind her and ran her fingers up the inside of my leg and over the front of my pants. "So it is," she said. "And you brought me another big package."

I slipped my hand under the side of her overalls and cupped her breast.

"I'm all sweaty and dirty," she said.

I kissed her behind her ear. "I love dirt and sweat. Good, honest smells. Earthy."

She turned, hooked an arm around my neck, and kissed me hard. "You smell good, too," she said. "Fish and seaweed and salt. Working in the earth makes me horny. Shall we give one of the Adirondack chairs a try?"

"Out here?" I said. "Under the open sky?"

"We wouldn't want to get the sheets dirty," she said.

The beers I'd brought out were lukewarm by the time we got around to drinking them, and the summer shadows had begun to lengthen inside the walls of our little backyard.

"It looks nice," I said to Evie, taking in the garden with a sweep of my hand. "You do good work."

She nodded. "I know."

"When I was a kid I did yard work for two bucks an hour," I said. "Under the broiling sun. Eight hours a day for sixteen dollars and maybe a glass of lemonade. My old man had plenty of money, but he believed a boy should work. So I mowed, I trimmed, I raked, I weeded. I had five customers, one for each day of the week. After four summers of it, I promised myself I'd never touch a rake or lawnmower ever again."

"That's why you don't help," she said.

"A promise is a promise."

"Well," she said, "I don't want help. I like weeding and stuff. I like the way it looks when I'm done. And it takes my mind off things."

"Any particular things?"

"Terrorism, global warming, genocide in Africa. A couple of gray hairs I found the other day." She touched her temple and smiled.

"That's it?"

"Sure," she said. "Tell me about your visit with your uncle."

So I told her about Uncle Moze and how he hadn't heard from Cassie in a year and a half, and I showed her the photo Moze had given me.

"She's really pretty," said Evie. "He hasn't talked to her for a year and a half?"

I nodded. "He figures he said something that alienated her. It's eating him up."

"How awful for him," she said. "So you're going to help, is that it?"

"I told Uncle Moze I'd try to talk with Cassie," I said, "see if I can convince her to reconcile with him, or at least to talk to him. Uncle Moze is a nice old guy. He was always good to me. Treated me like a man when I was just a kid. Now he's heartbroken. Cassie's pretty much all he cares about."

"So what're you going to do?"

"I'll do what anybody would do," I said. "I'll try to reach her on the phone, and if that doesn't work, I guess I'll head over to Madison and knock on the door."

I fished out the scrap of paper on which I'd scribbled Cassie's two numbers, picked up the phone, and dialed her cell phone.

It rang once. Then a husky female voice said, "Hi. It's Cassie. Sorry, I can't take your call right now. Leave a message and I'll get back to you, I promise."

There was a beep, and then another female voice, this one sounding mechanical, said, "I'm sorry. This mailbox is full. Please try another time."

I clicked the phone off and looked up at Evie. "No answer. Her voice-mail box is full, just like Uncle Moze said. I wonder what that means."

"Some people never check their voice mail," said Evie.

"It wasn't full a month ago, according to Moze."

Evie shrugged.

"Maybe she lost her phone," I said.

"That could be," she said. "Or it could be something else."

"Like what?"

"I don't know."

"It was kind of weird," I said, "hearing her voice. I still think of Cassie as a toddler. She couldn't have been more than two or three the last time I saw her. Not even talking in complete sentences. And now, suddenly . . . she's all grown up."

"And how old were you?" said Evie.

I nodded. "Thirteen, fourteen maybe." I checked the scrap of paper and started to dial the other number.

Evie reached out and grabbed my wrist. "Wait," she said.

I pressed the Off button. "What?"

"What are you doing?"

"I'm going to call the house."

"Let's think this through."

"What's to think through? I want to talk to Cassie."

She tilted up her beer bottle, emptied it, and handed it to me. "Why don't you fetch us another beer," she said. "And

38

while you're at it, bring out my cell phone. It's in my bag in the kitchen."

I went in, grabbed two bottles of beer from the refrigerator, found Evie's cell phone, and took them back outside.

Evie flipped her phone open. "What's the number for the dentist's house?"

I dictated it to her.

Evie pecked it out, then pressed her phone against her ear. She looked up at the sky for a moment, then said, "Yes, could I speak to Cassie, please? . . . Um, this is Evelyn Banyon. Is this Richard? . . . Me? I'm a friend of hers . . . Well, see, I knew her in San Francisco, oh, this was several years ago. I'm here in Boston now, visiting for a couple weeks, and I heard she was married, and I was hoping . . . Oh, I see. Well, when do you expect her? . . . Sure, okay, that would be great." She recited her cell phone number. "Right. Good. Thank you. And congratulations, Doctor. Cassie's a wonderful girl."

She took the phone from her ear, looked at it, and put it on the table. "He says she's not there. He's not sure when she'll be back. He'll tell her I called." She took another swig of beer. "He was lying about something."

"You think?"

She nodded.

I reached for her phone. "My turn."

She put her hand on it. "Use a different phone."

"Why?"

"What if he's got caller ID? If you call from the same phone five minutes after I did, he'll know something's up."

"Something *is* up, honey," I said. "Why should I pussyfoot around this fucking dentist? I want to talk to Cassie, that's all. It's pretty straightforward."

"You'd make a terrible hospital administrator," said Evie. "I don't know how you make a penny as a lawyer, I really don't.

Nothing is straightforward. Everything has angles and twists and shadows."

I smiled. "So what do you suggest, Signora Machiavelli?"

"Maybe the dentist is telling the truth," she said. "Maybe Cassie's in the shower or out shopping or away for the weekend. If so, he'll give her my message and she'll call back, wondering who the hell this old friend from San Francisco is whose name doesn't ring any bells, and I'll hand her over to you, and you can talk to her." Evie shrugged. "But, see, you might as well assume he's lying, in which case, actually talking to Cassie is going to be trickier. You've got to keep your options open, that's all. Try not to arouse his suspicion. Wait a couple hours, then call from a different phone. And you've got to decide whether you're going to be her long-lost cousin or a lawyer with confidential legal information for her."

"But I'm both of those things, more or less."

She rolled her eyes. "That's hardly the point. If one identity doesn't do the trick, you're going to need the other one."

I stared at her. "God, you're devious."

She grinned. "Thank you. That's very sweet."

After supper I went into my in-home office, sat at my desk, and dialed Richard Hurley's house number.

A woman answered with a cheery "Hello."

"Cassie?" I said. "Is that you?"

"No, I'm sorry. This is Rebecca."

"I'm trying to reach Cassie," I said. "I'm her cousin."

"Her cousin, huh?" Rebecca paused for a moment. "You better speak to my father. Hold on a sec, please."

A minute later, a man said, "Yes?"

"Mr. Hurley?"

"This is Dr. Hurley, yes." His voice was soft and cautious. "Who did you say was calling?"

40

"My name is Brady Coyne," I said. "I'm your wife's cousin. I'd like to speak with her."

"Well, I'm sorry," he said. "Cassandra's not here right now."

"It's quite important," I said.

"Well," he said, "she's still not here."

"When do you expect her?"

"Look, Mr.—what was it?"

"Coyne," I said. "Brady Coyne."

"And you're her cousin, you say?"

"That's right."

"Cassandra has never mentioned you."

"We've been out of touch."

"And now . . . ?"

"Now I need to be in touch with her."

"It's important, you say."

"Yes," I said. "It's urgent."

"I'll take a message if you want."

"Yes. Thank you. Just ask her to call me, if you don't mind."

He blew a quick, impatient breath into the phone. "What's your number?"

I gave it to him, and he repeated it back to me. Then he asked me to spell my name, which I did. "I'll see that she gets your message," he said.

"When?"

"Excuse me?"

"When will you give her my message?"

"First thing," he said. "As soon as she gets home."

"Tonight?"

"Look," he said. "I'm in the middle of something here. I'll be sure that Cassandra knows you called."

And with that he hung up.

I leaned back in my desk chair and looked up at the ceiling for a minute. Then I fired up my computer.

Ten minutes later the Internet Yellow Pages had given me both the home and the office addresses for Dr. Richard Hurley. His home, as Uncle Moze said, was in Madison. His office was in Cambridge.

Ten minutes after that I printed out the MapQuest driving directions from my town house on Mount Vernon Street in Boston to Dr. Richard Hurley's house on Church Street in Madison.

FOUR

Madison, Massachusetts, is a sleepy little community an hour's drive west of Boston when the traffic is light, as it was on Sunday afternoon. No significant highway violates the borders of Madison. Aside from a few pick-'em-yourself apple orchards, several horse farms, a general store, a couple of churches, and untold numbers of psychiatrists and accountants with offices in their homes, there is no commerce in the town. It's a green, moist, hushed place, famous for—and perversely proud of—its mosquitoes, with widely spaced expensive houses separated by stands of oak and maple and pine trees and manicured lawns. Madison is lushly populated with birds and deer and golden retrievers, a town where well-to-do people pay steep property taxes for the privilege of raising their animals and their children in insulated bucolic tranquillity.

I arrived in the center of town, such as it is, around two in the afternoon. A big white Congregational church overlooked the village green, and Church Street, not coincidentally, ran along beside it. It descended a gentle hill past an elementary school, and where it bottomed out, across from a complex of soccer and baseball fields, I spotted a white mailbox with Hurley printed on it.

43

I turned into the wide driveway and parked beside the four other vehicles—a new-looking Lexus SUV, a more elderly Chevy sedan with a baby's carseat strapped in back, a battered Dodge pickup truck, and a sleek red Saab—that were lined up in front of a three-car garage.

A dusty coat of tree pollen covering the Saab—but not the Lexus or the Chevy or the truck—suggested that the Saab hadn't moved for a while.

The house was a rambling contemporary featuring skylights, vertical cedar sheathing, fieldstone chimneys, and interesting roof angles. A curving walkway of big granite stepstones wound through azaleas and rhododendrons and thick groundcover to a double-wide front door.

I rang the bell, and a minute later a woman with an infant in her arms opened the door and peered at me through the screen. "Hi," she said. She was tall and lanky and wore a sloppy T-shirt and baggy jeans. She had bare feet and blond hair and a pleasant, toothy smile.

"I'm looking for Cassandra Hurley," I said. "Is this the right place?"

"It is," she said. "But Cassie's not here. Maybe I can help you?" She was about Cassie's age, I guessed.

I smiled perfunctorily at her baby. "I'm Brady Coyne. Cassie's cousin. You're Rebecca?"

She nodded. "I don't recall Cassie mentioning you," she said. The baby on her shoulder gurgled. She patted his back, then smiled at me. "You're the man who called last night, right?"

"That was me," I said. "Maybe I better talk with your father. Is he here?"

"Sure," she said. "I'll get him for you." She opened the screen door. "Come on in."

I stepped into a flagstone foyer. Beyond it was an open area

44

flooded with sunlight and bare of furnishings except for a giant Oriental rug.

Rebecca turned her head and yelled, "Hey, Daddy. There's somebody here for you."

She gave me a quick smile. "Don't know if he heard me. Old goat needs hearing aids, but he won't admit it. I'll get him for you." She turned and disappeared into the house.

A minute later a man a little shorter than I appeared. He had wire-rimmed glasses and curly steel-colored hair. He appeared to be in his early fifties. He was wearing a pale green golf shirt and khaki pants. His chest and shoulders bulged under the shirt, and he had a flat stomach and a splendid tan.

He held out his hand and smiled. "Richard Hurley," he said. "Becca said you wanted to talk to me?" Up close, I reestimated his age. Judging from the creases on his throat and the crinkles around his eyes, he was closer to sixty. But he had the teeth of a teenager, as any conscientious dentist should. His eyes were a washed-out blue behind his glasses. They peered at me with neither warmth nor hostility.

I shook his hand. "I'm Brady Coyne," I said. "I'm a lawyer, and I—"

"A lawyer, huh?"

"That's right."

He narrowed his eyes. "I thought you were Cassandra's cousin."

"I am that, too."

"You're the one who called last night."

"I did, yes."

"Cassandra isn't back yet," he said. "I know I told you I'd give her your message."

"That you did," I said.

"You don't believe me? Is that why you decided you had to show up here unannounced?"

45

"I don't know you well enough to believe you or not believe you," I said. "Where's Cassie?"

"She's not here."

"When do you expect her?"

"Look," he said. "I told you I'd deliver your message."

"When?"

"When she gets back."

"When will that be?"

"I'm not sure."

"Can you tell me where she is?"

"No."

"Can't," I said, "or won't?"

He pulled his head back and narrowed his eyes. "Look," he said, "maybe if you told me what was so urgent. . . ."

"It's private," I said. "Family business."

"I'm her husband," he said. "That, I believe, makes me her family. If there's some legal matter . . ."

I jerked my thumb over my shoulder. "Is that Cassie's Saab, by any chance?"

"So?"

"So where'd she go without her car?"

He folded his arms across his chest. "I will not stand here and be interrogated," he said. "I don't appreciate your tone, sir, lawyer or cousin or whatever you are. I said I'd give my wife your message, and I will do that, and now I'd appreciate it if you'd leave."

"I need to know what's happened to Cassie," I said.

"Nothing's happened to her."

I shook my head. "I don't believe that."

He took a step closer to me. "I will not put up with this—this harassment," he said. "Now, please—"

Suddenly another man shouldered Hurley aside and jutted his face close to mine. "You deaf or something?" he said to me.

"James," said Hurley. "Let me—"

James put his hand on my chest and gave me a shove. I staggered back against the wall.

He stepped forward, grabbed the front of my shirt, and showed me his fist. "My father asked you to leave," he growled. He was a big, strong, good-looking guy in his twenties. He wore a sleeveless T-shirt and blue jeans and work boots. "So get the fuck out of here."

I held his eyes with mine. "How much trouble do you want?"

"You don't scare me."

I smiled. "Okay. Punch me, then."

Hurley put his hand on James's shoulder. "James," he said, "for Christ's sake."

James turned and looked at him. "You going to put up with this guy's bullshit?"

"I don't need your help," he said.

"Yeah? Since when?"

"He was just leaving," said Hurley. "Let go of him."

James hesitated, then let go of my shirt and dropped his fist. He glared at me for a minute, then turned and disappeared into the house.

Hurley looked at me. "I apologize for my son."

"Don't worry about it," I said.

"Now," he said, "will you please leave."

"Sure. I'm on my way." I fumbled a business card from my pocket and held it out to him. "Would you give this to Cassie when you see her, ask her to call me? Or if you hear from her, tell her I need to—"

"Yes, okay," he said quickly. He took the card and stuck it in his pocket without looking at it. "Good-bye, Mr. Coyne."

"I had a root canal once," I said. "It wasn't half as bad as I'd expected. I swear the sonofabitch who did it was disappointed I didn't suffer more."

"Must I call the police?"

I held up a hand. "I'm leaving. I appreciate your family's hospitality."

I got into my car and pulled out of the driveway, and I had just started back up the hill when an elderly man with two dogs on leashes stepped into the middle of the road. One dog was an enormous Irish wolfhound. The other was a little cocker spaniel. If the wolfhound stood on its hind legs, it would've towered over the man. The cocker came up to his shins. It was a Mutt-and-Jeff pair of dogs.

The man held up his hand like a traffic cop.

I stopped, and he hobbled around to the side of my car. He moved creakily, as if his joints were stiff and painful.

In a conversational tone, he said, "Sit, fellas."

Both dogs instantly sat.

The man was wearing a shapeless canvas hat with a crimson band, and when he took it off to wipe his brow on his sleeve, I saw that his head was entirely hairless. I guessed he was close to eighty.

He bent to my window. "This is a one-way street, my friend. You're going the wrong way."

I laughed. "You've got to be kidding. A one-way street in Madison?"

He moved his hand from side to side, indicating the narrowness of the street. "On account of the school," he said. "As you can see, it's barely wide enough for a school bus. The question was hotly debated at a town meeting a couple years back. Most controversy we've had in this town since they voted to ban spraying for mosquitoes. One of these days I suppose they'll get around to putting up better signs. There's one down at the end, and another on the way in. When that big maple leafs out, it covers it up. Most people don't notice it. The town fathers and mothers, I guess they figure nobody but local residents would have any reason to travel on Church Street in the first place, and it's

48

their responsibility as taxpaying citizens to know the rules."

"Well," I said, "thanks for the heads-up."

"They'd give you a ticket in a heartbeat." He grinned. "Going the wrong way on our only one-way street? That's a major crime here in Madison."

I smiled. "You've lived here a long time?"

"Thirty-two years," he said. "Myself, I'm ready for that condo in Myrtle Beach. These New England winters are getting to me. But the missus, she likes her church and her flower gardens and her bridge club." He pointed to the house next door to Hurley's. "That's my place."

Through a screen of trees I saw a two-story farmhouse structure with a wraparound porch and a well-kept yard featuring a lot of stonework and rambling flower beds.

"Nice place," I said. "You know the Hurleys, then."

He shrugged. "Good fences make good neighbors, if you catch my drift."

"Robert Frost," I said.

"Howard Litchfield, too," he said. He jabbed his thumb at his chest. "That's me."

I stuck my hand out the car window. "I'm Brady Coyne. You saved me a motor vehicle violation."

He shook my hand. "Police stop you, you just tell them, hey, I *was* driving one way." He chuckled.

"I was hoping to see my cousin," I said. "Cassandra. Cassie. Mrs. Hurley. I haven't seen her in a long time. Her husband said she wasn't home?" I made it a question.

Howard Litchfield shrugged. "I haven't seen Mrs. Hurley around for a while."

"For how long?"

"Oh, I don't know. Don't recall the last time. Didn't notice."

"To tell you the truth," I said, "I'm kind of worried about her."

"You best talk to her husband, I guess."

49

"I just did."

He glanced at Hurley's house, then tilted his head and squinted at me. "Well, I'm sure he knows more about it than I do." He bent down and said something to his dogs, then straightened up and slapped the roof of my car. "We've got to be on our way. You drive safe, sir."

I backed into Hurley's driveway, turned, and headed out the right way on Church Street. In my rearview mirror I saw that Howard Litchfield was standing in the middle of the road watching me. His two dogs, the giant and the midget, were still sitting beside him.

I reached out the window and waved my hand. In the mirror I saw him raise his.

I wondered what he wasn't telling me.

"I think you were right," I said to Evie that night. We were sitting up in bed reading.

"Of course I was," she said. "I'm always right. What was I right about this time?"

"Hurley's lying. Something's going on with Cassie. She's gone, but her car's in the driveway covered with pollen, as if it's been sitting there for a month. The mailbox of her cell phone is filled up with messages. The damn dentist was evasive, and his son attacked me. The next-door neighbor knows something more than he's saying."

Evie laid her copy of *Smithsonian* magazine facedown on her lap, took off her reading glasses, yawned, and rubbed her eyes. "Attacked you?"

I shrugged. "I handled it."

"Of course you did." She smiled. "So what're you thinking?"

"I don't have any theories," I said, "if that's what you mean. Those people are hiding something, though. I'm sure of it. But mainly, I guess I'm thinking about Uncle Moze. He's worried about Cassie, and now I am, too. I'm worried that something has happened to her. And I'm especially worried about Moze, of course. This is eating him up, poor old guy. I've got to try to figure out what's going on."

She leaned her head against my shoulder. "Gonna go snooping, huh?"

"I guess I already started."

FIVE

Things slow down a bit in the law business in the summer. Or at least they do in my law business. Clients go on vacation. So do judges and other lawyers. For some reason, people are less inclined to file lawsuits or initiate divorce proceedings in July and August.

So in my office, which is, after all, a two-person office, just me-the-attorney and Julie-the-secretary/boss, we take Monday mornings and Friday afternoons off in the weeks between Independence Day and Labor Day. We arrive after lunch on Mondays and leave around lunchtime on Fridays, and nobody except us seems to notice.

Unfortunately, Evie didn't have the same deal at the hospital, so truly long weekends rarely materialized for us. That didn't stop me from taking the time off, nor did it make me feel the slightest bit guilty.

On that particular Monday morning, after a weekend devoted to Uncle Moze, I had some office work to catch up on. A few phone calls. Some paperwork Julie had slipped into my briefcase on Friday before I could make a clean escape. Nothing very challenging.

A little before noon, Henry and I went out to the kitchen, where, under his watchful supervision, I made a ham-and-Swiss-cheese sandwich with spicy mustard on pumpernickel, fished a dill pickle from the jar, added a handful of potato chips, and poured a glass of iced coffee.

I ate at the picnic table out in the garden so I could watch the chickadees and look at the flowers. A couple times I accidentally dropped a hunk of sandwich and a few chips on the ground, which Henry devoured. He seemed to like the spicy mustard, but after a tentative lick, he snubbed the bite of pickle I offered him.

I drank all the iced coffee myself. Caffeine keeps dogs up at night.

We had just gone back inside when the phone rang.

I guessed it was Evie, calling to tell me she loved me and to discuss options for dinner.

When I said hello, a woman's voice—not Evie's—said, "Have I got Mr. Brady Coyne?"

"Yes. This is Brady."

"You're Moses Crandall's nephew?"

"I am. Who's this?"

"Helen Meadows is my name. I'm your uncle's neighbor. Moses. Moses Crandall."

"Is something wrong? Is Moze all right?"

"Well, sir, I'm afraid they took him to the hospital this morning, and I ain't so sure how he's doing. Still alive, I believe. He's a tough old cuss."

"What happened, Miz Meadows?"

"It's Helen, young man." She paused. I heard her blow out a breath. "You see," she said, "Moze and me, we're both old-timers, and we kind of look after each other. He calls me at eight o'clock every night, just to see how I'm doing, and I call him, six thirty every single mornin' of the year, same thing. So today when I call he don't answer. I don't think too much of that. Figure he's probably in the bathroom. But when I call again fifteen minutes later, he still don't answer. Now I'm worried. He knows I'm going to call. We been doing it for years, and he always answers. So I go over to his house. That was our deal. If one of us don't answer the phone, it means something's wrong. When I get there I find him sprawled out on the floor wearin' his pajamas and lookin' pretty much like a goner. All grayish and still and clammy, breathing so soft and slow you can't see his chest move. So I call that 911 number, and the ambulance comes, and they work on him for a while, and then they take him off to the hospital with their sirens screaming, and when I get my wits about me, I remember how just yesterday he was talkin' about you, how you're helpin' him out with Cassie and all, and I didn't know who else to tell, but I figured somebody ought to know—family, I mean—so I looked up your number in his book, and here I am, tellin' you about it."

Helen Meadows paused. We both needed to catch a breath. "Moze," she said after a minute, "he can be terrible crabby sometimes, but he's a dear old bugger, and I don't know what I'd do if I lost him." She cleared her throat, and I guessed she was crying. "Anyways, I figured you'd want to know. You being family and all. Moze thinks the world of you, you know."

"I think the world of him, too," I said. "So where is he?"

"Pardon?"

"What hospital?"

"Maine Medical, up to Portland. Don't know why they took him there. The Portsmouth hospital's closer, but that's what they did."

Portland was a little under two hours from Beacon Hill, if the traffic was light. "So," I said, "how are *you* doing, Helen?"

"Me?" She hesitated. "I'm doin' how you'd expect, I s'pose, thank you kindly for asking. I'm scared, is how I'm doing. I tried calling the hospital, but they won't tell me nothing." She sighed. "You get old, you start losing your friends. Moze is my best

55

friend. I don't want to lose him. It'd be awful lonely around here without him, I'll tell you that."

"I'll check up on him, find out how he's doing," I said. "Why don't you give me your number and I'll keep you posted."

"God bless you."

She recited a phone number, which I wrote down.

After I hung up with Helen Meadows, I called information and got the main number for the Maine Medical Center in Portland. I called it, asked to be connected to the emergency room, which I eventually was, and they redirected me to intensive care. I said I was calling for information on a recently admitted patient, Moses Crandall, who was my uncle, and an apologetic-sounding woman told me they weren't allowed to give out patient information over the telephone.

"Can you at least tell me if Mr. Crandall is still alive?" I said.

"You're his nephew, you say?"

"That's right. Also his lawyer."

"Lawyer, eh?" She chuckled. "Okay. I'm scared."

"I didn't mean anything like that," I said.

"Oh, I guess you probably did." She hesitated. "All I can tell you, sir, lawyer or nephew or president of the United States, is that Mr. Crandall is here in intensive care."

"He is alive, then."

"I can't tell you anything else," she said. "Hospital policy. Sue us. You won't be the first one." She hesitated. "It may interest you to know, however, that it's against regulations to store dead bodies in the intensive care unit."

I smiled. "Thank you. We'll have to see about that lawsuit. Can I visit him?"

"Only family."

"Good," I said.

I called Julie, who'd already arrived at the office, and told her to go home, take the rest of the day off, because I wasn't coming in. She asked what was up, and I told her that I was going to visit my uncle in the hospital in Maine and that I'd tell her all about it.

She said she'd be happy to take the rest of the day off, though it would've been considerate if I'd mentioned it before she got dressed and drove into the city.

I said I was sorry, and if it would make her feel better, she could stay in the office until five.

She said thank you just the same. She hoped my uncle would be all right.

Then I snapped my fingers at Henry, who was curled up under the kitchen table. He scrambled to his feet, his toenails clacking on the tile floor, and plopped his chin on my knee so I could scratch his forehead.

"I'm off to Maine," I said to him. "You're going to have to stay here. Bark at that UPS guy. Lick Evie's face when she comes home."

Henry gazed at me out of those intelligent brown eyes of his, and there was no doubt he understood every word I said.

I called Evie's office. Gina, her secretary, said she was still off at a meeting, wasn't sure when she'd be out, but anyway, after that she had another meeting that it looked like she'd be late for, so could she take a message?

"Tell her my uncle's in the hospital," I said, "and I'm driving up to Portland to see him. Not sure when I'll be home. Tell her I'll have my cell with me. Tell her I love her."

"Is your uncle all right?"

"He's in intensive care. That's all I know. I don't know what happened to him."

"I hope he's gonna be okay," said Gina.

I found my cell phone in the bottom drawer of my desk. Evie had given it to me after I'd been very late getting home one night and had been unable to find a pay phone. She'd been worried, then angry, then frantic, and neither of us enjoyed that. I'd promised to carry it with me, but I was having trouble getting in the habit after resisting the idea of cell phones for all those years. If I didn't watch out, the next thing I knew I'd find myself standing in a trout stream casting to a rising trout with one hand and talking to a client on the damn phone with the other hand.

The image made me shudder.

I turned on the phone and shoved it into my pants pocket. Then I gave Henry a Milk-Bone, told him to behave, and walked down Mount Vernon Street and up Charles to the parking garage.

As I wended my way onto the expressway and headed north to Maine, I thought about Cassie. Wherever she was and whatever she was doing, I was certain she wouldn't want Moze to die thinking she was too angry to talk to him.

I just hoped both of them were okay.

A sign beside the closed door to the ICU at Maine Medical read, "VISITORS. Please ring the buzzer. A staff person will let you in."

Under the sign was a button. I pushed it. After a minute, a middle-aged nurse opened the door from the inside and arched her eyebrows at me.

"I'm here to see Moses Crandall," I told her. "I'm his nephew."

"Name?"

"Brady Coyne."

"Nephew?"

"Yes, ma'am."

She looked me up and down as if she were trying to determine how I could possibly be Moses Crandall's nephew. Then she shrugged and said, "This way." She turned and headed inside.

I followed her. The ICU was set up in a big square, with the patients' little cubicles lined up around the perimeter and the medical staff's desks and all the electronic monitoring devices clustered in the middle.

The nurse led me to a corner room. "Make it short, please," she said.

I had to take a deep breath when I saw Uncle Moze. He looked small and insignificant and terribly still, lying there under his white sheet. He appeared to have aged twenty years in the two days since I'd seen him. An oxygen tube was pinched on his nostrils. Transparent plastic tubes snaked from the back of his hand up to a cluster of plastic bags on a steel hanger. Wires coiled out from under his sheet and led to ticking monitors.

His eyes were closed. I had to look carefully to detect the faint, slow rise and fall of his chest.

I turned to the nurse, who had remained standing watchfully behind me. "How is he?"

"Stable."

"Is he in a coma?"

"No. He's sleeping."

"What do you mean, stable?"

"I mean," she said, "the doctors have given him medication. They can't tell yet how much damage was done."

"Damage," I said. "What happened?"

"Your uncle had a heart attack."

"Is he going to make it?"

"You'd have to talk to a doctor about that."

"Right," I said. "Yes. I definitely want to do that. How do I get to talk to a doctor?"

She smiled. "You ask me very nicely if I'll page him for you."

I returned her smile. "Please?"

She nodded, turned, and went to one of the desks in the middle of the big room.

I stepped to the side of Moze's bed and gripped his hand. "Uncle Moze," I said. "Hey, Uncle. It's Brady. How're you doin'?"

I saw his eyeballs roll under his lids, but he didn't open them. I gave his hand a squeeze. "Hey, old-timer. Can you hear me?"

He gave my hand a weak squeeze, and I saw his lips move.

I bent close to him. "Say it again."

His face contorted with effort, and his eyelids fluttered open. "That you, sonnyboy?" he said.

"It's me, Uncle Moze. I'm here."

"Cassie," he whispered. Then his eyes fell shut.

"I'll get her," I said. "I'll find Cassie. I'll worry about that. You concentrate on getting better."

He opened his eyes, blinked at me, and closed them. His lips moved.

I bent close to him.

"It . . . was . . . Cassie," he murmured.

"What was Cassie?" I said. "What are you talking about, Uncle Moze?"

But he was sleeping.

I sat there beside his bed for a few minutes, and then the nurse came back. "That's enough," she said. "He needs his rest."

I stood up, gave Moze's shoulder a squeeze, and told him I'd be back.

The nurse led me over to the ICU door. "I got ahold of Dr. Drury for you," she said. "He said he'd be up in a few minutes. There's a waiting room out there on your left. I'll make sure he sees you. Okay?"

"A few minutes?" I said.

She shrugged.

There were two cheap sofas and three upholstered chairs in the little waiting room outside the ICU. A small window on one wall looked out onto other hospital buildings. A scattering of magazines lay on the low glass-topped table in the middle of the room. *Today's Health, Good Housekeeping, Popular Mechanics,*

Downeast, Sports Illustrated. I looked through them. None was less than eight months old.

I was thumbing through the NBA preview issue of *SI* from the previous September when a deep voice said, "Excuse me? Are you Mr. Crandall's nephew?"

I looked up. He wore a white coat and brown pants. He had pale skin and a smooth, pink face, and despite the fact that his sand-colored hair was receding from his forehead, he looked about fifteen.

I stood up and put out my hand. "Brady Coyne," I said. "Mr. Crandall's my uncle, yes."

He took my hand. His grip was surprisingly firm. "Wilton Drury," he said. "I'm his cardiologist." He gestured to the sofa where I'd been sitting.

I sat down again, and he sat beside me.

"How is he?" I said.

"He's had a heart attack," he said. "He should recover. He was lucky. With that aneurysm of his, it's a miracle it didn't rupture and kill him. He's a—"

"Wait a minute," I said. "What's this about an aneurysm? Does he know about it? What kind of aneurysm?"

"It's an aortic aneurysm," Dr. Drury said, "and of course he knows about it. It was only a few weeks ago when we diagnosed it. He said he'd been feeling tired, listless, short of breath lately, and a friend of his finally talked him into seeing me."

"How bad is it?"

"He's had it for a while. It's getting bigger, the vessel walls are getting thinner." He looked out the window for a minute. "It's bad. It'll kill him. Probably within a year."

"Isn't there anything you can do?"

"Sure," he said. "We can operate."

"But?"

"You know your uncle," he said.

I realized I didn't know my uncle very well, but I could guess what Dr. Drury meant. "He refused?"

The doctor smiled. "Said he had a string of lobster pots to tend, didn't have time for no damn operation."

"I'll talk to him," I said.

"Oh, I talked to him," said the doctor. "I explained the situation as straightforwardly and graphically as I could. I told him how the walls of his aorta are being stretched with each beat of his heart. It's blowing up like a balloon. I told him how one of these days that thing'll just explode inside his chest, and then, just like that, he'll be dead." A little smile twitched at the corner of Dr. Drury's mouth. "Know what he said?"

I nodded. "I can guess."

"He said," said the doctor, " 'Sounds good to me.' "

"I was with him day before yesterday," I said. "He didn't say anything about any aneurysm to me."

"Of course he didn't."

I smiled. "If you've got to die," I said, "a ruptured aortic aneurysm sounds like a good way to do it."

"Yes, I suppose that's what he was thinking."

"Still," I said, "you could operate. Maybe if Uncle Moze felt that he had something to live for." I was thinking of Cassie.

"Well, actually," said Dr. Drury, "this heart attack complicates matters."

"It'd be risky?"

"Very risky. I wouldn't recommend it."

"But if he doesn't have that thing operated on . . ."

He shrugged.

"So," I said, "when you say he'll recover . . ."

Dr. Wilton Drury shrugged again. "I mean, he won't die of this heart attack. Mr. Crandall is in amazingly good physical condition given the fact that he smokes and drinks and pays no attention whatsoever to his diet. He's going to have to change his lifestyle."

I smiled. I couldn't imagine Uncle Moze changing a single thing about his lifestyle. "How long do you think he'll be here?" I said. "In the hospital, I mean."

"Hard to say. A few more days in ICU, at least. We've got to do some tests, keep a close eye on him, work out his medications. Then if all goes well, we'll move him over to the hospital floor for a few days, and if he's still doing okay, get him into rehab. Start his PT, build back his strength, see how it goes. That aneurysm complicates it."

"My uncle's a lobsterman," I said. "Every day he goes out on his boat, hauls his pots. He lugs heavy things. Hot sun beats down on him. He gets rained on."

"He can't do that anymore," said Dr. Drury flatly.

"Well, he probably will."

"It'll kill him," he said. "Guaranteed. If his heart doesn't get him first, the aneurysm will. If he'd been out on his boat when this happened . . ."

I nodded.

"His family's going to have to talk sense to him," he said. "You're not his only family, are you?"

"No," I said. It took me a minute to remember which of my mother's brothers and sisters were still living. "He's got a brother, Jake, and a sister. Faith's her name. Jake's still in Moulton as far as I know. I'm not sure where my aunt Faith is. And Moze has a daughter, if I can reach her. Cassandra. Cassie."

"Good. The family needs to be involved in some of our decisions." Dr. Drury cleared his throat. "Actually, I'm glad you're here, Mr. Coyne. There's something else you should know."

"What's that?"

"The ER doctor noticed it when they brought him in," he said. "Mr. Crandall had a fresh bruise on his chest."

63

I frowned. "A bruise?"

Dr. Drury patted the area over his left breast.

"He fell," I said, "hit something when he had his heart attack. Is that what you mean?"

He shook his head. "It looks like a fist hit him."

Six

I stared at Dr. Wilton Drury. "A fist," I said. "You saying somebody punched him?"

"That's certainly how it appears."

"A fist as opposed to some blunt object?"

He nodded. "Did you play baseball when you were younger, Mr. Coyne?"

"Sure. Third base, mostly."

"Ever get hit by a pitch?"

"Of course."

"The bruise a baseball makes on your ribs or shoulder or your leg? You can see the stitches."

"You can see the knuckles when someone punches you?" I said. "That what you're saying?"

"That's what your uncle's bruise looks like to me. Knuckles. He was lying on his back when they found him."

"As if he was punched and it knocked him backward," I said.

"Typically," he said, "when someone has a heart attack, if they're standing up, the pain causes them to bend over, and they fall forward."

"That is impressive forensic deduction, Doctor."

He smiled quickly. "It's speculative at this point, of course, but thank you. Unfortunately, your uncle's in no condition to tell us what actually happened. I reported it to the Moulton police, as I'm required to do. I'm expecting an officer to show up any minute now, as a matter of fact. If you want to join us . . ."

"I do. Definitely. What does 'any minute now' mean?"

He smiled. "Your guess is as good as mine."

Dr. Drury wandered away and I was left with that old *Sports Illustrated*. I flipped through it, looking at the pictures but not really noticing them. A jumble of thoughts was clanking around in my mind.

One thought was: No wonder Moze was suddenly so eager to track down Cassie. He'd just been given a death sentence.

Another—more disturbing—thought was: The words that Moze had struggled to whisper to me from his intensive care bed, if I'd heard them accurately, were "It was Cassie."

Did he mean that it was Cassie who had punched him in the chest?

What else could it mean?

It was nearly an hour later when the doctor came back. A woman was with him. She was medium-tall, slim, midthirties, I guessed, brownish blond hair in a ponytail, big silver hoop earrings, good tan, no makeup, and none needed. She wore a pale blue jersey and tight-fitting white jeans and dirty sneakers.

A badge was clipped to her belt. An automatic handgun sat in a holster on her hip.

Dr. Drury said, "Sergeant Staples, this is Mr. Coyne, Mr. Crandall's nephew."

She smiled and held out her hand. "Charlene Staples," she said. "Moulton PD."

I took her hand. "Brady Coyne."

She cocked her head at me. "You're a Crandall, huh?"

"That's right. My mother's side."

"You used to visit Mrs. Crandall on Harrington Street in the summer sometimes? Came in that big black Cadillac with Massachusetts plates?"

"Gram Crandall," I said. "My grandmother. Yes, I confess, that was our Cadillac. My father was a big-shot Boston attorney."

"I suppose that explains it," she said. "I grew up down the street from the Crandalls. My mother used to suck her false teeth whenever she saw your car go gliding past our house. She'd say, 'Just who do those people think they're trying to impress?'"

"We pretty much got the same reaction in our neighborhood in Massachusetts," I said.

She smiled. "About your uncle. It appears that somebody punched him. Any idea who'd do such a thing?"

"I should tell you," I said, "that until last Saturday, I hadn't seen Uncle Moze for about thirty years. I doubt if I'm going to be much help."

"Last Saturday, you say?"

"Yes. Went out on his lobster boat with him, helped him haul his pots, did a little trolling in the river. Then we went back to his house, had a beer."

"Why?" she said.

"Why . . . ?"

"Why after thirty years did you visit with him last Saturday?"

"It's kind of a long story, Sergeant."

"Why don't you call me Charlene." She smiled and sat down. "I'll call you Brady, okay?"

"Good," I said.

"So tell me your long story. I've got time."

"I haven't," said Dr. Drury. He looked at Charlene Staples. "Anything else I can do for you, Sergeant?"

"Just tell the nurses I'm going to want to try to talk to Mr. Crandall," she said. "Thanks for alerting us to this situation."

He gave her a little two-fingered salute and turned to leave.

"Doctor," I said. "Would you do me a favor?"

He stopped and looked at me with his eyebrows arched.

"Could you ask the nurses to talk to me if I call on the phone about my uncle?" I said. "They were fairly uninformative when I tried this morning."

"As they're supposed to be," he said. "Sure. I'll tell them. Give me your number, why don't you. If anything changes, I'll call you myself."

"Great," I said. "Thank you." I handed him one of my business cards. "You can call me anytime."

Dr. Drury left, and Charlene turned to me. "Okay. Let's have your long story."

I tried to condense it, but it amounted to my family history, what I knew of it anyway, and it took a while. I ended by telling her what Moze had whispered to me. "It was Cassie."

"And you think he meant that it was Cassie who punched him?" she said.

"I don't know," I said. "Yeah, I guess so. That's probably what he meant."

"Would that make any sense to you?"

"What would make more sense," I said, "is that he's just had a heart attack, he's heavily medicated, he's in a hospital for the first time in his life, he's disoriented, probably hallucinating, he's been thinking about nothing but Cassie for months . . ."

"On the other hand," she said, "as far as we know, Mr. Crandall's the only witness we have."

"If you ask me," I said, "he's the least reliable witness imaginable."

"A lawyer's opinion, huh?"

"Anybody would see it that way."

She shrugged as if she didn't necessarily see it that way. "Cassie Crandall was four years behind me in school. She had a reputation."

"That was a long time ago."

"She was gorgeous and sexy and smart," she said. "Terrific athlete. She ran track, played basketball and softball. Great singing voice. The boys drooled over her. She was always quite, um, mature for her age. The girls hated her. I never thought she deserved her reputation. It was all lies and envy. High-school stuff. Cassie was better than everybody else at just about everything."

"I didn't know her at all then," I said.

"So she and her father are estranged, huh?"

"I guess you could say that. She's the one who broke off communications."

"And you're trying to, um, reconcile them?"

I waved a hand. "I'm just trying to find Cassie, see if I can convince her to mend fences with Moze. Now, with him in the hospital, it feels way more important."

She cocked her head at me. "With him saying that she did it, it feels very important indeed."

"You can't take that seriously," I said.

"It's what we call a clue," she said. "When a victim IDs the person who assaulted him, we take it seriously, yes."

"Well," I said, "that's just nuts."

"Maybe." She looked at her watch. "You in a hurry to get back to Boston?"

"Nope."

"You feel like giving a police officer a hand?"

"Sure. What can I do?"

"You were inside your uncle's house last Saturday, you said, right?"

I nodded.

"I've got to check the crime scene, on the assumption that there was a crime, which the doctor believes there was. Come with me, tell me what you see. Will you do that?"

"I'm glad to help if I can."

She flashed me a terrific smile. Charlene Staples had green eyes, I noticed, and the corners crinkled when she smiled, as if she spent a lot of time squinting into the sun. "I'll be back in a minute," she said.

It was actually closer to fifteen minutes. I was getting pretty sick of that little hospital waiting room.

"Come on," she said. "Let's get out of here."

As we walked out of the hospital, she said, "I just talked to your uncle. He told me it was Cassie."

"You asked him who hit him?"

She nodded. "I said to him, I said, 'Mr. Crandall, I'm a police officer and I need to know who did this to you.' He was pretty out of it. I had to put my ear close to his mouth to hear him. But it was quite clear, what he said. He said, 'It was Cassie.' Like that."

I shrugged.

"That's what he said to you, too, right?"

"Yes," I said. "But—"

"So we've got an assault," she said, "and Cassie's our suspect. You tell me they're estranged. That probably means she's angry with him about something. That suggests a motive, doesn't it?"

"I suppose so."

"So what's her motive?" she said.

"I don't know."

We were in the parking lot. "Where are you parked?" she said.

I pointed to my car in the visitors' lot.

She smiled. "From a long black Cadillac to a sleek green BMW, huh? So now you're the big-shot Boston attorney." She pointed to an area beside the emergency room entrance where a cruiser with Moulton PD painted on the door was parked. "Follow me."

"I'm not that big of a shot," I said as she turned and headed for her cruiser.

She looked back over her shoulder and smiled.

Sergeant Charlene Staples exited the turnpike in Ogunquit and led me over some hilly two-lane back roads through Berwick, and we pulled into Moze's sandy driveway in Moulton a little less than an hour after we'd left the hospital in Portland.

She parked her cruiser in the shade of one of the big maple trees beside the house. I pulled up beside her.

As we walked up to the front door, she said, "Don't touch anything inside." She had one of those foot-long cop flashlights in her hand.

I nodded. "I've done this before."

She looked at me out of the sides of her eyes. "What kind of lawyer did you say you were?"

"Family law, mostly. Some litigation. I've been getting into divorce mediation lately. I sort of specialize in helping people."

"But you've been at crime scenes."

I smiled. "Oh, sure. Plenty of times."

She rolled her eyes. "I won't ask." She paused at the door and handed me a plastic envelope containing a pair of latex gloves. "You know what these are for, then."

I blew into them and slipped them on, and she wiggled her fingers into a pair, too.

Moze's front door was unlocked. Charlene turned the knob and pushed it open. We stepped directly into the living room. She put her hand on my arm, and I stopped. "Just look around," she said. "Tell me what you see."

71

The thin cotton curtains were pulled shut over all the windows, and the room was shadowy and musty. It felt unlived in, even though Moze had been found there only that morning. "It looks about the way it looked when I was here the other day," I said. "Kind of messy."

"Anything missing, out of place?"

I shook my head. "I'm not noticing anything."

"According to the EMTs, he was lying there." She flicked on her flashlight and shone it on the floor in the middle of the room, where the carpet was bunched up.

"In his pajamas," I said. "Could they give you any estimate of what time it happened?"

She turned off the flashlight. "They thought it would've been about an hour, maybe an hour and a half, before they treated him. They figured he would've died if they'd gotten here much later than that."

"And that was . . . ?"

"A little before seven this morning."

"So this must've happened around five thirty or six," I said. "Moze is sleeping in his bedroom. He hears something, gets up, it's just starting to get light outside so he doesn't bother turning on any lights. He comes here, into the living room, still half asleep, and somebody punches him. He falls backward. Has a heart attack. Maybe it was the punch. Maybe it was the surprise, the shock, the fright."

She nodded. "That's about how I figure it."

"It was probably still too dark for him to see anything more than shadows," I said.

"She might've said something. They might've had a conversation."

"She," I said. "Meaning Cassie."

Charlene shrugged. "She, he. If it was Cassie, and if she did

72

speak, Mr. Crandall would've recognized her voice, whether or not he got a good look at her."

"It could've just been some random burglar."

"Sure," she said. "We've been known to have random burglars here in Moulton. Kids, more often than not. Mr. Crandall says it was Cassie, but okay, sure. Unreliable witness. It could've been anybody. Maybe a female burgler that he mistook for Cassie. That's why I want you to look carefully, see if you notice anything missing. We'll start with this room. Then we'll move on to the others. Take your time."

I looked around slowly, consulting my mental picture of the place, trying to be methodical, taking each section of the room separately. When I finished, my eyes went back to the big console television in the corner.

"Okay," I said. "I got it."

"Got what?"

"Something missing." I pointed. "There were about a dozen framed photos on top of that TV. They were mostly of Cassie."

Now the top of the television was bare.

"Okay," she said. "Good. That's good. Anything else?"

"No. Nothing."

"You sure?"

I nodded.

"Were you in any of the other rooms?"

"No," I said. "We came in here, I sat over there, on the sofa. Moze went to the kitchen for beers a couple times. I stayed in here."

"You didn't go into the kitchen with him, use the bathroom, poke your head in the bedrooms?"

"No. The only thing I did was go over to the TV and look at the photos."

"Which are now gone," she said. She went over to the TV and

shone her flashlight around behind it. "No, they're not. Come over here. Take a look."

I moved beside her, and I saw a jumble of bent frames and torn photographs and broken glass strewn on the floor in the corner behind the television set.

"Look at this." She pointed with her latex-covered forefinger. There were dents and scratches and gouges in the wallpaper behind the TV.

"Somebody threw these photos against the wall," I said. "Threw 'em hard, too, judging by the size of some of those gouges."

Charlene looked at me. "Threw 'em with great anger, wouldn't you say?"

"Great emotion, anyway," I said. "You're thinking about Cassie, aren't you?"

"She's so angry at him she hasn't talked to him in a year and a half, you said."

"That's a different kind of anger from smashing her father's photographs and punching him in the chest hard enough to give him a heart attack."

She shrugged. "Maybe, maybe not."

"I'm just having trouble," I said, "thinking his own daughter could do this to him."

"I've seen way worse." She touched my elbow. "Come on." She steered me outside. "Why don't you wait out here."

"Wait for what?"

"I've got some work to do." She went over to her cruiser, opened the trunk, and came back with a camera. "I'll only be a few minutes." She went inside.

I sat on the front steps and looked at my watch. It was a little after five o'clock. I fished my cell phone out of my pocket and called Evie's office. After a few rings, the voicemail came on and Gina's recorded voice invited me to leave a message. I declined.

74

I tried our home number and got voice mail there, too. I told Evie I was still up in Maine, that Uncle Moze had had a heart attack and was in the ICU, that he was holding his own, that I wasn't sure when I'd be home, that I loved her.

I put my phone back into my pocket, and when I looked up, I saw an elderly woman shambling up the driveway toward me.

I stood up, and when she came near, she said, "Who are you?"

I smiled at her. "I'm Brady Coyne."

She nodded as if she already knew that. "I'm Helen Meadows. We spoke this morning. Do you have any news about Moze? I called the hospital but they wouldn't tell me a thing."

"I saw him a little while ago," I said. "He had a heart attack, but he's doing okay."

"Oh, dear," she said. "A heart attack." She was wearing overalls over a man's blue shirt, with red sneakers. She had white hair, cut short, and sharp blue eyes behind her thick glasses. "I was afraid it was something like that."

I pointed at the front steps. "Do you want to sit down?"

"Certainly not," she said.

I smiled. "The doctor says you saved his life," I said. "If you hadn't gone over when you did, called 911 right away . . ."

"That was our deal," she said. "We watch out for each other, Moze and me. I don't guess we ever really expected something like this would happen. Me, I just like the old cuss, enjoy havin' him as a regular part of my life, even if it don't amount to more than talkin' with him on the phone most of the time." She cleared her throat. "He don't have much to say, you know. Taciturn old coot. So he's going to be all right?"

"He'll be in the hospital for a while. But they expect him to recover just fine."

"You ain't patronizing an old lady, are you?"

"No, ma'am," I said. "I know better than that. I'll let you know if anything changes, okay?"

75

"That would be lovely," she said. She turned to leave.

"Mrs. Meadows?" I said.

She stopped. "It's Miss Meadows, young man. But you should call me Helen."

"Helen," I said, "I'd like to tell the rest of Moze's family about what happened."

"Jake and Faith," she said. "His brother and sister. That's about it, except for Cassie."

"Do you know how I could reach them?"

"Well, Jacob, he lives right in town here. He's got that real estate business, you know. Hangs out in the office most of the time, now that Millie—that was his wife—since she's been gone." She shrugged. "I suppose he'd want to know."

"You suppose?"

"Moze and Jake, they didn't have much to do with each other. Actually," said Helen, "the two of them weren't speaking to each other. Haven't been for years. There was some old grudge between 'em. Both of 'em, stubborn as mules."

I thought about Cassie and Moze, holding out, neither willing to give in to the other for all that time. "Any idea what the grudge was about?" I said.

"All I know is, it goes back a long ways. Moze never wanted to talk about Jake. Moze only talks about what he wants to talk about, if you follow me."

I nodded. "So what do you know about my aunt Faith?"

"Faith Thurlow's her name now," she said. She looked up at the sky. "Faith's gettin' on. She's a few years older than us. Me and Moze, I mean. Married a Greek fellow from Kittery right after high school. Name you couldn't pronounce, ended in 'opoulos' I seem to recall. He was a salesman of some kind. Harry. I think his name was Harry. They lived right here in town until Harry retired. Lord, that was twelve or fifteen years ago, I guess. Harry and Faith moved down to Florida, and before too long, Harry died. Next thing you know, Faith has found herself another man, this time a fellow named Thurlow who was somewhat younger than her. Faith always did have a way with men. So she married this Thurlow fellow and they settled in Rhode Island, of all places."

"Was Moze in touch with Faith?"

Helen Meadows shrugged. "He didn't say nothing about her one way or the other that I can recall. I didn't have the impression that they were on the outs the way it was with him and Jake, but I don't think they were especially close, either."

"So it's Faith Thurlow," I said, "and she lives in Rhode Island."

"Last I heard," she said. She held out her hand. "I've got to get back to my cats."

I stood up and took her hand. "I'll let you know what I hear about Moze," I said.

"I appreciate that." Helen Meadows nodded once, then turned and walked down the driveway. I watched her go. I was prepared to wave to her, but she never turned back.

A couple of minutes later Charlene Staples came out of the house with her camera hanging from her neck. She peeled off her latex gloves, stuffed them in her hip pocket, and sat on the steps beside me.

"What'd you learn?" I said.

"There's an old rolltop desk in his bedroom," she said. "The top was up. A bunch of bills and junk mail all jumbled up in there. A couple drawers were hanging half open."

"You think whoever hit Moze was looking for something?"

"Maybe," she said. "Or maybe your uncle was just disorganized."

"Judging by the living room," I said, "I'd vote for that."

"I found about two hundred dollars in fives and tens and twenties in the top drawer of his bureau," she said. "There was a box of woman's jewelry, must've been his wife's, in another drawer. A lot of heavy old gold stuff. Some of it's pretty valuable, I'd say. His watch and his wallet and the keys to his truck were sitting right there in plain sight on the table beside his bed."

"So this wasn't a burglary, you're saying."

"Not a very competent one, anyway," she said. "Of course, your burglar could've panicked when she—or he—hit your uncle, but it doesn't look like anything was stolen."

"Just those smashed photos."

She nodded.

"Helen Meadows just dropped by," I said.

"Who?"

"Moze's friend. She's the one who called 911."

Charlene nodded. "Oh, right. She's on my list. Did she have any idea who might've done this?"

"No. I didn't exactly interrogate her. She was pretty shaken up. I had the feeling that Moze is her only friend in the world."

Charlene nodded. "I'll have to talk to her." She jerked her head back at Moze's house. "The second bedroom in there," she said. "You didn't see it?"

"No."

"Pink bedspread. Ruffled curtains. Stuffed animals. Posters tacked all over the walls. Janis Joplin. Gracie Slick. Billie Jean King. The daughters from the Bill Cosby show. Sports trophies. Cassette tapes. Nancy Drew mysteries."

"Cassie's room," I said.

She nodded. "It looks like a shrine."

"Poor old Moze," I said. "She's always been the main thing in his life."

We sat there for a couple of minutes. Then I turned to Charlene and said, "So what happens now?"

She shrugged. "Until I can talk with Mr. Crandall, we don't really know what we're dealing with. I'll ask around, keep my ear to the ground, see what I can learn. Assuming your uncle makes it, all we've got is an old-fashioned breaking and entering and a simple assault. But if . . ." She waved her hand in the air.

"If he dies," I said, "we've got a homicide."

She nodded.

"And you'd consider Cassie a suspect."

"Cassie is a suspect," she said. She looked at her watch, then pushed herself to her feet. "Well, I'm outta here. Long day."

I stood up, and we walked over to our vehicles.

"Why don't you give me one of your cards," she said.

I gave her one. "You'll keep me informed?"

"Why not." She handed me one of her cards. "You do the same, okay?"

"Okay."

Charlene Staples got into her cruiser, wiggled her fingers at me, and drove out the driveway.

I slid into the front seat of my car and took out my cell phone. I figured I'd try one more time to reach Evie before I headed home.

She didn't answer at the house, and I didn't bother leaving another message. She didn't answer her cell, either.

I stuck the phone in my pocket and started up my car, and that's when the sleek red Buick sedan turned into Uncle Moze's driveway.

SEVEN

The red Buick pulled up behind my BMW and stopped right there, as if the purpose was to prevent my escape.

I stepped out of my car just as the guy got out of the Buick. He appeared to be in his late sixties, early seventies. He had a round, red face and a dramatic shock of thick snow-white hair. The stub of an unlit cigar was jammed into the side of his mouth. He reminded me of Santa Claus, minus the jolliness.

He strutted over, plucked the cigar from his mouth, and pushed his face close to mine. "Who the hell are you?" he said. He was quite a bit shorter than I, so he had to look up to glare into my eyes, which pretty much neutralized the aggressiveness he seemed to be going for.

"My name's Brady Coyne," I said. "Who the hell are you?"

He blinked at me as if it was unthinkable that I didn't know who he was. "I don't know any Coyne." He moved closer to me, so that his chest was nearly touching mine. "Whaddya want, anyway? What're you doin' here?"

I put my hand on his chest and took a step backward. His intrusion into my personal space felt like an attack. "This is my uncle's house," I said. "You didn't answer my question. Who the hell are you?"

"Yeah, well, this is my brother's house, smart guy." He paused, frowned, and looked me up and down. "Moses is your uncle? That what you said?"

I nodded. "Which means you are, too. Uncle Jake? Is that you?"

"Coyne," he muttered. "Coyne..." Then he suddenly grinned. "Hope's boy, right?"

"Right." I held out my hand.

He looked at it, then grabbed it and gave it a quick, limp shake. "Last time I saw you, you were just a kid," he said. "So what brings you back to this neck of the woods?"

"Uncle Moze is in the hospital."

Jake nodded. "I heard something about an ambulance. Figured I'd drop by, see what was up."

"He's in the hospital. Maine Medical in Portland. Had a heart attack."

"He gonna be all right?"

"I don't know."

"Heart attack," he muttered. "That's what the old coot gets for haulin' pots at his age."

"He'd probably appreciate it if you paid him a visit," I said.

"Doubt it," said Jake.

"Uncle Jake," I said, "do you know anything about Cassie?"

"Cassandra? Mary's girl?"

I nodded.

"Ain't seen her for years," he said. "Since she was in high school. Couldn't tell you what become of her."

"I thought maybe Uncle Moze might've mentioned something about her to you."

"To me?" He shook his head. "Not likely. Me and Moses, we don't mention much of anything to each other no more."

82

"Why not? What happened?"

He looked at me. "That's none of your damn business."

"Your brother came very close to dying this morning," I said. "Maybe it's time to bury the hatchet, before it's too late."

"You don't know nothing," he said.

"You're right," I said. "I don't. What about your sister? Aunt Faith? Are you talking to her?"

"Not much."

"Do you know how to reach her?"

He nodded. "She's down there in Rhode Island with her new husband. Fellow named Thurlow."

"Where in Rhode Island?"

"Tiverton, I believe. They got a place on the water."

"Have you been there?"

"Ain't been invited."

"But you've talked to her."

"Couple times."

"You should tell her about Uncle Moze."

"I should, huh?"

"Somebody should. She'd want to know, don't you think?"

He shrugged. "I suppose."

"Okay," I said. "I'm trying to catch up with Cassie. If you hear anything or think of anything, let me know, will you?"

"What makes you think I'd know something about her?"

I flapped my hand. "I don't know. But if you do . . ."

"Sure. Why not?"

I gave him one of my cards. "My numbers are there."

He looked at it, then looked at me. "Lawyer, huh?"

I nodded.

"Your old man was a lawyer. Hope thought she was hot shit, marrying a lawyer."

"Did she?"

"Drivin' around in that big Caddy. Him, all full of himself."

"They were my parents," I said. "They're both dead now."

"Meaning I ain't supposed to say the truth about them?"

"What's the truth, Uncle Jake? That you were jealous of them, of their success?"

"Nothin' to be jealous of," he said. "Me, I own my own company. I'm doin' good. I got plenty of money. Did it all on my own, too. I ain't jealous of nobody."

"Okay," I said. "Whatever." I looked at my watch, then held out my hand. "I've got to head home. It was good to see you again, Uncle Jake."

He shook my hand quickly. "Sure. You, too."

"You'll talk to Aunt Faith?"

"Don't worry about her," he said.

"Go visit Moses," I said.

"Yeah," he said, "we'll see about that." He turned and started back to his car.

"Hey, Uncle," I said.

He stopped and looked at me.

"I just figured out who you remind me of."

"Yeah? Who's that?"

"Gram."

"Huh?"

"My grandmother. Your mother. You look like the way I remember her."

He frowned and shook his head.

"Except," I said, "she was a lot more pleasant."

Uncle Jake Crandall rolled his eyes, then got into his red Buick and backed out of Moze's driveway.

As I drove home, I kept thinking about Cassie. Two days ago Uncle Moze had asked me to see if I could put him back in touch with her. I didn't know it at the time, but his sudden urgency was the result of learning that he had an aortic aneurysm, that he could die any minute. That was a good reason to want desperately to reconcile with his daughter.

Now he'd been punched in the chest and had a heart attack, and finding Cassie struck me as urgent, too.

Sergeant Charlene Staples thought Cassie was the one who'd punched him. Broke into his house at night and punched him and smashed all the pictures of her he kept on top of his television console.

Cassie, full of rage? Cassie, bubbling with hatred for the man whom she knew as her father, who brought her up, who fed her and clothed her, who taught her about the sea?

Maybe. Moze, in his druggy stupor, said she was the one who punched him.

But I wasn't prepared to believe it.

The next morning, Tuesday, a little after nine, I called Maine Medical in Portland, got connected to the ICU, told the nurse I was Moses Crandall's nephew, the one who'd visited him yesterday, and I wanted to know how he was doing.

"Stable," she said.

"Can you tell me any more than that?" I said.

"Not really. He's unchanged."

"Still basically unconscious, all drugged up?"

"Basically."

"You are not exactly brimming with information," I said.

"I'm telling you everything I know, sir," she said. "Mr. Crandall is resting comfortably. He is taking some nourishment intravenously. His vital signs are, um, stable. Like I said."

"Can you tell me if he's had any visitors?"

"I could tell you, yes."

I sighed. "Okay. Will you tell me, please?"

"Since you were here, Mr. Coyne, his only visitor was Sergeant Charlene Staples of the Moulton police."

"No others."

"No."

After I hung up from that informative call, I called Julie at the office.

"How's your uncle?" was the first thing she said.

"Stable, quote unquote. Look, I've got to do a few things this morning. What've we got?"

"The Sanborn mediation's at two," she said. "Want me to reschedule."

"No, no. I'll be there."

"Do what you have to do," she said. "I hope your uncle's going to be okay."

I told Henry to guard the house, then walked down to the parking garage on Charles Street and fetched my car. I drove out to Madison, and it was a little after ten when I turned onto Church Street. It was a drizzly summer morning, and the trees that lined the narrow street arched overhead. They hung heavy with moisture and formed a dripping green tunnel. I drove slowly past the school on the right and then Howard Litchfield's house on the left, and when Hurley's house came into sight, I saw, as I'd expected, that the Lexus SUV was gone. So were the Dodge pickup and the Chevy with the carseat.

Cassie's red Saab was still there, exactly where it had been two days earlier.

Hurley, I assumed, had driven to his dental office to inflict pain and poverty upon his patients. His son and daughter and grandchild had apparently returned to wherever they lived.

If Cassie had been away for the weekend, she'd be back now. I had no particular expectation that Hurley would give her my message, but even if he had, it wasn't a sure bet that she'd bother returning my call.

I didn't want to leave a telephone message with Hurley about Uncle Moze being in the hospital. I wanted to tell Cassie about it face-to-face, just the two of us.

If she was home now, she was home alone.

I pulled in beside the Saab. The soft rain dripping off the trees streaked the yellow pollen on the red car.

I sat there for a minute, looking for some sign of life from inside the house. When I saw none, I got out, walked up to the front door, and rang the bell.

I heard it chime hollowly inside. After a couple of minutes I tried again.

Nobody home.

I stood there at the front door and looked around. I could make out the roofline of Howard Litchfield's house next door through the screen of maple trees that separated the two properties. A thick stand of hardwoods and evergreens lined the other side of Hurley's property. Across the street, the soccer fields were mud-puddled and empty of players.

I felt sneaky and tricky and ready for action, the way I used to feel when I was a kid emerging from a darkened movie theater on a Saturday afternoon after a double bill of western gunslinging and World War II combat. Kid Coyne, fastest gun in Durango. Sergeant Coyne, sharpshooting jungle sniper.

I didn't know about the Madison cops. Maybe if they cruised down Church Street on this Monday morning and saw a strange BMW parked in Hurley's driveway, they'd stop and investigate. If so, I'd tell them the essential truth. I was Cassie's cousin, wondering if she was home. That was her car in the driveway, wasn't it?

I tried the front-door knob. It was locked, of course. I made a slow circuit of the house. There were two side doors, two sets of sliders off the back and side decks, a cellar door, and the garage doors. All were locked.

I shaded my eyes, peeked in several windows, and saw nothing but abstract paintings on the walls and modern furniture on the floors. It didn't look that comfortable.

I was prepared to slip inside and take my chances with an alarm system if one of the doors was unlocked. I didn't know what I was looking for, but I did want to look. I thought I'd know it when I saw it. Some clue to Cassie's whereabouts.

If the police came, I figured I could talk my way out of an entering charge.

But I wasn't about to break in. I was pretty sure I couldn't talk my way out of both breaking and entering.

I ended up back in the driveway. I walked slowly around the Saab. I saw no red blinking light under the dashboard or any decal on the window indicating that it was equipped with a car alarm, so I tried the door handle. It was unlocked. I guessed folks didn't bother locking their cars in Madison, where an out-of-towner going the wrong way on Church Street constituted a crime wave.

I pulled open the Saab's door and slipped into the passenger seat. There was no briefcase, no address book, no folder containing important documents, no homemade audiotapes. Nothing that might tell me about her, tell me where she was.

I did find some plastic CD cases in a pocket on the driver's-side door. Fleetwood Mac, Neil Diamond, Dolly Parton, the Bee Gees. Music from her formative years.

The glove compartment held the registration—the Saab was registered to Cassandra Crandall, not Hurley—and a few road maps. I opened the maps on my lap but saw no circles or routes outlined on them that might've struck me as clues to her whereabouts.

In the center console under a purse-sized pack of paper tissues, I found a cell phone. I hoped—and assumed—it was Cassie's, the one with the full mailbox. I hesitated barely one second before I slipped it into my pocket.

I found nothing else in Cassie's car. But the cell phone was an excellent start, I thought.

I got out of the Saab and closed the door, and when I turned to get into my own car, I saw Howard Litchfield with his Mutt-and-Jeff dogs standing in the street at the end of the driveway. He was wearing a yellow slicker with the hood over his head. The dogs were sitting patiently on the wet pavement.

Litchfield was looking at me with no expression that I could read—not curiosity, not disapproval, not amusement, not even interest, really.

I lifted my hand to him. He waved at me.

I went out to the end of the driveway. "I'm glad I ran into you," I said.

"Pretty hard not to," he said. "Since I retired, this is where I am, what I do, most of the time, rain or shine. Walking my dogs up and down the street."

I smiled.

"So you're back looking for Mrs. Hurley, huh?"

"That's right," I said. "I hoped I might find her at home this morning."

"I was thinking about what you said the other day," he said. He gazed up at the sky for a minute. "My wife was pretty good friends with the, um, the previous Mrs. Hurley. The new one, though, we haven't really gotten to know her."

"The previous Mrs. Hurley?"

He nodded. "Ellen was her name. God bless her. She died a few years ago. Lovely, quiet woman. She was sick much of the time. Asthma. That's what she ended up dying of, I understand. Poor woman had her hands full, raising those two children of his, never mind taking care of him."

"His children?" I said.

He frowned. "Pardon?"

"You said 'those two children of his.' They weren't hers?"

"No, no," he said, "that's right. A boy and a girl. Rebecca and James. They were with his first wife. The one before Ellen. She died, also."

"I met Rebecca and James," I said. "They don't live here with him, do they?"

"No, no. Not anymore. Rebecca, she's married, has a baby, and James moved out recently. They come to visit now and then." He looked at me. "You said you were interested in the, um, the third Mrs. Hurley. The present one. She's your cousin, you said."

I nodded. "I haven't seen her in a long time. Heard she'd gotten married and moved to Madison recently, and I thought I'd look her up. That's all. I happened to be back in the neighborhood this morning, so I thought . . ."

He arched his eyebrows. "Back in the neighborhood, eh?"

I smiled. "More or less." I lowered my voice conspiratorially. "It's very important that I talk with Cassie, Mr. Litchfield. If you have any idea at all . . ."

He looked up and down the street, then leaned his head toward me. "It's impossible not to hear the two of them," he said. "Her, especially."

"They argue?"

Howard Litchfield rolled his eyes. "She's got a mouth on her, that one. When they're going at it, my wife runs into the bathroom, turns on the ceiling fan, and shuts the door. She goes to church, my wife does."

"What do they argue about?"

He shook his head. "I couldn't tell you. I hear the tone of their voices, the occasional vulgarity out of her, that's about it."

"You wouldn't have picked up anything that might help me to track her down, would you?"

He shrugged. "I'm not one for gossip."

"Anything at all, Mr. Litchfield," I said. "It's really important."

"Well," he said, "there was something . . ."

"Whatever it is," I said, "it's strictly between you and me. I promise."

"This wasn't anything I overheard, exactly."

I smiled. "What happened?"

"Well, okay," he said. "It was two weeks ago last Saturday night, as I recall. Sometime after midnight. We always sleep with the windows open, and I heard voices and car doors opening and closing from next door. They weren't loud noises, mind you. My wife didn't even stir. More like voices that didn't want to be heard, and doors clicked shut, not slammed, if you know what I mean."

I nodded.

He smiled quickly. "Now, okay, I can't help it, but I'm interested in things. Call me nosy. My wife does. So I got out of bed and peeked out the window." He pointed up through the trees toward the roofline of his house, and I could make out the gray sky reflecting off some windows through the foliage.

"So you could see what was going on over here?" I said.

"Not clearly. There was a moon, but through the leaves all I could make out were shadows and now and then the movement of a light."

"A light," I said. "Like a flashlight?"

He nodded. "Maybe two flashlights. They kept turning them on and off."

"The shadows," I said. "They were people?"

"Two of them, I think," he said. "They were going in and out of the house. They were talking in soft voices. Not whispering exactly. Mumbling. As if they didn't want to be heard. Not like when the two of them are having one of their yelling contests. At one point it looked like they were lugging something out of the house, and after a minute or so, the vehicle drove away, and then everything was quiet again."

"Cassie and Hurley?" I said. "Is that who it was?"

He shook his head. "I didn't think so at the time, for some reason. It was how they seemed to be sneaking around, I guess."

"You didn't recognize the people?" I said.

He shook his head. "It was dark. Through the trees. Just shapes."

"Or their voices?"

"Like I said, they were whispering. I suppose it could've been Mr. Hurley and his wife. But I didn't think so at the time."

"You said they were lugging something out of the house?"

He nodded. "That's what it looked like. Something heavy. Took two of 'em to carry it. You could hear them grunting."

"Could you tell what it was?"

"It was hard to see. I wouldn't dare make a guess."

The thought hit me: a dead body. Cassie's body. Hurley and his son, James, maybe, lugging Cassie's body out to the car.

Whoa, I thought. Slow down, Coyne.

"These people," I said. "Their voices? Men, women?"

He shook his head. "Couldn't tell."

"What about the vehicle? Did you get a look at it?"

"Not clearly. I just saw the headlights flash on and then it backed out of the driveway."

"Dr. Hurley drives a Lexus SUV. Cassie drives that Saab. Was it either of them?"

He shrugged. "I really couldn't tell you."

"So what do you make out of what you saw, Mr. Litchfield?"

He blew out a breath and shook his head. "Dr. Hurley's kids visit sometimes. The daughter—Rebecca—she's over there a lot, especially since she had her baby. At the time I just thought it was them, leaving late, trying to be quiet so as not to wake the neighbors. Which is probably exactly what it was, though it did strike me as"—he looked up at the sky for a moment—"furtive, I guess. Sneaky. I don't know what to make out of it." He peered at me. "Now that I think of it, though, I don't recall seeing or hearing Mrs. Hurley since that night."

Since then, I was thinking, the voicemail box on Cassie's cell phone had filled up.

"Have you noticed anything else?" I said. "Since that night, I mean?"

He shrugged. "Can't say I have. Just, her car, the red Saab, it hasn't moved in two weeks. Other than that?" He shook his head.

"Well," I said, "I appreciate your sharing this with me." I fished a business card out of my pocket and gave it to him. "If you hear or see anything else, or if you see Cassie, or if you remember anything else, would you please call me?"

He looked down at the card, then up at me. "You're a lawyer?"

"Yes."

"You said you were her cousin."

"I'm that, too," I said. "This has nothing to do with being a lawyer. I want to see my cousin, that's all."

I had no intention of giving him any more information, and it didn't look as if I was going to learn any more from him. I glanced at my watch and frowned. "I've got to get going," I said. I held out my hand. "Thanks for your help, Mr. Litchfield."

He shook my hand. "No problem."

I turned to go.

"Oh, Mr. Coyne," he said.

I stopped. "Yes?"

"I won't say anything about seeing you snooping around over there."

"I wasn't really . . ."

He was smiling at me. "It's okay. She's your cousin. You're worried about her." He mimed locking his lips and throwing away the key.

I gave him a thumbs-up, went back to my car, backed out of

Hurley's driveway, and turned onto Church Street, heading in the right direction this time.

When I got to the end of the street, safely out of Howard Litchfield's sight, I pulled over to the side, turned off the ignition, and slid Cassie's cell phone from my pocket.

It was one of those square folding models, so small I could almost close my hand around it. The little display window on the front was blank, and when I opened it, the inside screen was blank, too. I poked some of the buttons and nothing happened.

Either the battery was dead or the phone was broken. The former, I hoped.

I slipped it back into my pocket and started up my car, and as I drove home, I pondered the significance, if any, of what Howard Litchfield had seen. I arrived at no conclusions.

I also wondered if the garrulous old fellow could, in fact, restrain himself from telling everyone he ran into how this Boston lawyer had been prowling around the Hurleys' house, poking around in Mrs. Hurley's Saab, asking questions.

I decided that if the dentist got wind of the fact that I'd been snooping around, it might not be such a bad thing. Sometimes you've got to stir things up.

EIGHT

I got home a little after noon. When I went into the living room, I found Henry curled up in the corner of the sofa, pretending to ignore me. He was sulking. He had every right to sulk. I'd gone off without him.

When I snapped my fingers, he slithered off the sofa, came over to where I was standing, and sat.

I knelt down and scratched the magic place in the middle of his forehead. He licked my hand. Instant forgiveness. You've got to love a dog.

I was feeling bad about leaving Henry home when I went to Madison. He could've come with me. He loves to ride in my car. "Want to go to work with me this afternoon?" I said to him.

His ears perked up. "Go-to-work" was one of the many English phrases that Henry understood. "Get-in-the-car," "go-for-a-walk," and "don't-sniff-that-man's-crotch" were some others.

The Inuit, I've read, have about a hundred different words for "snow." Henry had nearly that many for food and eating. Among them were "supper," "dinner," "breakfast," "lunch," "snack," "eat," "chew," "treat," "candy," "meat," "biscuit," "bone," "cookie," "Alpo," "steak," and "doggie bag."

Some people believe that dogs respond to intonation rather than pronunciation. They are wrong. I tested Henry. I said, "Henry! Want some broccoli?" using the same enthusiastic tone as when I said, "Henry! Want a bone?" The word "bone" caused him to scramble to his feet, trot over, poke me with his nose, and commence drooling. "Broccoli" barely elicited a quick, cynical arch of an eyebrow. Henry had tried broccoli once.

On the other hand, many times when Evie and I were sitting at the picnic table out in our garden toward evening sipping gin and tonics and sharing the mundane events of our workdays, I would say to Evie, without shifting out of our low-key conversational tone, "Well, I suppose I better go give him his supper," not even mentioning Henry's name, and he would leap to his feet, poke my leg with his nose, then trot to the kitchen door where it all happened, his ears perked up happily and his little stub tail a blur of wag.

So having heard me mention going to work, he would not let me out of his sight. He followed me to the bathroom and sat outside the door while I showered, and then trailed me to the bedroom and watched me climb into my lawyer outfit.

For courtroom appearances I always wore a suit, of which I owned a dozen in various weights and shades of charcoal. For mediation sessions such as today's, however, I liked to dress more casually—a pair of chino pants, a cotton shirt, moccasins, no necktie. I believed that my informality enhanced the relaxed, cooperative mood that was crucial for effective mediation, just as a pressed suit, silk tie, and shined shoes fit the intense atmosphere of the adversarial courtroom.

After I changed, Henry and I went down to my in-home office, which had originally been the back bedroom off the kitchen, where the hand-carved wooden sign on the door read Brady's Cave. Evie gave me the sign shortly after we moved into our townhouse. "Every man should have his own cave," she said.

Evie understood men—or at least me—better than any other women I'd ever known, which no doubt accounted for the fact that we had managed to share a home together for nearly two years in relative harmony.

My office was off-limits to everybody except me and Henry. Not even the cleaning lady was admitted. Evie could enter only upon invitation.

I kept my fishing gear and some outdoorsy clothes in the closet. My fly rods in their aluminum tubes were stacked in the corner. A wall of built-in shelves held my favorite books—mostly fly-fishing literature and novels and biographies. I had a twelve-inch television set for Red Sox and Patriots games, a CD player with powerful little Bose speakers, a reclining chair, and a minifridge loaded with juice and beer and Pepsi. There was a daybed for my naps and a dog bed for Henry's.

I had a desk in there, too, with a computer and a telephone. It sat in front of the window that looked out into our back garden. I'd been doing a lot of office work from home since Evie and I moved in. I liked watching the birds at the feeders while I talked on the phone with clients and other lawyers.

I sat at my desk. Henry lay down in the doorway, watching me, ever vigilant. I'd promised to take him to work with me, and he wasn't going to let me forget it.

I picked up the phone and dialed Roger Horowitz's cell phone.

It rang twice, then he grumbled, "Yeah, Horowitz."

"Got a minute?" I said.

"Christ," he said. "It's you."

"I need some information."

"This regarding a homicide?" Horowitz was a homicide detective for the Massachusetts State Police.

"I don't know," I said. "Maybe."

"Because if it ain't," he continued, "you might as well forget about it."

"Lunch at Marie's," I said. "You name the day."

"I got a lotta shit going on here, Coyne. I'm not your fucking research assistant, you know."

"Remember Marie's lobster ravioli, that nice cream sauce with the mushrooms?"

"Hard to forget," he growled.

"So have you got time to make one phone call for me?"

"One?"

"That's it," I said.

"It's always like that," he said. "One phone call, and next thing you know I'm rescuing you from a burning building or something." He blew a long, resigned breath into the receiver. "So who'm I supposed to call?"

"The police in Madison."

"Madison? Nothing ever happens in Madison."

"I want to know if they've got anything on a guy named Hurley. Dr. Richard Hurley. Lives on Church Street there. He's a dentist."

"A dentist, huh?" Horowitz paused for a minute. "I hate dentists. So what're we looking for?"

"Anything. Domestic-disturbance reports, 911 calls, hassles with the neighbors, wrong way on a one-way street." I hesitated. "Missing persons, maybe."

"Missing?" I heard a spark of interest in his voice. "Who's missing?" For homicide detectives, "missing" sometimes meant dead, and "dead" often meant murdered.

"It's my cousin," I said. "Her name's Cassandra Crandall. Or Cassandra Hurley, probably. She's married to the dentist, though I'm not sure she took his last name. And I don't really know that she's missing, but she might be. She seems to be."

"Sleuthing again, are we?"

I patted my pocket where I'd slipped Cassie's cell phone. "I found her cellular phone," I said.

"Whaddya mean, found?"

"It was in her car. I took it."

"Christ," muttered Horowitz. "You mean you stole it."

"It doesn't work," I said. "What do you know about cell phones?"

"I know you should put it back where you found it. Jesus, Coyne."

"I just want to talk to my cousin," I said. "It's pretty important."

"Don't steal anything else," he said. "I'll get back to you." And he hung up.

Roger Horowitz never said "hello" or "good-bye." He was all business and no courtesy. I liked that about him. Perfunctory gestures of courtesy are overrated.

I snapped the leash onto Henry's collar for our half-hour stroll to my workplace in Copley Square. There was absolutely no need to leash him. If I told Henry to heel, he'd stick by my side through an Alpo factory or a field full of pheasants. But Boston has a leash law, and it would be imprudent for a lawyer, an officer of the court, to flout the law, no matter how well behaved his dog happened to be.

When we walked into my office suite at ten of two, a midthirties man with thinning blond hair and a slender dark-haired woman of about the same age—Ed and Elizabeth Sanborn, my two o'clock mediation appointment, I assumed—were already there. Ed was sitting in the corner chair thumbing absently through my coffee-table copy of *American Angler*. Elizabeth was perched on the edge of the sofa with her knees pressed together and her purse on her lap, sipping coffee and staring blankly at the framed Ansel Adams print on the opposite wall.

Elizabeth had called me on the recommendation of Barbara Cooper, a lawyer she'd been talking with. She told me that Cooper thought she and Ed were good candidates for mediation, and they wanted to give it a try. She'd sounded skeptical, which was all right with me. I had more success with clients who didn't go into it thinking mediation would be easy.

I had met neither of them in person. From my brief conversation with Elizabeth, I knew they'd been married fourteen years, owned a house in Hingham, had two daughters and three cats, and kept a Boston Whaler moored in Scituate Harbor. He was a project manager for a building contractor in Braintree, and she was a part-time reading specialist in the local middle school.

I didn't know what issues had brought them to the point of divorce, nor did I care to know. For our purposes, those issues were irrelevant. Massachusetts is a no-fault-divorce state—although fault is never irrelevant to the two parties.

Julie introduced us. I shook hands with each of them, introduced them to Henry, ushered them into my conference room, and gestured to the chairs at the table. I told Henry to lie down on my old sweatshirt in the corner, which he did, offered the Sanborns something to drink, which they both declined, then went back out to the reception area.

"What's your take?" I said to Julie, who was peering at her computer screen. I jerked my head in the direction of the conference room.

"They arrived together. Talked a little. They weren't exactly holding hands. They seem more sad than angry."

"Odds?"

She cocked her head and looked up at the ceiling. "Sixty-forty."

"For or against?"

"For."

"So if it doesn't work out . . ."

"If mediation doesn't work out for them," she said, "it's because you screwed it up."

I smiled. "Won't be the first time." I took Cassie's cell phone

100

out of my pocket and put it on Julie's desk. "This doesn't work."

She picked it up and looked at it. "It's not yours. Where'd you get it?"

"It belongs to my cousin. My uncle's daughter."

"Your sick uncle?"

I nodded.

"How's he doing?"

"Stable." I shrugged. "Resting comfortably, as the medical professionals put it."

"So your cousin gave you her broken cell phone?"

"Sort of," I said. "Can you make it work?"

"What do you think I am?"

"You're a genius with electronic devices, among many other amazing things."

"True, true," she murmured. She flipped the phone open, poked a few buttons, closed it, turned it over in her hand. "Let's see what we can do." She looked up at me. "Meanwhile, you better get in there and mediate."

I flipped her a salute and went into the conference room.

Ed Sanborn was standing with his hands clasped behind his back rocking on his heels and gazing out the window. Elizabeth was seated with her hands folded on the table. When I entered, he turned around and she looked up at me.

I smiled at them. "Ready?"

Ed went over and sat across from Elizabeth. She looked at him for a minute, then dropped her eyes.

I took the chair at the end of the table, Ed on my left, Elizabeth on my right. "So what do you folks know about divorce mediation?" I said.

"You help us work it out," he said. He was looking at her. "It saves us from arguing in court. It saves us lawyers' fees. We don't end up hating each other. It's better for the kids." He looked at me and shrugged.

"That's about right," I said. "You're both committed to doing it this way?"

They looked at each other, then at me, and nodded. His nod was emphatic. Hers struck me as tentative.

"Elizabeth?" I said.

"I'm willing to give it a try," she said softly.

"It's not for everybody," I said. "A lot of couples who start with mediation don't complete the process. There's no shame in that."

"We understand," said Ed. "We can do it."

"To be clear," I said, "I am not a marriage counselor. This is divorce mediation, not marriage mediation. This is about making your divorce happen as smoothly as possible. I don't know what brought you two to this point, and for our purposes, not only don't I care, but I don't want to know. I certainly don't make judgments. People who have decided to get divorced from each other always have a lot of things they don't agree on. If they didn't, they most likely wouldn't be getting divorced. We will not mention any of those issues here, whatever they are. They are off-limits, against the rules. We have just one purpose, and that is hammering out a divorce settlement you both completely understand and agree to and that will satisfy the judge when you go to court. Okay?"

They nodded. They seemed a bit intimidated by my standard lecture on neutrality, which was part of my purpose. I'd learned early on that many people entered mediation hoping to find an ally who'd help them vindicate themselves. That attitude doomed the process before it began.

"There are just five issues we'll be discussing here," I said. "They are child support, spousal support, property, custody, and schooling." I held up five fingers, then bent down one of them. "The state has a formula for child support, and unless there's some unusual and compelling reason not to, we will comply

102

with the formula." I bent over a second finger. "Spousal support—alimony—is negotiable. Insurance is part of it. Health and life." I bent down the third finger. "Under most circumstances all property—all assets, and debts, too—held by the partners in a marriage are considered to be owned jointly. The usual division of marriage property is fifty-fifty. One of our most important jobs here will be to determine what everything you own is worth and then decide how we divide it all in half." I bent down my fourth finger. "As for custody, you have two daughters. Have you discussed it?"

"Joint custody," said Ed. He looked at Elizabeth, and she nodded.

"Okay, good," I said. "We'll have to decide precisely how that's going to work for you and your children. But it's great to have that settled in principle. Number five involves how you pay your kids' school tuitions. College and private school, if you go in that direction. That's about all there is to it. Those five issues. Now all we've got to do is work out the details." I paused, then said, "How does this sound to you?" I looked at each of them. "Ed?"

"Fine." He nodded quickly. "Good."

I arched my eyebrows at Elizabeth.

She shrugged. "Okay."

"And you're both committed to getting divorced, right?"

They nodded and shrugged some more.

"Because if you're not committed," I continued, "if one or the other of you has doubts or reservations, you should consider seeing a marriage counselor and trying to work it out. Or if doubts or reservations should arise during this process, if either of you starts to have second thoughts, it's important that you say so. We can suspend this process any time right up to the day you're scheduled to go to court. Understand?"

They exchanged glances, and I thought I detected the brief flicker of silent communication that married couples almost always develop regardless of the issues that divide them, the quick look that at a social gathering means, "Let's make an excuse so we can get the hell out of here," or, "I see the way you're ogling that slut. We'll deal with it later."

Elizabeth looked at me and gave a tiny nod.

Ed said, "We understand."

"Okay then," I said. "Your first homework assignment will be to list all your assets. Real estate. Personal property like furniture, appliances, cars, boats, jewelry. Investments, credit-card accounts, bank accounts, insurance policies. Write down everything. Every chair, every towel, every coffee mug and power tool, along with its value. Include your incomes and your debts. I'll give each of you some worksheets. I want you to fill them out separately. Omit nothing, even if there's something you think you don't own jointly. We'll use these lists to decide who ends up with what, how we divide the pie in half." I paused until they were both looking at me. "Full disclosure is important," I said. "It's also a legal requirement. If one of you owns something, has a secret bank account or some source of income, anything that the other one doesn't know about, and you leave it off your list, it not only violates each other's trust in this process—and mine, as well—but also you'll be breaking the law. Understand?"

More shrugs and nods.

"Okay then," I said. "The way it usually goes is, we meet once or twice a week for two or three hours. You pay Julie at the end of each session. No down payment or retainer or anything like that. For every session, each of you will have some homework to do. If all goes well, we'll finish up in four or five sessions. Do each of you have your own lawyer?"

"I thought you were our lawyer," said Ed.

"Part of my job is to explain the law to you," I said, "but I'm not your lawyer. I won't represent you in court. What I am is,

I'm your mediator. I require that each of you arrange to have a lawyer look over your agreement when we're done. I can give you some names if you want." I leaned forward. "Any questions at this point?"

Ed and Elizabeth Sanborn looked at each other. Then Elizabeth shook her head and pushed herself away from the table. "I can't do this," she said softly. She stood up, picked up her purse, and hugged it against her chest. Tears had welled up in her eyes.

Ed stood up and reached his hand across the table. "Honey, come on. We talked about this."

"Don't call me honey."

"But we agreed," he said.

She blew out a breath. "It's so . . . so cold. Our marriage comes down to who gets what?"

He put his hands flat on the table and leaned toward her. "So whose fault is that?"

"Hang on," I said. "Hold it right there."

They both looked at me.

"Sit down, Ed," I said.

He blinked at me, then sat.

"Elizabeth?"

She sat down, too.

"You two want to argue," I said, "okay by me. You want to do it in my office, that's fine, too. You're paying me by the hour. But I'm not interested, and I'm not going to listen to it. When you guys figure out what you want to do, let me know. I'll be in the other room."

I snapped my fingers at Henry, and he got to his feet and followed me out of the office. I closed the door behind us.

NINE

I poured myself a mug of coffee and sat on the sofa across from Julie's desk. Henry curled up on the rug beside her.

"They having second thoughts?" She jerked her head in the direction of the conference room.

I nodded.

"She cheated on him, you know," Julie said.

"Oh?"

"He's been cheating on her, too," she said, "except she doesn't know it."

"You overheard them talking?"

"Of course not. I'd never eavesdrop. They got here ten minutes before you. Their body language was unmistakable. She's racked with guilt. Thinks she still loves him. Hates the idea of divorce, what it would do to the kids, but believes she's unworthy. He's a hypocrite, playing the martyr, but feeling guilty, too."

I shook my head. "How do you know these things?"

"I'm a woman."

"You certainly are," I said. "So you give them better than even odds even with all that shit bubbling under the surface?"

"All that shit," she said, "her guilt, his secrets, it makes both of them highly motivated."

"Boy," I said, "I'm glad I'm not a marriage counselor." I looked at my watch. "What do you think? Five more minutes?"

"Not even," she said.

About two minutes later, the door to the reception room opened and Elizabeth poked her head out. "We're all set now," she said.

I stood up. "What about some coffee?"

"Sure," she said. "We both take milk, no sugar."

We finished up a little after four. I told Ed and Elizabeth Sanborn to take care of things with Julie on their way out. I made a few notes and slipped them into their folder, and a few minutes later Julie knocked on my open door.

"Come on in," I said.

She came in, put a fresh mug of coffee in front of me, and sat down. "How'd it go?"

"They were all business," I said. "We'll see."

"They made an appointment," she said. "Friday morning, ten o'clock. I think they're over the hump."

"There'll be more humps."

She put Cassie's cell phone on the table and pushed it to me. "I got it sort of working."

"Dead battery?"

Julie nodded. "It's the same make as mine. My jack fit it. When I plugged it in, it worked."

"Well, good. Thanks. So now what can I do with it?"

"Nothing. It won't work unless it's plugged in. The battery doesn't seem to take a charge. You'd have to get a new battery for it if you wanted to use it."

"I don't want to use it," I said. "I thought it would have some information."

Julie nodded and handed me a piece of paper. "I copied out all the numbers she had stored in her phone book."

I looked at the paper. There were two columns of codes and numbers, single-spaced. "A lot of numbers," I said.

"Fifty-eight," said Julie.

"When I tried to call this phone," I said, "I got a message that her voice-mail box was full. Did they automatically give that message because the battery was dead, or is it really full?"

"It's really full. I already tried calling it."

"You think of everything."

"Pretty much," she said.

"Is there any way we can get into her voice mail, listen to her messages?"

"Not without her password," she said. "Any idea what she might use for a password?"

I shook my head. "Wouldn't know where to begin." I skimmed down through the list of numbers Julie had written down, along with the names beside them. Many different area codes were represented. Most of the names were just first names or initials or what appeared to be nicknames.

One of them was "M. C." That was Moses Crandall. I recognized his number in Maine.

It occurred to me that most women would list their father's number under "Dad" or "Daddy" in their cell phone.

I noticed "James" and "Becca." I assumed they were Hurley's children. There was also a "Faith" with a 401 area code, which I knew was Rhode Island. Faith Thurlow, I assumed. Cassie's aunt. Mine, too.

I folded the piece of paper, stuck it in my shirt pocket, and said, "Thank you," to Julie.

"You planning to call all those numbers?" she said.

"Hell no. I was planning on having you call them."

"Now just a minute," she said. "I don't—"

I held up my hand. "That was a joke."

"Yeah. Funny." Julie rolled her eyes.

"I'm not sure what I'm going to do," I said.

"You pick out a couple numbers you want me to try for you, okay," she said. "You know I'm always happy to help. But fifty-eight . . ."

"I know," I said. "We'll see. Roger Horowitz didn't call, did he?"

Julie frowned. "Lieutenant Horowitz? Why would he call?"

"I asked him to check something for me."

She tapped Cassie's cell phone with her forefinger. "About this?"

I nodded.

"What's going on, Brady?"

"It's about my cousin. Uncle Moze's daughter. She's sort of missing." I told Julie about how Uncle Moze wanted me to help reconcile him with Cassie, and about my two trips to Madison, about meeting Hurley and his two grown kids, and about my conversations with Howard Litchfield.

When I was done, she said, "Wait a minute. You stole this phone?"

"I liberated it."

She rolled her eyes. "So what are you thinking?"

I spread out my hands. "Either Cassie took off or . . . or something's happened to her."

"You think the dentist . . . ?"

"I'm trying not to leap to conclusions," I said. "But Hurley was singularly unforthcoming, and his son was downright hostile, and the neighbor observed suspicious activity next door late at night." I shrugged. "I just want to catch up with Cassie and see if I can talk her into putting things right with Uncle Moze before it's too late."

"Well," said Julie, "those phone numbers should give you a start." She started to stand up, then snapped her fingers and sat down again. "Evie's secretary called. She's going to be late to-night. Said she'd take care of dinner."

"How late?"

Julie shook her head. "She didn't say. Can't be too late if she's bringing dinner."

"Did Gina happen to say why Evie was going to be late?"

"She said something about a meeting. I didn't ask."

I shrugged. "Okay."

Julie narrowed her eyes at me. "Is she all right?"

"Who, Evie?"

She nodded.

"What makes you say that?" I said.

"I don't know." She waved her hand in the air. "Nothing. I know how stressful her work is."

"Yes," I said, "she's been working too hard. Hospitals are going under left and right. She's pretty much responsible for keeping the place afloat."

"I'm sure that's it," said Julie.

Henry and I got home a little after six. I gave him a Milk-Bone, changed my clothes, mixed myself a gin and tonic, and took the house phone and the glass out to the back garden.

I sat in one of the Adirondack chairs, sipped my drink, and checked the phone's voice mail. I was hoping that Evie had left an I-love-you message for me.

She hadn't.

She got home a little after eight. I was on my second gin and tonic. I asked her if she wanted one, but she declined. "I'm starved," she said. "Let's eat."

She'd brought home a sausage-and-pepper sub for me and an

Italian for herself. We ate off waxed paper at the picnic table in the garden, with bottles of Sam Adams to wash it down and Henry under the table to collect errant crumbs.

I asked about her day. It had been busy, boring, and stressful. Didn't want to talk about it.

She asked about mine. I told her I had started mediation with a new couple. She nodded and didn't ask any questions about them, which wasn't like her.

We finished our subs, watched darkness seep into our little backyard, sipped our beers.

After a while, Evie said she wanted to take a bath. We brought the trash into the house. She went upstairs. I turned on the TV in the living room and found a Red Sox game.

A little while later Evie came downstairs. She was wearing a pair of my boxer shorts and one of my old extra large T-shirts. The neck was torn so that it hung over one bare shoulder. Her long auburn hair was damp. It flowed down her back like a waterfall. She was barefoot and bare-legged, and somewhere along the way she'd picked up a coppery all-over tan.

Wow.

I crooked my finger at her, and she came over, sat on my lap, and kissed my ear. "What's the score?"

"Six to four, good guys. It's the bottom of the ninth. Up to the bullpen."

"Our bullpen sucks," she said. She wiggled her butt in my lap. "I completely forgot to ask about your uncle. How's he doing? Any news?"

"Not that good," I said. I slid my hand under her T-shirt. Her skin felt soft and smooth and electric. When I slipped my fingers under the waistband of her boxer shorts, she shivered, and her breath caught in her throat. Then she sighed, touched my hand, and guided it safely up onto her hip. She patted it and held it there.

"Uncle Moze is stable," I said. "Resting comfortably, to be

precise." I experimentally tried to slide my hand up to her breast.

She gripped it and put it back onto her hip. "Don't," she said. "Okay?"

"Sure," I said. "No problem."

"Tell me what you've been up to," she said.

I told her about going to Madison, walking around the Hurley house with the full intention of entering if I'd found an unlocked door, finding Cassie's cell phone in her car, talking with Howard Litchfield.

"You stole her phone?"

"Why does everybody say that?" I said. "You, Julie, Horowitz. I took it, that's all. I didn't steal it. When I catch up with her, I'll give it back to her."

"Wait a minute," said Evie. "Did you say Horowitz?"

"It's not what you think," I said.

"Roger's a homicide detecive."

"Yes," I said. "This isn't about any homicide. I just asked him to talk with the Madison police for me, see what they knew about the dentist. Which reminds me. He didn't get back to me yet."

"He will," said Evie. "Roger always does what he says he'll do."

"Yeah," I said. "I told him I'd buy lunch for him. He loves Marie's lobster ravioli. He'll call."

About then the Oriole pinch hitter whacked a long fly ball that Trot Nixon caught at the edge of the warning track in front of the bullpen, and then all the Sox players swarmed out to the mound to shake the pitcher's hand and pat his ass.

Evie slid off my lap, kissed the top of my head, gave me a quick hug, and went back upstairs.

I let Henry out back to do his chores. Then I put together the next morning's coffee, let Henry back in, gave him his bedtime Milk-Bone, and turned off the kitchen lights.

By the time I slipped into bed, Evie was asleep.

TEN

Islept fitfully that night. Finally a little before five in the morning, just as the sky outside our bedroom window was beginning to fade from purple to pewter, I said the hell with it and slipped out of bed. Evie was sprawled on her belly, snoring softly. She was half uncovered, as if she'd been thrashing around. I pulled the sheet and blanket up over her, then went down to my office.

Henry, who'd been sleeping on the floor, followed me down. His toenails clicked on the steps.

I lay on my daybed and read a chapter of *Moby-Dick*. I'd been reading Melville's so-called classic for years, dipping into it here and there, it didn't seem to make any difference where, and no matter how wired I might've been, it never failed to put me to sleep.

Herman didn't let me down this time, either.

When I woke up, it was nearly eight o'clock. I showered, shaved, got dressed, poured the day's first mug of coffee, and went looking for Evie.

She was where I expected she'd be, sitting at the picnic table in our backyard garden with Henry lying on the bricks beside her eyeing the grosbeaks.

I didn't expect to see Roger Horowitz sitting there with them.

Evie was dressed for work—pale green knee-length linen skirt, off-white silk blouse, hair up in some kind of complicated bun. She looked terrific, as usual. Horowitz was wearing his standard dark suit. He looked rumpled, also as usual. They both were cradling coffee mugs in their hands.

Evie and I had gone to some Red Sox and Celtics games with Horowitz and Alyse, his wife, and we'd met for drinks and dinner a few times. He was an irascible son of a bitch. Dependable, loyal, honest, candid. Absolutely solid. But irascible.

Evie and Roger had always seemed to hit it off. She was a lot like him, though considerably less irascible. She got along with him a lot better than I did.

I assumed he was sitting at my picnic table having coffee with my girlfriend because he'd brought me information on Richard Hurley from the Madison police.

I started to open the back door to join them, but their body language made me hesitate.

As I watched, Evie said something that made Horowitz put down his mug, fold his arms, and shake his head.

Evie leaned across the table and said something to him.

He pointed his forefinger at her.

She shrugged and looked up at the sky.

I rattled the doorknob so they'd hear me coming, although it wasn't necessary. As soon as the latch clicked, Henry scrambled to his feet and trotted over. His entire hind end was wagging.

I scooched down to scratch his forehead, then went over to the table. I bent and kissed Evie on the cheek she tilted up for me, nodded to Horowitz, and sat down. "Am I interrupting something?"

Horowitz waved the back of his hand at me.

Evie shook her head. "Get any sleep?"

"Sorry if I disturbed you," I said.

116

"That's not what I meant."

"I apologize," I said. "Didn't mean to be snippy. That's how I am when I don't get much sleep."

She smiled quickly—acknowledging my effort to make a joke, but unamused, I thought.

"Melville finally did the job," I said. "It was around sunup. I could've slept till noon, I think." I looked at Horowitz. "You've got Marie's lobster ravioli on your mind, if I'm not mistaken."

"Exactly."

Evie stood up. "I've got to get to the office." She picked up her coffee mug, went around the table, and gave Horowitz a quick hug. "Say hi to Alyse for me. Tell her to give me a call. We'll plan something."

I got up, told Horowitz I'd be right back, and followed Evie into the house.

She was rinsing out her mug in the sink. "What's going on, honey?" I said.

She didn't turn around. "What do you mean?"

"Something's been eating at you lately."

"Nothing's going on, Brady. I'm late is all."

When Evie called me "Brady," it meant something was bothering her—most often me. Usually she called me "honey" or "big fella" or "sweetie."

I stood behind her, put my hands on her hips, and nuzzled the back of her neck. "So what's with you and Horowitz? What were you two talking about? It looked pretty intense out there. Any of my business?"

"Nothing. No." She twisted her head as if my nuzzling was annoying her and kept rinsing out the mug, even though it didn't need it. "Baseball. The Red Sox. How we should get together for a cookout or something sometime. We sure could use some rain. Like that. Nothing intense at all."

"Really."

She turned to face me. "Yes, damn it. Really. What, you think I'm lying to you?"

"I don't think you're telling me everything."

"You're right," she said. "There's a million things I don't tell you. What do you want to know?"

"I want to know that you're all right," I said. "That we're all right. That's all."

"I'm fine. We're fine. So cut it out, okay?"

"Are we?"

"Don't, Brady," she said sharply. "Please. Leave me alone, will you?"

"I worry about you," I said. "Sorry."

She shook her head, turned away from me, and mumbled, "Jesus Christ."

I held up my hands. "Fine. Okay. I care, that's all."

"It's nice that you care," she said. She gave me a quick smile. "Look. I'm sorry. I got a lot going on, that's all. Okay?" She looked up at the kitchen clock. "Oh, damn. I've gotta run. I can't be late. Not today." She brushed my cheek with her lips, gave my arm a squeeze, and she was gone.

When I went back outside, Horowitz was sitting at the table talking on his cell phone. I took the chair across from him. He held up a finger, mumbled something into the phone, then clicked it off.

He took a sip from his coffee mug and peered up at me from under those bushy black eyebrows of his. "You look like shit," he said.

"I slept lousy."

"Had a fight with Evie, huh?"

"Does it show?"

"You hide it pretty well," he said. "But I'm a trained detective."

"I suppose you wouldn't give me a hint about what you and she were discussing out here."

"We weren't discussing anything," he said. "We were just talking, you know? Waiting for you to get up. I came to talk to you, not her."

"That's it?"

"Yeah. That's it. You ain't jealous of me, are you?"

"You?" I laughed.

"Yeah. That's a fucking joke. Funny."

"Sometimes," I said, "I think that I'm just not cut out for a committed relationship."

"Nobody is," he said. "It ain't natural. It's too hard. You gotta work at it all the fuckin' time. Who wants to do that?"

"She's keeping something from me," I said.

"Everybody keeps things from everybody else," he said. "It's in our nature."

I smiled. "She said the same thing."

"You ever keep anything from her?"

I shrugged. "Sure. I guess so. Nothing important, though."

"What's unimportant to you might be very important to her. You ever think of that?"

"You're right," I said. "She's busy. She's under a lot of pressure. She doesn't like to talk about it."

"Give her space, Coyne," he said. "Trust her. She's a good kid. She loves you. What more do you want?"

I nodded. "You're right."

He took a sip from his coffee mug. "I talked to a cop out in Madison for you."

"What'd you learn?"

"Not much." He put down his mug, slid a hand-sized notebook from his jacket pocket, flipped it open, and glanced at it. "Nothing whatsoever on Hurley, there, your dentist, unless you're interested in a speeding ticket on Route 93 about six years ago. He's been

119

living in Madison for close to twenty years. They had a few 911 calls from the house. Medical emergencies. That's about it."

"Any details on the 911s?"

He shook his head. "Not really. It was Mrs. Hurley, the dentist's wife, each time. The last one, she ended up dying. This was a few years ago. I thought you were interested in recent domestic disturbances, that sort of thing."

"I was. I am." I hesitated. "So there's nothing on Cassie?"

He shook his head.

"He hasn't reported her missing?"

"If he had," said Horowitz, "I'd've known it myself."

"No complaints from the neighbors, nothing like that?"

"Nope," he said. "That's all I got for you, Coyne. It's pretty quiet out there in Madison, and I'd say this Dr. Hurley is as quiet as any of 'em. Pretty much a model citizen. You want to pursue this yourself, I can give you the officer's name."

"Let's have it," I said.

"I told him you were a persistent sonofabitch, he should expect you to harass him. He thanked me for the heads-up. Name's Hazen. Lieutenant Tony Hazen. Old friend of mine. We were cops together back when."

"Do you know every police officer in the commonwealth?"

"Just about." He scribbled in his notebook, ripped out the page, pushed it across the table to me, and tapped it with his forefinger. "Name and number."

I stuck the paper into my shirt pocket. "Thank you."

"You don't need to thank me," said Horowitz. "Just buy me a bowl of Marie's lobster ravioli."

"When?"

"Not today." He peered up at me. "You all right?"

"Let's see," I said. "Evie's grouchy with me, my cousin's missing, my uncle's in the hospital, and I need Herman Melville to put me to sleep at night. Otherwise, sure. I'm fine."

He rubbed his chin. "I lose perspective. All the shit I see."

"I can understand that."

"If it ain't a murder, it ain't important, you know?"

I smiled.

"That's pretty fucked up," he said. "Right?"

"Fucked up," I said. "Aren't we all."

"You should go fishing or something," he said.

"You're right."

"It'd relax you. Take your mind off things." He cocked his head and peered at me. "Fishing relaxes you, right?"

I shrugged. "Sort of. It's intense. Engrossing. Helps me forget things. When I'm fishing, that's what I'm thinking about. Fishing."

"Like this friend of mine," he said, "trooper out on the Mass Pike, the Lee barracks, name of Lynch. He's like that. One of those fanatical bass fishermen, right? Got a big boat shaped like a penis, goes a hundred miles an hour, and enough gear to stock an L.L. Bean store?"

I smiled.

"Anyway," said Horowitz, "Lynch, there, he was telling me how he went out a month or so ago. Remember that damn monsoon we got back the middle of June? It was then. So anyway, Lynchie gets up at like four in the morning, kisses his wife goodbye, off to some bass tournament in the Finger Lakes or something. His boat's all hitched up in the driveway, his gear stowed away, and when he goes outside, it's fucking pouring. I mean, coming down in buckets. Lynchie gets in his truck anyway, of course, heads for the Mass Pike, windshield wipers on high speed, turns on the radio, and they're promising a whole day of it. Driving rain, howling winds. Some kind of freak tropical storm, like a hurricane, the middle of June?" Horowitz looked up at me.

I nodded.

121

"Well," he said, "he keeps going for maybe half an hour, and the rain, it's just getting heavier, he can hardly see where he's going, and finally he says to himself, 'What the hell am I doing? This is stupid.' So he turns around and heads back home. Pulls in the driveway just about the time the sky would be turning light if the clouds weren't so thick. He sneaks into the house, quiet so as not to wake up anybody, undresses in the bathroom, and crawls back in bed with his wife. She's sleeping on her side, facing away from him, and he snuggles up to her from behind, kinda wiggles himself against her, puts his arm around her and sticks his face in her hair, and he whispers, 'You awake, baby?' And she mumbles and sighs and reaches around behind her, puts her hand on his hip, sort of pulls him up tight against her. He says to her, 'It's like a fucking hurricane out there. Never saw so much rain.' And she says, 'Yeah, and can you believe it? My dumbass husband, he's out there fishing in it.'"

I looked at Horowitz. "You never tell jokes."

"Joke?" he said. "What joke? I am absolutely humorless. I'm an officer of the law. I deal only in facts. Lynchie told me that himself. True story."

ELEVEN

After Horowitz left, I went into the kitchen to refill my mug. Henry followed along, ever hopeful. I gave him a Milk-Bone. Hope, I believe, should be rewarded now and then. Life without hope isn't worth living.

I went into my room. It was a little after nine. Julie would be at the office. Julie was never late.

I called her. When she answered, I said, "I'm home. It looks like I'm going to be working from here today. Anything I need to know?"

"Define working," she said.

"Oh, cleaning up our paperwork, catching up on our phone calls. What we lawyers do when we're not wowing juries."

"You haven't found your cousin, huh?"

I smiled. Julie knew me too well. "Well, true," I said. "I'm kind of concerned."

"Do what you've got to do, Brady," she said. "I'll take care of things at this end."

Even when she was being supportive and agreeable, Julie had a way of making me feel guilty. Actually, every woman I've ever had any kind of serious relationship with could make me feel guilty just by arching an eyebrow or putting emphasis on an unexpected syllable.

Evie was a master at it. She said this guilt thing was *my* problem, *my* insecurity, *my* paranoia. Stemmed from my relationship with my mother, she theorized. She said it revealed a deeply rooted mistrust of women in general, not to mention the fact that I probably did have things to feel guilty about.

I told her I could manage to feel guilty even when I was innocent, which, in fact, I almost always was, and I didn't really trust anybody, regardless of gender, race, religion, political orientation, sexual preference, or national origin. It had nothing to do with my feelings for women or whether my mother breast-fed me.

Evie pointed out that I was also a master of denial.

I did agree with her that it was my problem, even though I firmly believed that women—or the women that I seemed to be attracted to, anyway—or maybe it was the women who were attracted to me—were genetically endowed with an uncanny instinct for, and took sadistic pleasure in, sticking sharp objects into the vulnerable places in my psyche.

Julie was masterful at it.

During our divorce, Gloria, my ex-wife, told me that I needed guilt, thrived on it, sought out women who fed it to me. It drove Gloria nuts when she realized that she'd been trying to please me—and to keep our marriage together—by subconsciously laying guilt trips on me. When she finally figured out how this unhealthy dynamic between us actually worked, she couldn't divorce me fast enough.

So now Julie, by a subtle inflection in her tone, had made me feel guilty about taking the day off from my law practice to help my ailing uncle get in touch with his wayward daughter. This was, I believed, an eminently worthwhile thing to do. Noble, even. Certainly nothing to feel guilty about.

I felt guilty anyway.

When I hung up with Julie, I realized I was feeling guilty about picking a fight with Evie, too.

I thought about calling her, apologizing, telling her I loved her. But when I played it out in my head, I saw how it would most likely just rekindle the conflict.

So instead I dialed the number Horowitz had given me for Lieutenant Tony Hazen, the Madison cop.

The officer who answered said that Hazen didn't come on duty until four that afternoon and asked if there was something he could help me with.

I said no, it was Hazen I needed to talk with. I mentioned that I was a lawyer, left my name and number, and asked to have him call me.

The cop said he'd be happy to deliver my message, but if I really needed to talk to Lieutenant Hazen, my best bet would be to drop by the station. "Truthfully," he said, "he's not much for returning calls. He talks to who he wants to talk to."

"Sort of like the phone company," I said. "When they're trying to sell you something . . ."

He chuckled. "Electricians, plumbers, doctors. Anybody you really need to talk to. Hazen figures, if you need to talk to him bad enough, you'll keep trying, and if he's lucky you'll end up either talking with somebody else or giving up. He's got an in-box overflowing with messages. Every now and then he throws them all away and starts over."

"Is that true?" I said.

"Nah," he said. "I exaggerate. He looks 'em over, answers the ones that interest him. But he takes his time about it. Not good at returning phone calls."

"What if I said it was about a missing woman?"

"Then you should tell me," he said, "not Hazen."

"Is that your department?" I said. "Missing women?"

He laughed. "We don't have departments here in Madison. There aren't enough of us. We're all just cops. No, you should tell me because I'm here and Hazen's not, and it doesn't matter what you say on any message to him, because he most likely won't even read it. You got a missing woman?"

"I don't know," I said. "So if I drop by the station at four, he'll be there?"

"He's on the desk 'til midnight. He'll be here."

Next I tried Dr. Richard Hurley's home phone and, as expected, got his answering machine. I didn't want him to think he could make me go away by ignoring me, so I left a message. "It's Brady Coyne, Cassie's cousin, again," I said. "I'm still trying to contact your wife. It's imperative that I talk with her, and I've got a couple questions for you. Please get back to me." I recited my home, office, and cell phone numbers for him, even though he had my business card.

Then I called his office. A young-sounding woman answered. "Dr. Hurley's office," she said. "May I help you?"

"I'd like to speak to him," I said.

"I'm sorry, sir. He's with a patient right now. Did you want to make an appointment?"

"I need to speak with him directly."

"I'll be happy to give him a message," she said, "ask him to return your call, if you want."

"Does he have any openings today?"

She laughed. "Our first opening is . . . hang on, I'm looking . . . how's October third?"

"No," I said. "That doesn't work."

"Is this an emergency, sir?"

"Yes."

"I mean, a dental emergency?"

"Would he see me if it was?"

126

"If it were an emergency," she said, "I would refer you to one of Dr. Hurley's associates."

"Just ask him to call me," I said. I gave her my name and numbers. "Use the word 'emergency,' " I added. "Tell him it concerns Cassandra, his wife."

She promised to deliver my message. I detected no reaction when I mentioned Cassie.

I hung up.

I was getting nowhere.

Evie was still on my mind.

The hell with it. I called her office.

Evie's secretary answered. "Evelyn Banyon's office," she said. "May I help you?"

"Hey, Gina," I said. "It's Brady. Is Evie—?"

"Oh, shit," she said. "She's gonna kill me. She asked me to give you a call. I was just about to like a half hour ago when the goddamn phone rang, and then I sorta forgot. Good thing you called."

"She's not there, then?"

"Nope. She had to run off to a meeting. Wanted me to tell you she's gonna be late tonight. That's why I was supposed to call you."

"Late again," I said. "How late?"

"She didn't say. Just late."

"Another meeting?"

"I guess so." Gina hesitated. "She also wanted me to tell you she was sorry she snapped at you."

"Snapped," I said.

"That's a quote." She giggled. "She said you had a sort of argument, and she was feeling bad about it. She *was* feeling bad. I could tell."

"Well," I said, "that's why I called. Because I was feeling bad about it, too. Will you tell her that?"

"Sure."

"Have her call me if she gets the chance, okay?"

"Well," she said, "I'm looking at her schedule. She's pretty much tied up all day. But I'll give her the message."

"Tell her I'll have my cell phone with me. Tell her I love her."

"Absolutely." She hesitated. "Uh, Brady?"

"What, Gina?"

"Would you do me a favor?"

"You want me to tell her you called me," I said. "Right?"

"Smart you," she said. "I probably would've remembered anyway, eventually. But I'd just as soon she didn't know I screwed up, you know? So will you?"

"Sure," I said. "You tell her the same thing. I'd rather she didn't know I called. She might think I was checking up on her. We should keep our stories straight, you and I."

"You got it," she said.

After I hung up with Gina, I felt a little better, knowing that Evie felt apologetic, even if she'd commissioned her secretary to communicate her feelings to me instead of finding a minute to do it herself.

I took out the paper on which Julie had typed the list of numbers from Cassie's cell phone. Two full columns, single-spaced. Names, nicknames, initials. It was daunting. No way I could call all of them.

I moved my finger down the list. They were alphabetical, the way, I assumed, she'd found them in the cell phone.

I stopped at "Grannie." Moze had mentioned that Cassie's boyfriend, the one before she married Hurley, was called Grannie. There were two numbers. "Grannie-cell" and "Grannie-work."

At Grannie-work, the recorded message said, "This is Professor Grantham Webster, English Department, Cabot College." Webster had a deep, rumbling voice with the hint of the Smoky Mountains in it. "Please leave a detailed message and a number where I can reach you. If you want to see me in person, my summer office hours are Monday, Wednesday, and Thursday, two to four. I don't schedule appointments. You're welcome to just drop in."

Okay. Thank you. Today was Wednesday. Maybe I would.

I didn't bother leaving a message.

I tried Grannie-cell, got his voice mail, and left no message there, either.

I went back to the list. Mostly first names, a few last names, nicknames, and initials that meant nothing to me. A diligent investigator would start at the beginning, and he'd call them all, and he'd interrogate everybody intensely, on the assumption that any one of them might have the answers he was looking for, and he'd make a note of those he didn't reach so he could call them again.

Not me. I couldn't do that. There had to be a better way.

I went back to the list. There were numbers for "Becca" and "James" and "Richard." The Hurleys, I supposed, although there were also numbers for "Becky" and "Jimmy" and "Dick." And there were numbers for people named Carla, Liz, Donna, and Sue. Numbers for Digger and Tipper and Flip. Numbers for Smith and Osborne, Grapelli and Bratonio, Shwartz and Grabowski. Numbers for Pizza and Chinese, Auto and Bank, Oil and Electric. There were initials. More names and nicknames and commercial places. More initials.

There was that number for "Faith" in Rhode Island. My aunt, I assumed. According to Uncle Jake, Thurlow was Aunt Faith's current married name.

I called her number. It rang five times. Then a woman's voice said, "You have reached the Thurlows. Please leave a message." Aunt Faith's voice, I guessed, a soft, breathy, elderly voice. She sounded nervous and sad. It made me want to see her, see what my aunt looked like after all these years, see if she really was nervous and sad, and if so, why.

I didn't leave a message. Uncle Jake had said she lived in Tiverton, which was just over the Massachusetts border. About an hour's drive from Boston. I could find her. I decided I didn't want to talk to her on the telephone. I wanted to sit across from her, watch her face, pat her hand, give her a hug.

I leaned back in my chair, blew out a breath, and stretched my arms over my head. I'd been sitting there for about an hour, had made five or six calls, and I was exhausted. How the hell did the private investigators do it, hour after boring hour, day after excruciating day, year after interminable year?

Gordon Cahill, the best PI I knew, once told me that investigating was like selling encyclopedias door-to-door. You could knock on a hundred doors and get every one of them slammed in your face, and then the next ten, bingo. Ten sales. You never knew. All you knew was, if you just kept staking out people, making phone calls, calling them again, following up leads, just keeping at it, sooner or later you'd get a hit.

You'd sell a set of World Books.

You'd find what you were looking for.

If you didn't do it, guaranteed you'd never get anywhere. So you just kept doing it.

You had to have that kind of mentality, Gordie said. You had to thrive on drudgery. That's why PIs, contrary to the movies and the novels, were notoriously boring people.

Boring or not, I knew I didn't have that kind of mentality.

TWELVE

I got up, went to the kitchen, refilled my coffee mug. Henry wanted to go out, so I went out with him. I sipped my coffee at the picnic table and watched the chickadees at the feeders while Henry poked around.

After a while we went back inside. I went into my office and was looking over that list of numbers from Cassie's cell phone, wondering if I had the fortitude to start calling them, when the phone rang.

I picked it up, said hello, and a male voice said, "Is this Mr. Coyne?"

"Yes," I said. "Who's this?"

"James Hurley?" He made it a question.

"Yes, James. Sure. What's up?"

"I, um, wanted to apologize."

"Apologize," I said. "Why?"

"Why what?"

"Why do you bother to apologize?"

"I feel bad."

I said nothing.

"I was out of line the other day," he said. "It was stupid. I'm sorry."

"Okay," I said. "Apology not necessary, but accepted. Forget about it."

"I've got a bad temper," he said. "Sometimes it gets me in trouble."

I waited, and when he didn't say anything else, I said, "That's why you called? To apologize? That's it?"

"Mainly, yes." He cleared his throat. "I was wondering if you found out what happened to Cassie."

"You think something happened to her?"

"I didn't mean that. I just—"

"You're friendly with Cassie," I said. "Isn't that right?"

"Friendly." He hesitated. "What's that supposed to mean? Friendly."

She had your number in her cell phone, for one thing, I wanted to say. Except I didn't think that telling him I'd snatched Cassie's phone from her car was a good idea.

"Maybe I was mistaken," I said instead.

"No, no," he said. "Cassie and I get along pretty well. You could say we're friends. We were, anyway. I don't see much of her anymore."

I said nothing.

"Since she married my father, I mean."

"Why not?"

"It's awkward, that's all."

"Wait a minute," I said. "Are you saying that before she married your father, you and Cassie—?"

"Oh, jeez, no." He laughed quickly. "Nothing like that. We were just friends. I don't get along so well with him, that's all. My father."

"You mean since he married Cassie?"

"I don't like how he treats her."

"How does he treat her?"

"Look," said James Hurley. "It's none of my business. Yours,

132

either. She married him. She knew what she was getting into."

"Is your father abusive?"

"He doesn't beat her, if that's what you mean."

"But?"

I heard him blow a breath into the telephone. "Nothing. Forget I said anything, okay?"

"So what do you think happened to Cassie?" I said.

"I suppose she just had her fill of him, you know what I mean?"

"You think she left him?" I said.

"I don't think anything," he said. "I have no idea. It's just, the way he treated her, I wouldn't blame her."

"What about Rebecca?"

"My sister? What about her?"

"Where does she fit into the equation?"

"Becca gets along with everybody," he said. "She's pretty much preoccupied by her baby. She's kind of oblivious to everything else. Look, I've got to go."

"James," I said, "if you talk to Cassie, please tell her I need to speak with her. Tell her it's important. Ask her to call me."

"There's no reason I'd be talking to Cassie," he said.

"But if you do."

"Should I say what it's about?"

"It's about her father," I said.

"Really? Her father?"

"That's right," I said. "Why?"

"Oh, nothing," he said. "I was under the impression that Cassie didn't have any family left, that's all."

"What gave you that idea?"

"I don't know. I probably misunderstood."

"She has a father," I said, "and he wants to talk to her."

"Sure," he said. "Anyway, sorry about the other day. I didn't mean to scare you."

"I wasn't scared," I said.

After I hung up from talking with James Hurley, I called the hospital in Portland. When I told the nurse who answered at the ICU my name and asked about Uncle Moze, she told me he'd had "a good night," that he was "resting comfortably," and that his condition was "still serious, but stable."

No, I couldn't speak with him. He was heavily medicated. Yes, Dr. Drury had put me on their list and they had my number and would call me if there was any change.

Henry and I had lunch in the garden. Leftover pepperoni pizza, reheated in the toaster-oven, and iced coffee. Henry got the pizza crusts.

I sat there in the Adirondack chair, tilted my head back, and looked up at the sky. I thought about Uncle Moze, the taciturn old bird, secretive about his aneurysm, desperate to reconcile with Cassie. And now he'd had a heart attack. A bad one, it seemed.

And so I was feeling the urgency. I had to get in touch with Cassie, tell her about Uncle Moze.

I pushed myself to my feet, went into the kitchen, and put my plate and glass in the dishwasher. I looked at the clock. Almost two in the afternoon.

I headed for the front door.

Henry trailed behind me, looking hopeful.

"Not this time," I said to him. "You stay and guard the house. I'll be back in time to give you supper."

He lay down, put his chin on his paws, and watched me out of the tops of his eyes.

It was hard to leave him there. Dogs are at least as skilled as women at making a man feel guilty.

Cabot College was a small liberal-arts school bordering the Brookline Golf Course near Larz Anderson Park. I'd driven past it many times, but this was the first time I'd ever turned into the entrance and followed the long curving driveway between the rows of hundred-year-old beech and maple trees to the Greek Revival building that, according to the sign, housed Student Services.

The lawns were lush and freshly mown and utterly empty of poetry-reading and sunbathing and Frisbee-throwing summer-school students. In fact, the campus struck me as deserted. The only signs of life were the half dozen vehicles in the visitors' lot.

I parked there, went into the building, and followed the sound of a muffled voice to an open office door. I peeked in, and a pretty young woman—she might have been a student, she looked that young—peeked out at me. She was talking on the telephone, but she smiled and curled a finger at me.

I went in and stood far enough back from her desk to give her privacy. She looked me up and down as she talked on the phone. When she hung up, she leaned back in her chair and said, "Hi. Can I do something for you?"

"Can you tell me how to find Professor Webster's office?" I said.

"Sure. I doubt he'll be there, though."

"His office hours are two to four today, I thought. Monday, Wednesday, and Thursday. Today's Wednesday and it's, um"—I glanced at my watch—"it's a little after two."

"We're between sessions," she said. "We have two summer sessions. The first one ended last week, and the next one doesn't start 'til next week." She shrugged. "On the other hand, Professor Webster is very dedicated. I could call, see if he's there, save you a ten-minute walk, if you like."

"A ten-minute walk wouldn't hurt me," I said, "but thanks. That would be a help."

She pecked out a number on her phone, put it to her ear, and gazed up at the ceiling. Then she looked at me and said, "Professor

Webster? It's Mary Beth over at Student Services . . . Oh, fine. Quiet." She laughed softly at something he said. "Look, I have someone here for you." She nodded, put her hand over the receiver, and looked at me. "He wants to know who you are and what you want."

"Tell him my name is Brady Coyne and I'm a lawyer."

Mary Beth repeated that information for Webster, listened for a minute, then nodded, smiled, and said, "Okay. Sure. Thanks," and hung up.

She looked at me. "He says, that's what he gets for keeping office hours during break. Lawyers coming after him. Professor Webster's got a great sense of humor. Anyway, he's waiting for you. Come on. I'll show you how to find the English building."

I followed Mary Beth outside, and she pointed across a broad expanse of lawn to a brick building nestled among several other more-or-less identical brick buildings. "His office is on the second floor," she said. "Number 203. He's probably the only person in the entire building."

Less than ten minutes later I'd crossed the lawn, entered the English building, mounted a flight of stairs, and stopped outside the open door to room 203.

Grantham Webster—"Grannie"—was seated in a high-backed leather chair at his desk with his back to the doorway, pecking away at a desktop computer.

I stood in the doorway, cleared my throat, and said, "Professor Webster?"

He swiveled around. He had skin the color of dark maple syrup, short curly black hair with flecks of gray in it, and half-glasses perched down toward the tip of his nose. He was small and wiry. I guessed he was about my age. He was wearing a white shirt with the sleeves rolled up over his elbows and a striped necktie pulled loose at his throat.

136

He lowered his head and looked up at me over his glasses. "You're the lawyer?" he said.

I nodded. "Brady Coyne."

"I'm Grantham Webster." He turned back to his computer, ejected a CD from it, put it into a plastic case, and slid the case into a wire rack on his desk. Then he swiveled around, took off his glasses, stood up, and smiled. "Come on in. Tell me what I've done this time."

I went over and held out my hand. "Thanks for seeing me, Mr. Webster."

"Grannie," he said. "Everybody calls me Grannie." He shook my hand. His was long and bony. He had a firm, confident grip. He pointed to the wooden chair in front of his desk. "Have a seat."

I sat, and Webster resumed his seat in the high-backed chair across from me. His desk was a jumble of papers and books. There was one framed picture with its back to me, a mug with a college seal full of pens and pencils, and a green-shaded desk lamp. "I'm Cassie Crandall's cousin," I said.

He nodded as if he already knew that. "Cassie in trouble again?"

"I don't know," I said. "I can't seem to locate her."

He blew out a breath. "You've come to the wrong man, I'm afraid," he said. "I'm not with Cassie anymore. You should talk to her husband."

"I did. He doesn't seem to know where she is. Either that or he's not telling me. I've tried calling her. The mailbox in her cell phone is full. I'm a little concerned."

"Let's see," said Webster. "You're Cassie's cousin, and you're a lawyer. So which is the operative role here?"

"Cousin. Her father—my uncle—is in the hospital. He and Cassie have been out of touch. I want to put them back in touch."

"Out of touch, you say?"

I nodded.

"Hm," he said. "That's very odd. Cassie adores her father. Talked about him all the time. Old Moze. Raised her all by himself. He's a lobsterman." He smiled. "I guess you know that. Anyway, Cassie made a point of speaking with him on the telephone regularly. Every Sunday evening, no matter where she was, what she was doing, she'd give him a call. If they are, as you say, out of touch, that's most worrisome. I know she'd want to know that he's hospitalized."

"Do you think something could've happened to her?" I said.

"Sir," he said, "I have no idea what Cassie's up to these days. All I know is, we're together for nearly four years, and then one day she tells me she's decided to marry this dentist who's old enough to be her father. We were living together. Committed. Or at least, that's what I thought. She moved directly from my house to the dentist's house. Just like that. Hello, good-bye, have a nice life."

"That must've been a punch in the gut for you," I said.

He plucked his glasses off his nose and leaned toward me. "Nicely put," he said. "That's how it felt. I never saw it coming. A sucker punch." He lifted one hand, then let it fall on his desk. "But that's how it goes. You get over it. The earth keeps spinning. People are still starving in Ethiopia. What are you going to do?"

"If Cassie were to go away somewhere . . ."

"Leave the dentist, you mean?" He shook his head. "I don't—" A sudden buzz stopped him. He fumbled among the papers on his desk and came up with a cell phone. He glanced at its little screen, frowned, flipped it open, pressed it against his ear, and said, "What do you want?"

He gazed up at the ceiling as he listened. Then he said, "Wait. Stop. Hold on." He looked at me. "Give me a minute, okay? Close the door?"

I nodded, stood up, went out into the hallway, and shut the office door behind me. I leaned against the opposite wall, trying not to listen. From inside Webster's office I could hear the occasional murmur of his side of the conversation, though I couldn't distinguish his words. Mostly, it seemed that he was listening.

At one point his tone suddenly shifted, and his voice was louder, and I heard him say, "Forget it. It's not going to happen."

A few minutes later his door opened and he stuck his head out. "Sorry about that. Come on in."

He returned to his chair behind the desk. I sat where I'd been sitting.

"I've got an ex-wife," he said, as if that explained everything.

I nodded.

He picked up his cell phone, frowned at it, put it down, pushed it to the side. "Where were we?"

"I was asking you where you think Cassie might go if she decided to leave her husband."

"Cassie doesn't leave one thing unless she's got something else lined up," he said. "Cassie's never without options."

"You don't think she'd leave him?"

"That's not what I'm saying," he said. "But if she did, she'd have a plan."

"Well," I said, "where might she go?"

"Go? Anywhere. She's got friends all over the country. She has lots of friends. Cassie collects friends. Everybody loves her. She's one of those people, no matter how she treats you, you're always ready to forgive and forget and take her back."

"How about you?"

"What, forgive and forget? Take her back?"

I nodded.

He rolled his eyes. "You've got to be kidding."

"When was the last time you talked to her?"

"Not since she dumped me and moved in with the dentist. Over a year."

"She has your numbers in her cell phone," I said.

Webster cocked his head and narrowed his eyes at me. "What's that supposed to mean?"

"Generally the numbers you enter in your cell phone are the ones you call on a more or less regular basis."

"You think I'm lying to you?"

"The thought crossed my mind."

He frowned at me for a moment. Then he leaned back in his chair and laughed. "I like that," he said. "Straight from the shoulder. Pull no punches." He ran the palm of his hand over his face. "Okay, in the spirit of pulling no punches, you want to know what I think?"

I nodded.

"I think you should question the dentist as directly as you're questioning me here."

"Why?"

"I don't trust him," he said, "and I don't like him. I don't think he's a kind or loving man."

"You've met him, then."

"Only from what Cassie told me."

"But you think Hurley's capable of . . . ?"

He shook his head. "I don't know what he's capable of. Look. I'm completely prejudiced, I know. But I'm willing to bet he knows more than he's saying."

"I bet you're right," I said. "I bet you know more than you're saying, too."

Grantham Webster grinned. "I like that," he said. "Your candor, Mr. Coyne. Wonderful."

"Thanks," I said. "Does the name Faith Thurlow mean anything to you?"

140

He narrowed his eyes for a moment, then shook his head. "No. Should it?"

"It's Cassie's aunt," I said. "I wondered if Cassie has been in touch with her."

"As far as I know," he said, "not when I was with her. Aside from her father, she never had much to say about her family. For example, I didn't know she had a cousin who was a Boston lawyer. I don't recall her ever mentioning an aunt named Faith . . . what was it?"

"Thurlow," I said.

He spread his hands. "Look, Mr. Coyne. I don't know where Cassie is. What can I tell you?"

I shrugged. "Tell me about her."

He looked at me. "Sure," he said. "Why not." He leaned back and laced his fingers behind his neck. "Where to start? I was an adjunct professor in Boulder working on my PhD. Taught a creative-writing seminar in the continuing ed program. Cassie was a part-time student. Older than the others. Smarter, more . . . more worldly. She was a terrific writer. She had real stories to tell, stories she'd lived, and she wasn't afraid of spilling her guts out on the page." He smiled. "Not to mention, she was about the sexiest woman I ever laid eyes on." He waved a hand in the air. "You see where I'm going here."

"I think so," I said.

"I was totally smitten with her, I don't mind telling you. And she was . . ." He smiled. "We did things that . . . well, that could've wrecked my career. I didn't care. I figured she'd get sick of me sooner or later. When I got this appointment here"—he waved his hand around his office—"I asked Cassie if she'd come with me. I was shocked when she said yes. I mean, what's a woman like Cassandra Crandall want with someone like me?"

"Rhetorical question, I assume," I said.

"Poor-as-dirt untenured professor? Not to mention, an angry black man twelve years older'n her?"

"Are you angry?"

He smiled. "We live in a racist society, Mr. Coyne."

"I don't know about Cassie," I said. "But a lot of women would find those qualities irresistible."

He nodded. "She did. For a while, anyway. Turned out, I was just a step along the way for Cassie. She always had an agenda. Oh, I think she liked me well enough. But for the long term, you can't beat a rich white suburban dentist."

"You make her sound pretty cold."

"Oh, no. Not at all. Cassie's way more complicated than that. She loved her freedom, loved her wild times, and she and I, we did have a lot of fun. But she had a profound need for security, too. Money, family, status, stability. All that American Dream stuff. She wasn't ever going to have that with some scrawny middle-aged African American from the hills of western Carolina, an assistant professor at a little second-rate college who has to teach summer courses to keep up with his credit-card payments." He blew out a breath. "I worry about her. Cassie wants it all. She hasn't figured out, you can't have it all." He looked at me. "That's my story, Mr. Coyne."

"I'm sorry," I said.

He nodded and smiled. "She's special, that's for sure. I do miss her."

"Can you think of anything else?"

"Nothing that will help you track her down, if that's what you mean. I have no idea what's she's up to." He shrugged. "Never did."

"If you think of anything else, or if you hear from Cassie, would you give me a call?" I stood up and put one of my business cards on his desk.

He picked up my card, looked at it, then dropped it back on his desk. "I don't expect to hear from Cassie," he said. "But if I do . . ."

"Thanks." I held my hand across his desk.

He half stood to shake it.

"I guess I was lucky to catch you here," I said. "Mary Beth says you're very dedicated."

"Dedicated." He laughed quickly. "I should get a life, is the truth of it."

THIRTEEN

I left Cabot College and slid into the westbound lane on Route 9, bound for Madison. As I crept along with the rest of the afternoon traffic that was emptying the city, I pondered what Grantham Webster had said . . . and I wondered what he hadn't said. He'd made no effort to disguise his scorn for Richard Hurley. He was harder to read on the subject of Cassie. I was convinced that he knew more than he'd revealed to me.

Route 9, with traffic lights every quarter of a mile, was stop-and-go—a lot more stop than go—all the way to 128, and then in Waltham they'd closed down all but one northbound lane to rebuild an overpass.

Route 2, when I finally got there, was jammed all the way from Crosby's Corner to the Concord Rotary without any help from construction work.

I never could understand why they called it "rush hour."

By the time I pulled up in front of the police station in Madison, it was a little after five. I sat in my car for a few minutes, taking deep breaths, rotating my head on my stiff neck, and giving thanks that Evie and I lived in the city within walking distance of our offices.

145

The Madison police station was a dormered Cape Cod structure with weathered shingles, green shutters, window boxes, flower gardens, foundation plantings, and flagstone pathways. If you didn't notice the discreet sign in front and the two cruisers parked in the side lot, you'd mistake it for another suburban house, which was probably the whole point.

Immediately inside the front door there was a little enclosed lobby area with a bulletproof glass window. A gray-haired woman wearing a pink blouse and a pleasant smile sat behind the window like a ticket taker in her booth. I bent to the round vent at the bottom, gave her my name, and told her that I'd come to see Lieutenant Tony Hazen.

She nodded, spoke into a telephone, then looked up at me and said, "You can go on in, sir." The door beside her window buzzed. I turned the knob and stepped into a small waiting room furnished in oak and glass and stainless steel.

I looked at the Wanted posters that were thumbtacked to the corkboard, and a minute later a tall fortyish guy wearing chino pants and a green checked shirt appeared. He had thinning sand-colored hair and sharp blue eyes. "You're Coyne?" he said.

I nodded.

"Hazen," he said. "Your friend Horowitz asked me to cooperate with you. This way."

He led me down a short corridor to his office. He sat behind his standard-issue gray metal desk—its top was utterly bare except for a telephone and a computer—and I took the metal chair across from him. Behind him, a big window looked out on some woods.

"You're interested in Hurley on Church Street, Horowitz tells me," he said.

"Yes. His wife, really. Cassandra."

"Horowitz said you seem to think she's missing."

"Well," I said, "I don't know about missing. But she's not

home. Hasn't been for a couple weeks, anyway. Either her husband doesn't know where she is or he's keeping it a secret. I've tried calling, I've dropped by the house, I've left messages. It's got me worried."

"Worried how?"

"That something's happened to her."

"Such as . . . ?"

I shook my head.

"People travel," he said. "They visit relatives. They take vacations."

"It's him," I said. "Hurley. There's no reason he shouldn't tell me if Cassie's away visiting somebody or taking a vacation or something."

He shrugged. "Maybe he thought it was none of your business."

"Cassie's father—my uncle—has been trying to reach her. The voice-mail box on her cell phone is full."

"Like she stopped answering her phone, returning her calls."

"Yes."

"Hm," he said. "That's interesting. How do you know?"

"How do I know . . . ?"

"About her cell phone."

"Simple," I said. "I tried to call her."

He cocked his head, looked at me for a moment, then smiled. "Sure, okay. And why was it you said you wanted to talk to Mrs. Hurley?"

"Does it matter?"

He shrugged. "It might."

"Her father had a heart attack," I said. "It happened Monday morning. He's in the ICU at Maine Medical in Portland."

Hazen shrugged. "Okay. Let's take a look." He pecked on his computer keyboard for a minute, sat back and watched his monitor, and then looked up at me. "Well, this is interesting."

"What's that?"

"Two weeks ago yesterday Dr. Hurley reported a missing handgun."

I arched my eyebrows.

Hazen peered at his computer screen. "It's a Smith and Wesson thirty-eight. Chief's Special, two-inch barrel, stainless-steel finish. Current registration. Hurley has a license to carry."

"I have a Chief's Special," I said. "Mine has a three-inch barrel and a blue finish. I keep it in my office safe."

He nodded. "Common weapon. I don't know any chiefs who actually have one."

"So this one was stolen?"

"Missing." He smiled. "Most of the time it turns out that a missing gun has just been misplaced. It's in a lockbox, and the cleaning lady moves it. The wife doesn't like the looks of it, sticks it in the back of a closet or something. Hurley said he usually keeps it in a drawer in the bedroom. Madison has a lot of expensive homes. We have our share of burglaries. A lot of our citizens register handguns."

"He reported it when, did you say?"

"Fifteen days ago. But he said for all he knows it might've been missing for months. Claimed he never thinks about it, never had occasion to use it. Doesn't practice with it or anything."

I was thinking that Hurley could've decided to use his gun to kill Cassie. Report it missing, then shoot Cassie, then dump the gun. If it somehow turned up and ballistics linked it to Cassie, Hurley would claim that he couldn't have done it because he didn't have the gun.

Well, that was a pretty old trick, and I didn't mention it to Lieutenant Hazen. I assumed the same thought had occurred to him.

"What else do you have?" I said. "Horowitz mentioned there'd been some 911 calls from the Hurley address."

"Those go back quite a few years," he said. "Before the present Mrs. Hurley lived there."

"Can you tell me about them?"

"It's public record. The reports were published in the police blotter in the local paper at the time. You can go to the library, look 'em up."

I smiled. "Roger Horowitz a friend of yours?"

He peered at me. "We started out together at the academy. I didn't know him that well. He was pretty gung ho, I remember that. We went in opposite directions. Me, I like it safe and peaceful. You can't get any safer or peacefuller than Madison. Horowitz, he's easily bored. He's not happy unless he's tracking down dangerous killers." He shrugged. "He's a good cop. He was called in on a homicide we had out here a couple years ago. I had it figured all wrong. He saved my ass on that one."

"He's saved mine a few times, too," I said.

Hazen looked at me for a minute, then nodded and squinted at his monitor. "There've been, um, four 911 calls from that address on Church Street over the space of . . . nine years. First three, they were severe asthma attacks. Hurley's wife. His previous wife, I mean. Ellen Hurley. EMTs attended her at the scene, she was taken to the ER at Emerson Hospital, examined, treated, kept overnight, released the next day. The fourth time, she died before they got there."

"What did she die of?"

"Asthma."

"She died of an asthma attack?"

"Not that uncommon, I understand," he said. "I heard the other day, Massachusetts is the asthma capital of the nation. Something to do with the pollen."

"She didn't have medication?" I said.

"She did. She kept those whatchamacallits. . . ."

"Inhalers?"

"Yes. She kept them all over the house." He peered at his monitor. "This time? The time she didn't make it? It was April.

She was outdoors. Washing windows or something, had one of her attacks, didn't have an inhaler with her, fell off her stepladder. Dr. Hurley called it in when he got home from work, found her there on the ground. Hard to tell how long she'd been there." Hazen looked up at me. "You're thinking he had something to do with it?"

I nodded.

"I guess it's possible he did. No reason to think so at the time, though. At the time, it seemed like this woman had an asthma attack. Just the way it looked. When he called 911, Hurley said he found a pulse but she wasn't breathing. He did all the right things. Covered her, didn't try to move her, tried to get her to use an inhaler, gave her CPR. When the EMTs got there, they did whatever they do, but I guess it was too late."

"Was there an autopsy?" I said.

Hazen looked at his computer. "Yes. At the request of the next of kin."

"The husband?"

"Hurley. Right."

"Why?"

"Why what?" he said. "Why'd he request a PM?"

"It was obvious, wasn't it?" I said. "Another asthma attack, except this time she didn't make it?"

"You'd have to ask him about that, I guess."

I smiled. "Good idea."

Hazen leaned back in his chair, laced his fingers behind his head, and looked at me. "You seem to want to make something out of this."

"I'd rather not, actually."

"Most of the time," he said, "things are exactly what they appear to be, you know? They teach you that first day of cop school. Don't try to complicate something that's simple. Don't overlook the obvious. The commonest things most commonly happen. If it looks like a duck, quacks like a duck? Looks like the woman died of an asthma attack? Odds are good she died of an asthma attack."

"I'm just thinking," I said. "Two wives die, so he marries another one, and now she's . . . whatever. Missing."

"Sure." He smiled. "And the dentist murdered all three of 'em." He leaned forward, planted his elbows on his desk, and said, "Look, Mr. Coyne. You come up with something more than an unfounded suspicion that some crime has been committed in my little town here, you let me know, okay?"

"Okay," I said. "I'll definitely do that." I hesitated. "What about James Hurley?"

"What about him?"

"Do you have anything on him in your computer?"

"Horowitz didn't say anything about James Hurley."

"I'm asking."

Hazen sighed, pecked at his keyboard, then frowned at his monitor. "Don't see how this is relevant."

I shrugged.

"Okay," he said. "There were a couple of juvie things. They're sealed. And, um, a DUI two years ago. Resisted arrest." He looked up at me. "Gave the officer a shove, used abusive language. Lost his license for six months. Five years' probation. That's it."

"Do you know him?" I said.

"Sure. It's a small town. He's not a bad kid. Immature, quick-tempered, that's all. He'll be fine." Hazen glanced pointedly at his watch. "Any other citizens I can help you out with?"

"No, that's fine." I stood up and reached my hand across his desk. "Thanks for your time."

He shook my hand without standing. "I meant what I said. You learn anything, you let me know."

"Sure," I said. "I will."

"You can find your way out okay?"

I nodded. "Don't get up."

He smiled and waved. "I wasn't planning to."

From the Madison police station I headed back to the town common and turned onto Church Street. I slowed down as I approached Hurley's house. His Lexus was not parked in front of the garage, but his daughter Rebecca's Chevy sedan was.

Cassie's red Saab hadn't moved.

I turned into the driveway, parked beside the Chevy, and went to the front door. The screen door was closed, but the inside door was open.

I rang the bell.

"Just a minute," came Rebecca's voice from the bowels of the house.

A minute later she appeared on the other side of the screen. She was wearing jeans and a T-shirt, no makeup, bare feet. She was wiping her hands on a dish towel. She blinked at me, then smiled. "Oh, hi. What's up? Cassie's not here."

"I was actually hoping to speak with your father."

"He's not home yet," she said. "He has late appointments on Wednesday evenings. Some of his patients can't get away during the day, you know?"

"That's very flexible of him," I said. "Maybe you—"

She held up her hand. "Hang on a sec." She darted away.

She was back a minute later with her baby in her arms. "Sorry about that," she said. "What were we saying?"

"I was just hoping—"

"Look," she said. "Why don't you come on in. I've got dinner in the oven and a hungry baby here."

"Really," I said. "That's all right. I'll come back another time."

"No, no," she said, "come in." She smiled and nodded, then

reached out with her free hand and clicked the lock on the inside of the screen door.

I pulled it open, stepped into the dim coolness inside, and followed Becca Hurley through the living room into a big country kitchen. It had skylights and exposed beams and hardwood floors and stainless-steel appliances. Copper-bottomed cookware and bunches of dried herbs and braids of garlic hung from the beams. The back wall was all window.

She gestured at the kitchen table by the window. "Have a seat." She slid the baby into a high chair and dropped a small handful of Cheerios on the tray.

I sat, and she sat across from me. The aroma of roasting lamb and garlic was in the air. A small television on the counter was reporting the news. "Something smells good," I said. "Your father's a lucky man to have you to cook for him."

"Oh, usually I don't. But since Cassie . . ."

"You're staying here while she's . . . away?"

She gave me a quick frown, as if I'd said something unbelievably stupid. "Danny and I have our own little place in Westford. It's close by."

I noticed that Becca was wearing a wedding ring. "What about Danny's dad?"

She smiled. "He's in the Middle East right now. He's a reporter. He's always overseas." She shook her head. "Wherever there's danger, that's where he wants to be. I keep telling him, now that he's a daddy . . ."

"That's got to be hard," I said.

She nodded. "It is. Danny's hardly even seen him. But it's not as if I didn't know what it was going to be like. So it's nice to have family close by, you know?"

"Like your brother?" I said.

"James?" She flapped one hand in the air, apparently dismissing James. "I hardly see him. Once in a while I run into him

153

here. Like the other day when you were here. He's got his own life now. He's got an apartment in Chelmsford."

"Since when?"

"Since Cassie moved in. Is that what you mean?"

I nodded. "Was that his idea?"

"What, moving out, getting his own place?"

I nodded.

"Why are you asking?"

I shrugged. "No particular reason."

Becca smiled. "James pretty much lost his cool the other day when you were here."

"He apologized. Not a problem."

"He thought you were harassing our father."

"I suppose I was."

"Well," she said, "I think it was just a mutual thing. Him moving out. Cassie made it pretty clear that she was uncomfortable with him."

"And your father went along with that?"

"What Cassie wants, Cassie gets." Becca frowned. "I'm sorry. I forget my manners. Can I get you an iced tea or something?"

"Sure," I said. "Iced tea would hit the spot."

She went over to the refrigerator. "You're still trying to catch up with her, huh?" she said over her shoulder.

"I am," I said. "I'm concerned. I've been talking to everybody I can think of."

"Oh, I'm sure she's fine." She was pouring from a pitcher into a tall glass filled with ice cubes. "Cassie can take care of herself."

"You don't have any idea where she might be, do you?"

"Me?" She smiled. "Not a clue." She muted the TV, then came over and put the glass of iced tea in front of me. She sat across from me, picked up a Cheerio off the baby's tray and put it into his mouth.

154

"Your father doesn't seem to know anything about his wife, either," I said.

"I try to keep my nose out of my father's marriages," she said. "So who've you been talking to? Besides Daddy, I mean."

"And you," I said.

"Right." She smiled. "And me."

"Well," I said, "her former boyfriend, for one."

She frowned. "He was a, um, black man, wasn't he?"

"Yes. Do you know him?"

She shook her head. "Cassie mentioned him a couple times. He's a college professor, I think. I always wondered if she still had a thing for him."

"After marrying your father, you mean?"

"I guess I was just feeling overly protective. You know, being suspicious of my daddy's pretty new wife." She popped another Cheerio into Danny's mouth. "It's not that I think Cassie was being unfaithful or something."

"I wondered about that," I said. "I just came from the Madison police station."

She frowned at me. "The police?"

I nodded.

"Wow," she said. "You really are worried, huh?"

"I am," I said.

"You think something . . . ?"

"I don't know what to think." I took a long gulp of the iced tea. "So your father. How's he dealing with it? With Cassie being gone?"

"Oh," she said, "I don't think I should talk about anything like that. That's pretty personal. You'll have to talk to him."

"I'm sorry," I said. "I suppose you're right. What about you?"

"Me?" She shook her head. "It's upsetting to me because it's upsetting to him. It's none of my business, really, except I want my father to be happy." She put her elbows on the table and her chin on her elbows, and she leaned toward me. "So how come you're doing all this?"

"Looking for Cassie, you mean?"

She nodded.

"Her father's in the hospital. I want her to know about it."

"What's wrong?"

"Heart attack," I said.

"I'm sorry," she said. "Cassie's your cousin, so, um, he's your uncle, right?"

"Yes. He's in pretty bad shape. Keeps asking for Cassie."

"Is he gonna make it?"

"They think so. He's still in the ICU."

"Well," she said, "I hope he's okay."

I drained my glass of iced tea. "When do you expect your father?"

"Well, like I told you, he works late on Wednesdays. He should be here around eight."

"And he's going to have a nice lamb roast waiting for him," I said. "Lucky guy."

"Oh, he's a good old dad," she said. "And with his wife not here . . ." She waved her hand in the air. "Who wants to get home after spending ten hours inside people's mouths and have to open a can?"

I looked at my watch. It was a little after six. I pushed myself back from the table and stood up. "Tell your father I dropped by and I'd appreciate it if he'd give me a call, would you?"

"Sure. Of course." She started to stand up.

I held up my hand. "Relax. I can find my way out. Thanks for the iced tea."

"Any time," she said. "Good luck with Cassie."

"Thank you." I picked up a Cheerio from Danny's tray and held it up so he could see it.

He looked at it cross-eyed, and I flashed on my two boys back when they were infants in high chairs. Two or three lifetimes ago. They were men now.

Danny opened his mouth. I dropped the Cheerio on his tongue. He gummed it, swallowed, then laughed.

I turned to leave.

"I hope your uncle's going to be okay," said Becca.

"Thank you."

She followed me to the front door and held it for me. "If I hear anything about Cassie or something," she said, "I'll let you know."

"That would be great," I said.

I went out to my car, and as I backed out of the Hurley driveway, I saw that Becca had stepped out onto the porch. She was smiling and waving at me.

FOURTEEN

After I pulled into the traffic on 128 I took out my cell phone and called Evie at home.

She picked up after several rings.

"It's me, babe. On my way home."

"Oh, good. Where are you?"

"In Lexington. I should be there in half an hour. Just wanted you to know."

"I picked up a couple of nice ribeyes at Deluca's," she said. "If you'll grill 'em, I'll bake the potatoes and throw together the salad."

"Sounds great," I said. "Gin and tonics first, though, huh?"

"Goes without saying." She hesitated. "Is everything okay?"

"Yep. You?"

"Oh, sure," she said. "Everything's great."

I rubbed the steaks with kosher salt and fresh-ground pepper and grilled them over mesquite charcoal outside, aiming for medium-rare. While the steaks sizzled, Evie and I sipped our gin and tonics. I asked her how things were at work.

She said, "Busy," and waved her hand in the air. She really didn't want to talk about it, she said.

She asked about Uncle Moze and Cassie. I told her about my conversations with Grantham Webster and Lieutenant Tony Hazen and Rebecca Hurley, and Evie watched my face and nodded . . . and I had the profound impression that she hadn't heard a word I'd said.

We ate at the picnic table in the garden. I'd learned to love ribeyes above all other cuts of beef on a weeklong fishing trip in Montana many years ago. Henry loved ribeyes, too. There's a lot of fat on a good hunk of ribeye. Henry got the fat. Cholesterol didn't worry him.

By the time we finished eating, night had fallen and our little walled-in garden was awash in moon- and starlight.

"How about another drink?" I said to Evie.

"No, I don't think so," she said.

"Ah, come on," I said. "Here we are, just the two of us—well, Henry counts, making it three—here we are, a beautiful summer's night, stars and moon and all. Let's have a brandy or something."

"I don't want a drink," she said. "Thanks anyway." She stood up. "I need a bath." She turned and headed for the back door. Then she stopped. "There's a message for you in our voicemail. I meant to tell you earlier."

"Who's it from?" I said.

"A man calling himself Grannie," she said, and she went into the house.

I went in, found the phone, and got our voicemail. One message. I clicked to hear it.

"Mr. Coyne," he said, "it's Grannie. Grantham Webster. I am wondering if you could meet me tomorrow at four o'clock in my office. That's Thursday afternoon. I think I might have something to report to you. No need to confirm. I'll be there anyway."

I went into my office and dialed the two numbers for Grannie on my list from Cassie's cell phone. No answer at either his cell or his office. I left no message. He'd be there at four, and so would I.

At nine o'clock on Thursday morning I called the hospital. Uncle Moze was still "stable" and "doing as well as could be expected" and "resting comfortably" and, no, he wasn't able to talk on the telephone yet. I couldn't persuade the nurse to elaborate on her platitudes, nor could she tell me when they might move him out of the ICU. I asked her to have Dr. Drury give me a call, and she promised to give him my message, though she didn't promise that he'd actually call.

I walked out my front door about nine thirty, headed for my office. I was about halfway down Mount Vernon Street when someone came up behind me and grabbed hard onto my left arm, just above the elbow.

I whirled around. My right fist was clenched, and I was about to take a swing at him when I saw that it was James Hurley.

"Let go of my arm," I said.

He let go and held both hands up in the air. "Sorry," he said.

"What the hell do you think you're doing?"

"I want to talk to you," he said.

"So you sneak up behind me and grab me?"

"Shit," he said. "I'm sorry. I did it again. I just wanted to talk to you." He shrugged. "But I heard you've been asking questions about me, and I don't like that. It makes me a little mad."

"What are you talking about?"

"Tony Hazen. The cop. You were asking him about me."

I looked James Hurley up and down. "You want a cup of coffee?"

"Huh?" Then he smiled. "Sure. Why not."

We walked down to the Starbucks on the corner of Charles and Beacon. James ordered some kind of fancy brew with froth on top. I got black coffee, house blend. We took our cups across the street to the Common and found a bench.

"I didn't go to Tony Hazen to ask about you," I told him. "I was asking about your father."

"I heard it was about me."

"How'd you hear that?"

He shrugged. "It's a small town. I got friends on the force."

"Well," I said, "your name did come up. I learned some things about your family."

"What business is it of yours?"

"I'm just trying to find Cassie," I said. "She's my cousin, and she's your stepmother. So you might say we're all family."

He laughed. "What did you find out?"

"Your mother died," I said. Howard Litchfield was actually the one who told me that, but I didn't want to bring him into it. "Then your stepmother died, too."

He looked out over the common. The angled morning sunlight filtered down through the trees, spreading patches of light and shadow on the grass. "What's that got to do with Cassie?" James said.

"I don't know."

"It's really none of your business," he said. "What happened to my mother."

"It must have been rough on you and your sister."

"More for her than me," he said. "I was pretty young when our mother died. It didn't really hit me the way it did Becca. I was sad about Ellen, but, you know, she wasn't really our mother. Becca took it pretty hard."

"Ellen's death, you mean?"

162

"Both of them."

"She seems to be doing pretty well now," I said. "She's got her baby and her husband, and now that Cassie's gone, she's got her father to take care of."

James laughed.

"What's so funny?"

"Becca doesn't have any husband," he said.

"She said—"

"What, the foreign correspondent? The brave globe-trotting reporter who travels from one war zone to another writing prizewinning stories? Is that what she told you?"

I nodded. "Something like that."

"Look," he said, "Becca doesn't even know who Danny's father is."

"None of my business," I said.

"I agree," he said. "Just, her stories, you know?"

"Well," I said, "I guess you can't blame her for lying about that to a stranger." I drained my coffee cup. "Was there anything else you wanted? Because I'm going to be late for work if I don't get going."

James Hurley shrugged. "I just wondered what you were doing, talking to the police."

"Why? You got something to hide?"

He shook his head. "Nope. Nothing that they don't know. I just don't like people snooping around my family." He smiled. "But like you say, you're sort of family, too."

"I'm just trying to track down Cassie," I said. "It had nothing to do with you."

He nodded. "If I hear anything, I'll let you know."

We stood up and shook hands. Then he started down the pathway leading to the Park Street T station, and I turned and headed in the opposite direction, to Copley Square.

When I got to the office, Julie said that Evie had called. Her message was that she loved me, she was sorry for being so grouchy lately, and she'd made reservations for dinner tonight, eight o'clock.

"Nola's," she said. "She's taking you to Nola's."

"It's in the North End," I said. "Italian place."

"I know. Isn't that nice, Evie making the reservation like that? Saying she's sorry?"

"It is nice," I said. "It makes me happy."

Julie was smiling expectantly. She liked to see me happy, and she liked knowing that my relationship with Evie was harmonious.

But mainly, Julie wanted me to tell her what it was exactly that Evie was sorry about.

I would've told her if I'd known.

Lieutenant Horowitz had also called, Julie said, asked what my schedule was for the day, and then insisted that she schedule me for lunch with him at Marie's for twelve fifteen. It was, he'd said, a matter of extreme urgency.

Julie said she knew Horowitz better than to believe what she called his "extreme-urgency bullshit" and that we had a law practice here.

I told her that he was just collecting a debt, and anyway, Roger Horowitz was not the kind of guy who lingered over lunch no matter who was buying, but after lunch I had an appointment and wouldn't be back to the office, so she might as well take the afternoon off.

Julie opened her mouth, then closed it. She nodded. "Okay," she said. "I will."

When I got to Marie's, I looked around the crowded dining room and saw an arm wave from a booth in back. I went over and slid in across from Horowitz. He was talking on his cell phone. He held up a finger at me, mumbled something into the phone, then clicked it off and stuck it in his jacket pocket.

He craned his neck and looked around, and Sophie, our regular waitress, a dark-eyed business management major at Northeastern, appeared almost instantly at our table. "Ready to order now, guys?"

Horowitz, of course, ordered the lobster ravioli. I asked for a spinach salad.

When Sophie left, Horowitz said, "Spinach salad? You turning into some kind of vegetarian freak?"

I shrugged. "I grilled ribeyes last night, for your information. I happen to like spinach salad. Besides, it's got bacon in it."

He shook his head. "Since Evie came along," he said, "I hardly know you."

"Same old me," I said. "Maybe marginally healthier."

"Yeah," he said, "and all settled down, verging on henpecked. You still go fishing whenever you want?"

"I never went fishing whenever I wanted. I want to go fishing all the time. And I'm not henpecked."

Sophie put a basket of bread on our table. Horowitz fished out a slice, ripped it in half, poured a little olive oil on his bread plate, swabbed the bread in it, and stuffed it into his mouth.

I broke off a piece of bread and dipped it in oil for myself. The oil had rosemary and another herb I couldn't identify in it. I decided I could make a meal on Marie's bread and oil.

We talked about the Red Sox until Sophie brought Horowitz's lobster ravioli and my spinach salad. We ate in silence for a few minutes.

Then between bites Horowitz said, "You know your cousin is the dentist's third wife?"

I nodded. "The previous one died of an asthma attack. He had another one before her who was the mother of his two kids."

"Hazen told you about the second one, died in Madison, huh?"

"Yes. I got the details. Hazen was very cooperative."

"He was?"

I smiled. "He was okay. Answered my questions. He seems to respect you."

"You don't know what happened to the first wife?"

"She died, too. Hurley has bad luck with wives."

He shook his head. "The first wife committed suicide. Hazen didn't tell you that?"

"No, he didn't. Suicide, huh?"

Horowitz consulted his sheet of notes. "Hurley and his family were living in Arlington at the time. This was back in eighty-four. One Tuesday morning in October after the dentist went off to work and the kids left on the school bus, the wife—her name was Loretta—she closed the garage door, started up her soccer-mom van, sat behind the wheel, and swallowed half a bottle of Valium. The daughter—Rebecca—she found her mother when she got home from school. Called her father. Hurley. The dentist. He went home, then called the cops."

"There was an investigation, of course," I said.

"We investigate all suicides," he said. "As you know."

"And?"

"And the ME signed off on it. No question it was a suicide."

"Was there a note?"

"Yep."

"What'd it say?"

He shrugged. "I don't have those kinds of details, Coyne."

"So you don't know why she did it?"

"Why do most people?"

"Most people don't," I said.

He smiled. "Depression. Despair. What I understand from reading the studies, it's more what's inside their heads than what's going on in their lives. Bad brain chemistry. Almost anything can set it off."

"I'd like to know what set off Loretta Hurley."

"Too late to ask her," he said.

Sophie cleared away our plates and brought our coffee. We declined dessert.

"So Hurley's had three wives," I said, "and two of them are dead."

Horowitz looked at me.

"At least two," I said.

"I didn't say that," he said.

FIFTEEN

I walked home from Marie's through the heavy smoggy city air, and by the time I got there I was drenched in sweat. Henry feigned indifference to my arrival until I fished a Milk-Bone out of the box in the kitchen cabinet. Then he ambled over and sat in front of me and gazed up at me with adoring eyes.

I opened the back door, and Henry took his Milk-Bone out to the garden. Then I climbed out of my law-office suit, showered, and put on my college-campus outfit—chino pants, light cotton shirt, sneakers.

By now it was quarter of three. My appointment with Grannie Webster was at four. I figured by the time I walked down Charles Street to the parking garage, picked up my car, and navigated the midweek, midafternoon city traffic, it could take close to an hour to get to Cabot College in Brookline. It was only over on the other side of the city, but there were no shortcuts to Brookline. No matter how you went, there were traffic lights and taxicabs and delivery trucks and commuting automobiles evacuating the city.

I snagged a bottle of water from the refrigerator and went out back. Henry was lying on the cool flagstones in the shade of the picnic table, watching a downy woodpecker hammer at the suet feeder.

"You want to come with me?" I said to him.

His raised his head and perked up his ears and stared at me, as if he couldn't quite believe what he'd heard.

"Come on," I said. "Let's go."

He didn't hesitate. He scrambled to his feet, trotted to the back door, and pushed at it with his nose.

I didn't know if Grantham Webster liked dogs. But I was pretty sure he'd like Henry.

I overestimated the time it would take to get there. Typical. I've squandered many weeks of my life sitting in my car waiting for the time of an appointment to arrive because, to be on the safe side, I'd given myself an extra fifteen or twenty minutes that I didn't need just in case I had a flat tire or ran into a detour.

I pulled into the visitors' parking lot next to the Student Services building at Cabot College a little after three thirty. The campus, if anything, appeared more deserted than it had been the previous day. This time there were just two other cars in the lot.

I let Henry out and told him he could run around if he wanted provided he stayed close and came when I called him. He gave me his look that meant "You got it, boss," and proceeded to squirt on every shrub and tree trunk he could find.

I followed the diagonal pathway across the rolling green lawn to the building that housed the Cabot College English Department, and when I got there I called Henry in and told him to heel.

The English building, like the rest of the campus, was hushed and apparently deserted. We climbed the stairs to the second floor and turned down the corridor to Webster's office.

His door was half open, and I could see that he was seated in his high-backed desk chair facing his computer with his back to the doorway, just as he had been the first time I was there.

I rapped lightly on the door and said, "Mr. Webster? Grannie? I know I'm early. If you're busy, I can wait."

I noticed that the computer screen that he was looking at was blank. Odd.

I pushed the door open, stepped in, and said, "Hey, Grannie, are you okay? I can—"

And that's when, more or less simultaneously, Henry growled, I sensed a movement beside me, something hard smashed against the back of my skull, a sudden piston of fiery pain slammed through my brain and into my eyes, and Henry yelped. The room swirled around me, and I stumbled and fell forward, and I banged my forehead against something hard on the way down.

Behind my eyes a white light flashed with the suddenness of an explosion, followed instantly by a sharp, jarring, echoing pain in the center of my brain. Then the light dimmed into a kind of pink afterglow, and my brain turned to cottony fuzz.

My cheek lay on the scratchy carpet. I didn't want to breathe. I knew it would hurt too much.

I was aware of movement near me. Then something hard pressed against the back of my head. I wanted to pull away from it, but I had no will to move.

I heard the unmistakable snick of a revolver's hammer being cocked next to my ear.

I could only wait.

Then the pressure of the gun barrel went away.

A minute later I heard the door close.

The next thing I knew I was lying facedown on the carpet with both the front and the back of my head throbbing and Henry licking my cheek.

I touched my forehead. My hand came away with blood on it.

I pushed myself onto my hands and knees, tried to shake the dizziness out of my head, and crawled over so I could sit back against the wall. I closed my eyes against the pounding pain in my head, and when I did, my stomach churned. I opened my eyes and forced them to focus on a painting on the wall. I took a deep breath and swallowed back the bile that kept surging up in my throat.

Henry lay down beside me and plopped his chin on my lap. He looked up at me with worried eyes. I patted his head and he turned up his face to lick my hand.

I noticed that the wooden chair in front of the desk had tipped over onto its side. That, I guessed, was what I'd hit when I fell forward.

I wondered, vaguely, how Grannie Webster had moved so fast from behind his desk that he could whack me on the head when I stepped into his office. Come to think of it, why would he want to hit me? And why hadn't he pulled the trigger when he had his gun pressed against my head? Okay, I was early for our appointment, but . . .

I wasn't thinking straight, I realized that.

Then I noticed that Webster was still sitting in his chair looking at his blank computer screen.

I pushed myself to my feet. My head began to spin. I took a gulp of air and steadied myself against the wall until the dizziness passed. Then I went around the desk to where Webster was seated.

He was slouched in his chair with his chin on his chest. A splotch of red the size of a tea saucer glistened on the front of his shirt.

Oh, shit.

I knelt in front of him. His eyes were open and unblinking. I pressed two fingers against the side of his neck. There was no pulse.

172

I touched the blood on his shirt with my fingertip. It came away wet.

My head still throbbed, but my mind, suddenly, was very clear.

I fished my handkerchief from my pocket, used it to pick up Webster's desk phone, and called 911. When the woman answered, I said, "My name is Brady Coyne. I'm at Cabot College. The English department building, second floor, office number 203. A man is dead. Grantham Webster's his name. He's a professor here."

"Are you sure he's dead?"

"He was shot in the chest. I couldn't find a pulse. His eyes are open. I've seen dead people before."

"Okay, sir," she said. "You wait there, please. Don't touch anything. This is an office, you say?"

"That's right."

"Wait outside in the hallway, then. Somebody will be there right away."

"This happened recently," I said. "The blood is still wet."

"Right," she said. "Sit tight."

I replaced the phone on its cradle and went out to the hallway. Henry followed behind me. I noticed that he was favoring his left hind leg. I sat on the floor with my back against the wall, and Henry sat beside me. I moved my fingers over his left leg and hip, and when I touched a spot on his upper joint, he flinched and yelped. There was a little swelling there. I prodded around gently. Henry looked at me and whined, then turned his head and licked my hand where I was touching him.

The son of a bitch must have kicked Henry. Hit me on the head, okay. Fair enough. But you better not kick my dog.

I fished out my cell phone and dialed the secret number that Roger Horowitz had given me. It was his cell phone number, and he'd admonished me to use it only in emergencies. He'd made it clear that it was a great honor and privilege to be made privy to this special phone number, and I better not abuse it.

He answered with a growl. "What?"

"It's Coyne," I said. "Got a homicide for you. Guy was shot in the chest, and not very long ago."

"Where are you?"

"Cabot College. It's in Brookline. English Department building, second floor. I called 911 already. Guy's name is Grantham Webster. Cassie Crandall's ex-boyfriend. I had an appointment with him at four. He said he expected to have some news for me. I got here early, and he was dead when I got here. Whoever did it was still here. Whacked me on the head and kicked Henry and thought about shooting me but didn't. He got away."

"He kicked Henry?"

"Yeah."

"Bastard," muttered Horowitz. "Don't suppose you saw who it was, huh?"

"Sorry. I didn't see anything."

"How long ago did this happen?"

I looked at my watch. It was ten after four. "Fifteen, twenty minutes ago."

"It took that long for you to call it in?"

"I was out for a minute. Then I was, um, groggy. Disoriented. Still am a little."

"Well, shit," he said.

He was thinking that in fifteen or twenty minutes, whoever had shot Grannie and hit me would be long gone.

"I'm okay," I said. "Thanks for asking."

"Yeah, good," said Horowitz. "If the local cops get there before me, just tell 'em what happened and they should wait for me. I'm on my way."

As it turned out, three or four uniformed Brookline cops plus a middle-aged woman with an automatic weapon holstered on her hip and a badge on her belt, who I assumed was a local detective; two EMTs pushing a collapsible gurney; Roger Horowitz and Marcia Benetti, his partner; and two people from the medical examiner's office all arrived at the same time about ten minutes later—a dozen or so people hustling down the narrow carpeted corridor.

They all stopped outside Webster's office door where Henry and I were sitting. Everyone looked at Horowitz. This was a homicide, and the state police were in charge.

He took one look at me and said, "Somebody attend to this man."

One of the EMTs, a Will Smith look-alike who told me his name was Arthur, knelt beside me, took my blood pressure, listened to my heart and lungs, shone a miniature flashlight in my eyes, asked me my name and what day it was and who was the current president of the United States. He swabbed the wound on the back of my head and the gash on my forehead with something that stung like hell, then bandaged both places.

"You've got a hard head, sir," said Arthur.

"Yes," I said. "People keep telling me that."

He smiled. "How do you feel?"

"Not that bad. A little dizzy. My head hurts."

He nodded. "You got a couple nice bumps. How'd you manage to get two bumps, if you don't mind me asking?"

"I don't mind," I said. "Somebody hit me on the back of the head. I fell forward and I guess I smashed my forehead on the chair or the desk or something."

"They bled quite a bit," said Arthur. "I put some butterflies on the one on your forehead. You'll probably end up with a scar. You might want to get stitches."

I touched my forehead. A bandage ran from my hairline diagonally down toward my left eye. "I guess it'll be all right," I said.

"I don't think you got a concussion," he said. "Still, wouldn't be a bad idea to get you to the hospital."

"No hospital," I said. "I'm fine."

The EMT shrugged. "Up to you," he said. He looked at Henry. "Your dog okay?"

"I think he got kicked," I said. "Left hind leg, up on his hip."

He scratched Henry's forehead. "How you doin', poochie?"

"His name's Henry," I said. "He doesn't like being called a pooch. He's a purebred Brittany."

"Sorry." Arthur fingered Henry's leg, which elicited a soft whine, then looked up at me. "Just a contusion, I'd say. I'm no vet, but I don't think anything's broken. When you get home, give him an aspirin." He patted Henry's head, stood up, and smiled. "You'll want some aspirin, too." Then he turned and went into Webster's office.

A minute later Marcia Benetti came out of the office and scooched down beside me. "Roger wants me to babysit you until he's ready to talk to you."

"I don't need babysitting," I said. "I'm not going anywhere."

She cocked her head and frowned at me. "Listen, are you okay?"

"Me? Sure. I'm fine."

"You don't look so good."

"Yeah," I said. "People tell me that all the time."

The team from the ME's office, a paunchy man wearing a short-sleeved white shirt and a younger Asian woman with two cameras around her neck, were waiting outside the office door. Horowitz and the Brookline officer were inside with the EMTs.

The uniformed local cops, I assumed, had been dispersed to search the building and to secure the perimeter of the crime scene.

A short time later, the EMTs came out of the office. Horowitz poked his head out and said something to the ME and his partner, and they went inside.

The EMTs headed down the corridor and disappeared around the corner. Going outside for a smoke, maybe.

"You've been with Horowitz how long now?" I said to Benetti.

"Five and a half years," she said.

"That has to be a record for him."

She smiled. "He's a grouchy bastard, but he's the best. We get along. We've worked it out."

Flashbulbs were going off in Grantham Webster's office. Marcia Benetti sat on the floor beside me. Henry slept between us. She absentmindedly stroked his back.

After a while the ME and his partner came out of the office and went down the corridor.

Then the EMTs returned. They went into the office.

They came out a few minutes later with a plastic body bag on their gurney. They pushed it down the hallway. One of the wheels squeaked, and I could hear it even after they turned the corner and disappeared.

Sixteen

Horowitz and the female Brookline officer came over to where Marcia Benetti and I were sitting against the wall. Horowitz squatted down in front of me. The officer remained standing.

"This is Detective Cohler, Brookline PD," Horowitz said, jerking his head at her.

I looked up at her. She was, I guessed, around forty. She had dark curly hair, cut short, an angular face, and thin, cynical lips. "Nice to meet you," I said.

"Me, too." She held out her hand and smiled quickly. It was a pleasant smile.

I shook her hand.

Horowitz jabbed my arm with his forefinger. "You don't have any idea who did this?"

"No."

"You didn't see anything?"

I shook my head.

"He's black," said Horowitz. "The vic."

"African American," I said.

"Right," he said. "So how'd your uncle feel about his daughter dating a black man?"

"My uncle?"

He nodded. "Ignorant Maine lobsterman, right?"

"Less ignorant than you might think," I said. "Anyway, Uncle Moze told me he never met Webster. He wanted to, but Cassie kept putting it off. I don't think Moze had any idea what color his skin was."

"As if Cassie thought he'd be upset if he knew?"

I shrugged. "Maybe."

"You believe him?" said Horowitz. "Your uncle?"

"Sure I do," I said. "It's irrelevant, anyway. My uncle's in the hospital. I kinda doubt that he snuck down here in his hospital johnny and did this."

"Sure. Okay." Horowitz sighed. "Start at the beginning, then. Bring us up to the time when you poked your head in there and got it whacked."

"You know some of it already."

"That's okay," he said. "I want Detective Cohler and Marcia to hear it, too."

I started with my visit to Uncle Moze the previous Saturday. I told them how Moze had apparently been punched in the chest and how he was hospitalized with a heart attack. I recounted my return to his house with Charlene Staples, the Moulton police officer. I told them about my two trips to Madison, about my encounter with Dr. Richard Hurley, about how I filched Cassie's cell phone from her car, about Howard Litchfield and what he might have seen, about Hurley's children Becca and James, about the deaths of his two previous wives. I told him about my two visits with Grantham Webster.

In other words, I told them everything I could think of.

Horowitz didn't interrupt. Benetti was taking notes. Cohler was staring down at the floor. I had the sense that she would remember every word I said.

180

When I was done, each of them asked me some questions, either to clarify or to elaborate on something I'd said.

Then Horowitz said, "Okay, Coyne. You didn't see anything. But I bet you got a theory."

I shrugged. "Hurley's the obvious one."

"Because you don't like him?"

I smiled. "Not just that. Cassie's missing. He didn't report it. He's the spouse. Grannie Webster was her old boyfriend." I paused. "Besides, Hurley owns a handgun."

Horowitz's eyebrows shot up. "Huh?"

"Your friend Hazen," I said, "the Madison cop, he told me that a couple weeks ago—which would be sometime around when Cassie disappeared—Hurley reported his gun was missing. It's a Smith and Wesson Chief's Special. Thirty-eight."

"Missing," he said.

"Convenient, huh? Report your gun missing before you go shoot somebody with it. Then throw it in the river."

"An old trick," said Cohler. "A staple on TV cop shows."

"The one he held against my head was a revolver," I said. "He cocked the hammer right next to my ear."

Horowitz and Benetti exchanged glances. "There's another obvious suspect," he said.

"I know," I said. "Cassie."

He nodded. "Say she took the gun."

"If she's even alive," I said. "And assuming you can conjure up a motive for her to kill Grannie."

"She and Webster were together," Horowitz said. "Then they split. There's a motive in there somewhere."

"You think Cassie's the one who punched her father, too?" I said.

"That Maine cop you talked to seems to think so, huh?" He

shrugged. "You said yourself that your uncle said it was Cassie who hit him."

"He was drugged up, confused, semicomatose. He'd been obsessing on Cassie. Hardly a reliable witness."

"You got a better suspect?"

"Besides Hurley?" I shrugged. "You can probably come up with motives and scenarios for any number of people. Think about all the people in Webster's life that have no connection to Cassie. Family, colleagues, students, old lovers, college roommates. You don't know anything about him."

"True," said Horowitz. "But I will. I'll know everything about him. But the thing of it is, he called you, set up the appointment for four this afternoon, said he expected to have information for you. Information about your cousin."

"He didn't actually say it was about Cassie," I said. "I inferred it."

"What else could it be?"

"Maybe he just wanted to hire a top-notch attorney."

"Right," said Horowitz. He didn't bother smiling. "So he had another appointment right before yours. I'm thinking that was when he expected to get the information he intended to pass along to you. That's why he wanted you to wait till then."

"If I'd gotten here earlier," I said, "he would've still been alive."

"As it was," said Horowitz, "you were early enough to bump into the shooter. What you got for being early was a whack on the head. That'll teach you."

"Yes," I said. "A good lesson."

"Lucky he didn't plug you, too."

I nodded. I'd already thought of that. "Did you find an appointment book on his desk?"

"Oh, sure." He rolled his eyes. "A clue. Just like in the movies."

"I just thought . . ."

"Mr. Coyne," said Detective Cohler, "you visited Webster here in his office yesterday, you said?"

"That's right."

"I wonder if you'd mind taking a look in there, see if you notice anything, before forensics gets here." She glanced at Horowitz, and he nodded.

"Sure," I said. I pushed myself to my feet and braced myself against the wall until a moment of dizziness passed.

Henry scrambled to his feet, gave himself a shake, and looked up at me expectantly.

"He might have to pee," I said to Cohler.

"Ask him if he can hold it," she said.

"He's got a sore leg," I said. "Who'd kick a dog?"

Cohler shook her head.

"Lie down," I told Henry.

He shrugged and lay down.

I went across the hall and stood in the doorway to Webster's office.

"Put your hands in your pockets," said Horowitz. "Don't touch anything."

I shoved my hands in my pants pockets and stepped into the office. The smell of burned cordite was strong. I hadn't noticed it before.

I closed my eyes and tried to remember how it had looked when I'd dropped in on Webster the previous day. I tried to play out the scene step by step, beginning at the moment I looked in and saw him working at his computer to the time I stood up and we shook hands and I walked out.

Then I opened my eyes and looked slowly around the office. At first, the only difference I noticed was the chair that had tipped over when I hit my head on it.

Then I said, "Okay."

"Okay what?" said Detective Cohler.

183

"There was a wire rack right there beside his computer." I pointed. "It held about a dozen CDs. It's gone. When I got here the other day Webster was working on his computer. When he stopped to talk with me, he copied whatever it was onto a CD. Then he ejected it, slid it into its plastic case, and put it in a rack. It looked like a little vertical bookcase."

"So our killer stole the rack of CDs," said Horowitz. "He was looking for information."

"Or else he just didn't want anybody else to have it," said Cohler.

"There's something else," I said.

The three of them turned and looked at me.

"Did Webster have a cell phone in his pocket?" I said.

"No," said Horowitz. "No cell phone. In his pocket or anywhere else."

"The other day he had a cell phone on his desk," I said. "It rang once when I was talking with him. It was his ex-wife. I went out into the hall and closed the door. It was obviously a private conversation."

"Ex-wife, huh?" said Cohler. "I suppose you didn't, um, overhear his end of the conversation."

I squeezed my eyes shut for a minute. "When he first answered and heard who it was, he said something like, 'What do you want?' Not exactly bubbling with friendliness. Then he asked me to give him some privacy. I went out and closed the door and tried not to listen. Mostly it was murmuring that I couldn't understand, but at one point he raised his voice and I heard him say something like, 'Forget about it. It's not going to happen.' When I went back in he apologized, said it was his ex-wife, as if that explained it."

"You didn't catch a name, did you?" said Marcia Benetti.

I looked at her.

"The ex-wife," she said. "Did he call her by name?"

"No, I don't think so."

Benetti turned to Horowitz and arched her eyebrows.

He shrugged.

"What?" I said.

"Marcia's thinking it might've been the ex-wife who shot the professor and hit you on the head today."

"I got hit pretty hard," I said.

"What?" said Marcia. "You don't think a woman could hit you hard enough to hurt you?"

"I didn't—"

"A gun butt is a pretty hard object," Horowitz said. "Do a number on the manliest of men, even when wielded by a slight person of the distaff persuasion." He grinned. "No shame in being bested by a woman, you know."

"I'm not ashamed," I said. "And I wouldn't say I was exactly bested. I was taken unawares. That's different."

Cohler, I noticed, was smiling.

"So you're thinking the killer took Webster's cell phone?" said Horowitz.

"If it's not here. Most people carry their cellulars around with them. He had it with him the other day. It would have the names and numbers of people he knew stored in it. That might be useful to somebody."

Horowitz was looking up at the ceiling. I hadn't said anything he hadn't already thought of.

"Mr. Coyne," said Cohler, "I'm wondering if in that instant before you got hit maybe something registered. A scent, perhaps? The rustle of clothing?"

I tried to think. "No," I said. "I didn't even notice the cordite odor until just now. It happened too quickly to notice anything. When I got here, the door was half open. I saw him sitting there with his back to me. I didn't know he was already dead. I spoke his name and pushed the door open and started to go in and . . ."

"Maybe something will occur to you," she said.

"If it does," I said, "I'll let you know."

She glanced over her shoulder toward the open door, where Henry was waiting. "You think your dog might've bit him?"

"Henry?" I shook my head. "He's the most trusting, least vicious dog in the world."

"Even when somebody hits his master on the head?"

"That," I said, "would provoke a growl. Not a particularly fearsome growl at that."

She shrugged. "Too bad."

Horowitz had wandered over to the corner of the room. "Hey, Coyne," he said. "Come here. Something I want you to take a look at."

I went over to where he was standing.

He pointed at the floor.

I squatted down.

"Don't touch," said Horowitz.

It was the broken remains of a small framed photo, about a five-by-seven. The wooden frame was splintered. The glass was shattered.

The photograph was lying faceup on the floor. It pictured Grantham Webster and Cassie Crandall, their heads and the top halves of their torsos. They were standing side by side. Cassie was leaning against him with her arm slung casually around his neck. They appeared to be about the same height. They were squinting into the sun showing a lot of white teeth. They looked happy. Carefree. Stoned, maybe.

Webster was bare-chested. He had sloping shoulders and a narrow chest. Cassie wore a skimpy lime-colored bikini top that showed plenty of cleavage. She had a slender model's body. She was so deeply tanned that her skin was almost as dark as Webster's.

In the background a flat turquoise sea—certainly not the Atlantic of New England—stretched away to the horizon. There was no foreground in the photograph. They could've been on a boat or on a beach.

"That's your cousin," said Horowitz. It wasn't a question.

I nodded. "Webster had this photo on his desk. It was facing away from me, so I didn't see who was in it when I was here the other day."

"So what do you think?"

"I think Webster must've still loved Cassie," I said. "Keeping this photo on his desk."

"Even though she dumped him," he said.

"I also think," I said, "that whoever did this was the same one who punched my uncle."

Horowitz nodded and pointed to a fresh triangular gouge on the wall. "Threw the photo," he said. "Just like you were saying happened in your uncle's house. Lots of anger there."

"Or jealousy," said Cohler.

"Anger and jealousy," said Marcia Benetti. "They go together."

There were voices out in the hallway. Benetti stepped out of the office. A minute later she poked her head in. "Forensics is here," she said.

Horowitz, Cohler, and I went into the hallway. Four new people were there, two women and two men. Each of them was carrying a big satchel. They wore white jumpsuits with FOREN-SICS stenciled across their backs and a Massachusetts State Police emblem stitched on the shoulder. One of them was squatting down patting Henry.

Horowitz went over to talk to them. When he came back, he said, "Okay, we're done here." He looked at me. "Let's go."

I looked at him. "Go where?"

"You know how it works," he said. "We need you to go over

what happened again for us so we can get it on tape."

"Wait a minute," I said. "I told you everything. Gave you several useful clues, even."

He shrugged.

"It's Thursday night, for Christ's sake, and—oh shit." I looked at my watch. It was ten after seven. "How about we do this another time."

Horowitz gave me his humorless Jack Nicholson grin. It meant: Fuhgeddaboudit.

"I gotta call Evie, then," I said. I pulled my cell phone from my pocket.

"Wait'll we get outside," he said. "I want to clear the area."

Marcia Benetti stayed behind with the forensics team. The rest of us trooped down the hallway and descended the flight of stairs. Henry took the lead. He was limping. When we got outside, he stopped and looked at me.

I waved my hand. "Okay."

He hobbled over to some shrubbery that he'd obviously had his eye on.

I sat on the steps and pecked out our home phone number.

It rang twice. Then Evie picked it up.

She said, "Yes?"

"Honey," I said. "It's me."

I heard her blow out a breath. "Where are you? I made a reservation. Julie told you, right?"

"She did," I said. "Dinner. Nola's. Terrific. Look. Something came up. It's kind of a long story. Right now I'm with Horowitz, and he insists—"

"Horowitz?"

"There's been a homicide."

"What?"

"A homicide, honey. A murder."

"Jesus Christ," she muttered. "Are you all right?"

"I'm fine."

"Who—?"

"Nobody you know. I'll tell you about it when I get there."

"When will that be?"

I looked at Horowitz. "How long is this going to take?"

He shrugged. "Hour, hour and a half."

"I should be home around nine," I told Evie. "Why don't you call Nola's, see if you can reschedule for, say, ten."

"You gonna be up for this?"

"Absolutely," I said.

"Ten," she said. "Sure. Okay." She hesitated. "You sure you're all right?"

"I'm fine."

I heard her blow out a long breath.

"You're upset with me," I said.

"Nope."

"I can tell," I said.

"Not upset," said Evie. "I was worried. We had a date and you weren't here. Now that I know it was only some silly homicide, I feel ever so much better."

I decided this wasn't the best time to tell her I'd been whacked on the head, never mind that Henry had been kicked. Evie understood cruelty to humans. She didn't like it, but working in hospitals, she saw it every day.

Cruelty to animals bewildered and infuriated her.

I followed Horowitz and Cohler to the Brookline police station, where I repeated everything I'd told them before. They asked me a lot of questions and caught me in a few contradictions and several memory lapses.

When they finished with me, Horowitz walked outside with me to the parking lot beside the station. It was a little after

189

eight thirty, and darkness had fallen over the city. The tall lamps that lit the lot threw orange pools of light onto the blacktop.

"You okay?" Horowitz said when we got to my car.

"I'm fine."

He looked at me and nodded. "Keep your nose out of this case, Coyne. You hear me?"

"I hear you."

He grabbed my arm and pulled me close to him. "I mean it. This is a fucking murder here."

"Gotcha, Roger. Don't worry about it. I know you'll solve it quickly."

He peered at me for a moment, then shrugged, turned around, and headed back into the police station.

At Cohler's insistence, Henry had waited for me in the car. A police station was no place for a dog, she said, even a particularly nice one such as Henry.

When I slid in behind the wheel, he uncoiled himself from where he'd been snoozing in the backseat and licked the back of my neck.

"How's the leg?" I said to him.

He gave me a couple more licks.

"Hungry?" I said.

Magic word. He sat down and began to drool. It was way past his supper time.

Mine, too.

Evie and I got home from Nola's in the North End a little after midnight. We sat side by side in our Adirondack chairs out in the garden in the soft yellow light of a full July moon. Henry curled up in the narrow space between the chairs.

We talked about the food we'd eaten, and the food we wished

we'd had room in our stomachs to eat, and then we tilted back our heads to the night sky and didn't talk at all.

I kept seeing Grannie Webster slouched in his chair, a splotch of wet blood on his chest, his dead, staring eyes already glazing over.

Evie reached over and groped for my hand. "You okay?" she said.

"Sure," I said. I gave her hand a squeeze.

"Your head feel all right?"

"Fine. I little wine helps, you know?"

She chuckled softly. "You think Henry's all right?"

"He ate a good dinner. When dogs eat heartily, it means they're all right."

After a while, we went inside, unplugged all the telephones in the house, went to bed, and made love.

Evie went to sleep almost instantly.

I lay awake for a long time.

SEVENTEEN

Friday morning. I got to the office at five of ten. Ed and Elizabeth Sanborn, my ten o'clock divorce mediation appointment, were waiting for me. They were sitting side by side on the sofa sipping coffee. Two very large people could've sat between them without feeling crowded, but still, the fact that they were sharing the same sofa spoke a kind of body language that I took as a positive sign. The previous time when they were waiting they'd put as much space between each other as the size of the room allowed.

I said hello and shook hands with each of them, then went over to Julie's desk, where she was squinting at her computer monitor.

She looked up and frowned at me. "What happened to your head?"

I touched the butterfly bandage on my forehead. "I fell down, banged it on the edge of a chair."

Julie opened her mouth, then thought better of it. "You had a call while you were gone.

"Who called?"

"Dr. Richard Hurley."

"What's he want?"

"Wouldn't tell a lowly secretary. Just said it was important. He sounded agitated. Wanted you to call him right away." She handed me a slip of paper. "Here's the number. He's at his office. Said to give the receptionist your name. She'll interrupt him."

"Agitated how?" I said.

Julie shrugged. "Eager. Anxious."

"Okay," I said. I turned to Ed and Elizabeth, who were sitting there watching me, and said, "I'll be with you in a minute." Then I went into my office.

I sat at my desk and poked out the number Julie had written down. When the receptionist answered, I told her it was Brady Coyne, returning Dr. Hurley's call.

"Oh, yes, sir," she said. "Please hold on. I'll get him for you."

A minute later Hurley said, "Mr. Coyne?"

"Yes. Returning your call."

"Sir," he said, "I don't appreciate your lurking around my house and harassing my daughter."

"Lurking," I said. "Harassing."

"I'm tempted to report you to the police."

"This is why you called me?" I said.

I heard him blow out a breath. "No," he said. "I'm sorry. We're both after the same thing, I guess. I'd like to talk to you."

"I've got clients waiting for me right now."

"Yes," he said. "And I've got a patient in the chair. I didn't mean now. Not on the phone. What about this afternoon? Can you free yourself up? Let me buy you a drink?"

"What do you want to talk about?"

"Cassie," he said.

When I suggested we meet at two in the Oak Bar at the Copley Plaza, he agreed instantly. This struck me as significant. For me, it was a three-minute stroll from the office. For him, it meant a drive or a cab ride into the city from Cambridge in Friday afternoon traffic or, even worse, stuffing himself into a standing-room-only subway car.

I wondered if he knew that he was a suspect in Grannie Webster's murder.

Come to think of it, I wondered if he had actually done it.

Well, maybe I'd find out. As Yogi Berra would say, Richard Hurley had something on his mind that he wanted to get off his chest.

Without being told, Ed and Elizabeth Sanborn took the same seats across from each other as they had the previous time.

I sat at the end of the table between them. "Did you both do your homework?" I said.

They nodded.

"Did either of you run into any problems?"

"Ed's got an IRA and a 401(k)," said Elizabeth. "Are those considered joint property?"

I nodded. "Investments, insurance, retirement plans. Both of you. Just assume that everything is jointly owned." I glanced at Ed. He was staring down at the top of the table. "Ed? You with us on this?"

He looked up. "Can I say something?"

I nodded.

"It's about our marriage," he said, "not our divorce."

"I tried to make it clear last time—"

"I can't go on until I say what I've got to say."

"You want to talk to me," I said, "or Elizabeth?"

"Elizabeth."

I stood up. "I'll leave the room. Let me know when you're done."

"Please stay," said Elizabeth.

I looked at Ed.

He nodded. "Yes. Please."

I sat. "I'm not a marriage counselor," I said. "I don't give advice. I don't take sides."

"We understand," said Elizabeth. She looked at Ed. "What do you want to say?"

He cleared his throat, then looked at me. "This all started because Elizabeth—"

"Don't talk to me," I said. "Talk to your wife."

He smiled quickly and turned to Elizabeth. "This all started," he said, "when you told me about your . . . your affair with Harry. It was like a kick in the balls. I didn't have a clue. I felt stupid. Betrayed, sure. But mainly stupid. Stupid and naive. I didn't think you'd keep a secret from me. I just . . . trusted you. My first reaction was to say I was getting a divorce. I expected you to argue with me. But you didn't. That was the worst part. That you just said okay."

Elizabeth's eyes were brimming with tears. "And what the hell did you—?"

"Let me finish," said Ed. "See, it was all about my ego. Macho me. No woman cheats on Ed Sanborn." He looked up at the ceiling for a moment, then returned his gaze to Elizabeth. "I don't want a divorce, honey."

Elizabeth's cheeks were wet. But she stared evenly at him and said nothing.

"There's something you need to know," Ed said.

"I do know," she said softly.

His head jerked back. "You know what?"

"I know about you and Celia Franklin."

"Oh, Jesus," he said. "How long have you known?"

"Over a year."

"So is that why you and Harry . . . ?"

"I don't know," she said. "Maybe. It wasn't even so much the—the infidelity. It was the fact that you carried it off so smoothly.

You had this giant secret, and I didn't have a clue. First it made me feel stupid, and I hated you for that. Then it made me feel like I ought to have a secret, too."

"Why didn't you say something?"

"I was waiting for you," she said. "To tell me. To admit it. I thought—"

"Hold on," I said. I stood up. "This has nothing to do with me. You guys take your time. Use this room for as long as you like. You're off the clock." And I walked out.

When I closed the door behind me, Julie looked up. "What's going on?"

"You're amazing," I said.

"I know. What this time?"

"You had the Sanborns pegged. Elizabeth was having an affair. Ed just confessed that he was having one, too."

Julie nodded. "So what're they going to do?"

"I guess that's what they're talking about in there. What do you think?"

"They're going to go for it."

"The divorce?" I said.

"The marriage, dummy."

Twenty minutes later my office door opened, and Ed and Elizabeth came out. They said they were going to try to make their marriage work.

I shook their hands and wished them luck.

After they left, Julie said, "Told you so."

I stuck my tongue out at her.

I keep my .38 Smith & Wesson Chief's Special revolver in the safe in my office. I leave it loaded, except for the empty chamber

197

under the hammer. I've killed two men with that gun. Both were evil men who would have killed me. I've never regretted killing either of them. Not that I don't think about it sometimes.

After Ed and Elizabeth Sanborn left, I went back into my office, opened my safe, and took out my Chief's Special. I was remembering Grannie Webster sitting in his office chair, a splotch of red on his chest.

I was remembering the quick pain and the slow, spinning blackness when I got whacked on the head.

What I was mainly remembering was the cold hard muzzle of a gun pressed against the side of my head, and the sharp, evil snick of the hammer being cocked beside my ear.

I hefted my revolver in my hand, ran my thumb over its smooth blue barrel, crooked my finger around the trigger, raised it in both hands, and aimed it at a bus that was creeping down Boylston Street outside my office window.

"Bang," I whispered.

Then I lowered it, wiped the finger smudges off with my handkerchief, and put it back into the safe where it belonged.

I called the ICU at Maine Medical a little after noontime, and when I gave my name, said I was Moses Crandall's nephew, and asked how he was doing, the nurse said, "Oh, hello, Mr. Coyne. I have some good news for you today."

"Excellent," I said. "I need some good news."

"Dr. Drury was in this morning," she said, "and he put in an order to move Mr. Crandall to the floor."

"The floor," I said.

"The regular part of the hospital. He'll be out of intensive care."

"That means he's getting better, right?"

198

"It means . . . well, yes. In essence, that's what it means. It's good news."

"Today?" I said. "Will they move him today?"

"As soon as a bed opens up. Today or tomorrow."

"Thank you," I said. "And if you don't mind me saying so, I hope we never have to talk again."

She laughed. "I don't mind at all."

I'm never late. When I was in school, I always wrote my papers a few days early so I'd have time to revise them. I pay my bills when they come in. I show up early for appointments.

I don't consider this a virtue. It's a neurosis, the vestige of some old Puritan ethic that nowadays is quite dysfunctional. In a world where being "fashionably late" is a sign of status, my compulsive promptness just ends up aggravating me. As regularly as it happens, I still have no tolerance for people who mean "one o'clock" when they say "twelve thirty."

Julie keeps telling me it's the way of the world, and not only should I get used to it, but I should get in step with it. People mistrust the motives of someone who's on time, she says.

If you ask me, being late, trying to control a situation by making somebody wait for you, is pure hostility. Passive aggression.

I can be as aggressive as the next guy. I understand and respect active aggression. But not the passive kind. Passive aggression is for cowards.

So it took all my willpower to wait in my office until two thirty—a half hour after the time we agreed to meet—before I walked across the plaza from my office to the bar in the Copley Plaza Hotel, where, judging by the agitation I'd heard in his voice on the phone, Dr. Richard Hurley would already be waiting for me.

199

The Oak Bar was dim and hushed and less than half full in the middle of a Friday afternoon. In a few hours it would be mobbed and noisy and swirling with cigar smoke.

I stood in the doorway for a moment to let my eyes adjust from the bright afternoon sunshine outside. I spotted Hurley at a table against the wall.

I went over and sat across from him. He was wearing a green blazer over a pale blue shirt with a paisley necktie. An untouched martini sat in front of him.

"Thanks for meeting me," he said. His eyes slid up from mine and focused on my forehead for a moment. I waited for him to ask about the little butterfly bandage, but he just blinked and looked down at his drink.

I had to swallow my knee-jerk impulse to apologize for keeping him waiting. "What's your mind?"

"You want a martini?" he said. "The martinis are excellent here."

"Why not," I said.

He lifted a finger, and a waiter appeared. "A martini for my friend," said Hurley.

When the waiter left, I said, "We're friends?"

He picked up his martini glass, looked at it, then put it down. "Look," he said. "You and I got off to a bad start. I'm sorry. And I'm sorry about James."

"James already apologized," I said.

Hurley arched his eyebrows, then shrugged. "Well, I do, too. It's just, when your wife leaves you . . ." He picked up his glass again, and this time he took a sip. "You don't like to acknowledge that. Especially to strangers. It's embarrassing."

"You saying Cassie left you?"

"So it seems. I was at a convention in Springfield that weekend. When I got home Sunday afternoon, she wasn't there. She left me a note. All it said was, 'Please don't try to look for me.'" Hurley tried to smile. "No explanation. No apology. Nothing. I didn't see it coming. Even now, over two weeks later, I still can't figure it out. I thought we were doing okay."

"So," I said, "you're doing what she asked? You're not looking for her?"

"Would you?"

I shook my head. "I don't know. It would depend."

He shrugged. "Even if I wanted to, I wouldn't know where to start." He shook his head. "It's up to her. I'm trying to reconcile myself to the fact that she's gone for good. If she decides to come back, of course, I'll welcome her with open arms."

"The note. It was her handwriting?"

He blinked. "Well, sure."

"Do you still have it?"

"Hell no," he said. "When I read it, I was furious. I ripped it up and threw it away."

"Furious," I said.

"Wouldn't you be? I mean, okay, if your wife's going to pack up her clothes and leave you, wouldn't you think she might at least have the courtesy to tell you face-to-face?"

"She took some clothes with her?"

He nodded.

"Anything else?"

"I don't know. Whatever she might've taken, it was just her stuff. I haven't tried to figure it out. There were a bunch of empty hangers in her closet, that's all."

"She takes clothes," I said, "but she didn't take her car?"

"I know. Taking some clothes makes me think she'll be gone for a while. Leaving the car makes me think she'll be back." He smiled quickly. "She might not love me, but I always thought she loved that car."

"You think she doesn't love you?"

"I wish I could think of some other way to explain what she's done."

201

"Why do you suppose she didn't take her car?"

He shrugged. "Maybe she figured if she had her car with her, someone could use it to trace her, find her. Cassie's a very shrewd person."

She didn't take her cell phone with her, either, I almost said. But then I'd have to explain how I knew that, and I didn't want to get into it with this guy.

The waiter arrived with my martini on his tray. He set it in front of me and looked at Hurley. "Another, sir?"

Hurley shook his head. "Not now."

The waiter slid away. Hurley leaned across the table toward me. "I know you've been looking for her. Have you had any luck? Do you know where she is?"

I shook my head. He could take that to mean I didn't know, or that I wasn't going to tell him. I didn't care.

"I imagine you've thought about what might've prompted her to leave when she did," I said.

"Oh, I've thought about it. I've thought, if I just didn't go to that damn convention in the first place, or if I decided to come home Saturday night rather than staying over for the Sunday-morning brunch . . ."

That didn't answer my question, but I let it go. There was no reason to expect he'd answer it truthfully anyway.

Neither of us said anything for a minute. Then Hurley said, "My first wife committed suicide. I didn't see it coming. Didn't understand it. Still don't. And then Ellen, my second wife . . . she died. An asthma attack. Just a . . . a random thing. I didn't really understand that, either. Now Cassie . . ."

"You've bad luck with marriages," I said.

He looked at me and laughed quickly. "That's it," he said. "Bad luck."

I took a sip of my martini. "Cassie's a lot younger than you," I said.

202

He smiled. "Believe me, I was as shocked as anybody when she agreed to go to dinner with me that first time. And then when she said she'd marry me?" He shook his head. "I guess I shouldn't be surprised that she decided to move on. She's a beautiful woman, Mr. Coyne, as you know. She's extremely smart. She's got a wonderful, earthy sense of humor. She's had a lot of life experience. She's worldly. Cosmopolitan, you might say. She reads. She likes art. She knows how to dress."

"What do you mean, life experience?" I said.

"Oh, just that she's traveled a lot, lived in many different places. You know Cassie. She's one of those people who's instantly comfortable, makes friends no matter where she is."

Actually, I didn't know Cassie. I hadn't seen her in about thirty years. All I knew about her was what other people told me, and I knew enough to take all of that with a grain of salt.

I leaned forward on my elbows and said, "Has it occurred to you that something might've happened to her?"

Hurley blinked. "Of course," he said. "Anybody would."

"What do you think might've happened to her?" I said.

He shook his head. "I don't know. I don't like to think about it."

"For example."

He sat there breathing for a few seconds. "For example," he said softly, "she might've left me for another man. She had a boyfriend when we met. I know she was . . . very fond of him."

"Okay," I said. "A boyfriend. Any other thoughts?"

He waved his hand in the air. "Of course. Awful thoughts. You can imagine."

"Yes," I said. "I can imagine." I leaned back in my seat and sipped my martini.

"I do wish you hadn't brought my daughter into this," Hurley said after a minute.

I shrugged. "I didn't bring her into anything. She answered the door when I knocked on it. She invited me in."

"What did she tell you?"

I shrugged.

"Rebecca doesn't know anything," he said.

"Did you ask her?"

"If she knew anything, she'd tell me."

"She seems to be a good mother," I said.

"It's rough on her," he said. "Her husband's away all the time."

"A foreign correspondent, she told me," I said.

"Yes," he said. "That's right."

I didn't tell him that James had revealed to me that Becca had no husband, that she didn't even know who had fathered her child.

Clearly, Richard Hurley wasn't going to mention it, either.

He was swirling his martini in his glass, studying it. "You also came around the house the other morning." He looked up at me. "Tuesday, I believe. When no one was home."

"Yes," I said. "I was looking for Cassie."

He cocked his head and peered at me. Then he smiled. "You're not going to tell me a thing, are you?"

"No."

"You're not even going to tell me whether there is something to tell me."

I shook my head.

He blew out a breath. "Okay. Fair enough. Maybe I can ask you to do one thing for me."

"You can always ask."

"If you find Cassie," he said, "ask her to call me? That's all I want. I want to talk to her."

You and Uncle Moze, I thought.

"I'll tell her that," I said. "Next time I see her."

Evie and I were sitting out in the garden. The sun had set behind the town houses that surrounded us, and the evening air was cool. Henry was standing beside me with his chin planted on my thigh, lest I forget that he hadn't eaten yet.

We were sipping gin and tonics and sharing the events of our days, as we did most evenings when we got home. Evie's day had been a series of meetings which she called boring and stressful. She didn't want to think about them.

I told her I was interested in her work.

She said please, she really didn't want to talk about it.

I told her they were moving Uncle Moze out of ICU. It looked like he was going to be all right.

She said that was wonderful news and wondered if I planned to go back and visit him.

I told her I intended to see him as soon as they had him settled in his new room.

She asked if there was any news on the man who had kicked Henry and hit me on the head and killed Grantham Webster.

I told her that I hadn't heard anything, but there was no reason why I would. It was Horowitz's case. If it ever came to trial, I'd probably have to testify. Otherwise, it was none of my business.

I told her how the Sanborns, my mediation couple, had decided to give their marriage another try. I told her how they both had secrets, how mistrust had corroded their relationship, and how, now that they had told each other their secrets, they thought maybe they could put things back together.

And as I told Evie about the Sanborns, I finally realized what I had not been allowing myself to think: Evie had a secret, and it was causing me to mistrust her, and it threatened to corrode our relationship.

I watched her face as I talked.

She gave nothing away.

I got up and refilled our gin-and-tonic glasses. When I returned, I told her about meeting Cassie's husband at the Oak Bar.

"So you didn't tell him anything?" said Evie.

"Hurley?" I said. "Nope. He wanted me to, but I didn't. Not that I had much to tell him anyway. He told me some things, but I have no idea which of those things, if any, are true."

"So what are you thinking?"

"I'm thinking," I said, "that he's pretty damn philosophical about the whole thing. Hey, he goes. She left me. Oh, I was angry at first. But I understand. Can't blame her. Good luck to her."

"Like he's accepted it. Like he's moving on."

"Like that's what he wants me to think."

"You're not buying it."

I shrugged. "His first wife committed suicide. His second wife fell off a ladder and died of an asthma attack. Uncle Moze got punched in the chest and ended up in the ICU. Grannie Webster got shot. I got whacked on the head. Henry got kicked in the ribs. It all seems to revolve around Cassie."

Evie was peering at me. "You think this Hurley . . . ?"

"I don't know. Yeah, maybe. I don't trust him, I know that."

We sipped our drinks in silence for a few minutes. Then Evie said, "So that couple, they're going to give it another try?"

"Looks like it."

She smiled. "Good for you."

"Me? I didn't do anything."

"But if it hadn't been for the mediation . . ."

"I'd like to take credit for it," I said. "But I really can't."

"You should," said Evie. "It's ˌ lovely story."

"What," I said, "two people going behind each other's backs, cheating on each other?"

"You know what I mean."

"Yeah," I said. "Julie reacted the same way."

"It's a happy ending," Evie said. "Boy wins girl, boy loses girl, boy wins girl back. We women love those stories."

I watched Evie's face as she talked about love and happy endings, and I didn't detect the slightest hint of irony.

"Hard to say where they're going to end up," I said. "But you're right. It's a nice story so far. They've suspended the mediation, which is more than okay by me. They're going to work on the marriage. They're going to try to rebuild trust. Good luck to 'em."

Evie lifted her glass. "Good luck to them," she repeated.

I clicked my glass against hers. I wanted to say, "Good luck to us." But I didn't.

EIGHTEEN

My father was sprawled on his Barcalounger in the living room of my boyhood house. His chest was soaked in blood, and his eyes were open and empty, and I was thinking that if I could just drag his body down to the basement everything would be all right, and that's when the red and blue lights suddenly started flashing and a siren began bleating right outside the window. I put my arms around my father's chest and tried to lift him from his chair, but he was a dead weight, and I had no strength in my arms, and I ended up lying on top of him with my arms around him and my head on his shoulder and my legs wrapped around his waist, exactly the way I held on to him when Daddy would carry me upstairs to bed after I fell asleep in the car. And then the siren went off again, and I knew I was going to get caught, and then I woke up and the phone beside the bed was ringing.

I took a deep breath and let it out slowly. The specific images from the dream dissipated almost immediately. But the feeling— it was desperation, the fear of being caught, not guilt or sadness or grief—lingered.

The phone rang again.

Beside me, Evie thrashed around. "Answer the damn telephone," she mumbled.

I picked it up and said, "Hello?"

"Mr. Coyne?"

"Yes."

"It's Wilton Drury here at Maine Medical."

It took me a minute to realize who Wilton Drury was. "Oh, Doctor. Yes. Hi." I sat the edge of the bed with my back to Evie. "What time is it?"

"It's, um, six twenty."

"Bad news, right?" I said. "You wouldn't be calling at six twenty in the morning unless—"

"Your uncle is going to be all right," he said quickly. "He's just had a little setback is all."

"Setback? What do you mean, setback?"

Beside me, Evie had rolled onto her side. She put her hand on my arm.

"I believe it's a reaction to the medication. We've been trying to wean him off the strong stuff, and maybe we moved too fast on that. Every patient's a little different."

"The medication, huh?"

"We believe so. Yes."

"But it might be something else?"

"I'm quite sure," the doctor said, "once we get his medications worked out—"

"What exactly is wrong with him?" I said. "This setback? Is he unconscious? Did his heart stop beating?"

"He's, um, a little fuzzy. That's all." Dr. Drury chuckled. "Technical term. Fuzzy."

"Mentally, you mean? Fuzzy mentally?"

"Yes. Mentally. He was quite alert yesterday. Sitting up, eating, joking with the nurses, walking around a little. His vital signs were all good. When I told him we were going to move him over to the floor, he became quite animated, started talking about going home, driving his truck, hauling his lobster pots. He joked about smoking cigarettes and drinking beer."

"He probably wasn't joking," I said.

Dr. Drury laughed quickly. "I suppose you're right. Anyway, last night—"

"Is it permanent?" I said. "This fuzziness?"

"I don't think so," he said. "I think it was just a reaction to the new regimen of medication. I think he's going to be all right."

"Explain fuzziness to me," I said.

"The nurses had trouble rousing him," he said. "And when they did, he didn't seem to know where he was."

"A stroke," I said. "It sounds to me like he had a stroke."

"I'm quite sure it was the meds, Mr. Coyne."

"It's temporary then, right?"

"I think so, yes. Temporary."

"So you've seen improvement since you adjusted his meds?" I said. "Is that what makes you think it's temporary?"

"It's, um, premature to say that," he said. "We'll certainly know a lot more in the next twenty-four hours."

"I was hoping to visit him today."

"It would be better to give him a day or two," said the doctor. "Let us get him adjusted to his meds, get reoriented. I don't think it would do either of you any good to see him today."

"I'll be up tomorrow regardless," I said.

"Sure," he said. "Don't blame you."

"What can I expect when I see him?" I said. "What about his memory?"

"That's hard to say, Mr. Coyne."

"You'll let me know if anything changes?"

"I will," he said. "You know you can call anytime. I've instructed the nurses to share information with you."

211

I thanked Dr. Drury, hung up the phone, and sat there on the edge of the bed. A setback. That didn't sound good, no matter how Dr. Drury spun it. Moze was old. He had an aortic aneurysm. He'd already had one heart attack. It didn't sound good at all.

I thought about Cassie. If Uncle Moze was going to die, I thought it was very important to get him and Cassie together. Important for him, and important for her, too.

Evie slid her hand under my T-shirt and rubbed my back. "What's going on?" she said.

I told her what Dr. Drury had told me.

"I'm sorry," she said.

"I know," I said. "What are your plans today?"

"I thought I told you. I've got to go to the office."

"You didn't. It's Saturday."

She shrugged. "What about you?"

"I'm going to drive down to Rhode Island and visit my aunt. Aunt Faith. My only surviving aunt."

"That's nice," said Evie. "Reconnecting with your family."

"Sure you don't want to come along?"

"Like I said," she said. "I've got to go to the office."

I went on the Internet, accessed the white pages for Tiverton, Rhode Island, and found Orville Thurlow at 20 Shade Street, listed with the same phone number as the one for Faith in Cassie's cell phone.

MapQuest told me how to drive from Mount Vernon Street in Boston to Shade Street in Tiverton. It was a straight shot down Route 24. It would take one hour and four minutes. On a Saturday morning, with no commuting traffic, I thought that estimate would be about right.

I waited until after lunch, sort of hoping that Evie might spend

212

only half of this Saturday in July at her office and that she'd come home for lunch and agree to ride with me to Rhode Island.

But she didn't.

I asked Henry if he wanted to go for a ride. He jerked up his head, scrambled to his feet, sprinted to the door, and sat there with his ears cocked.

I took that for a yes.

It actually took a little less than an hour to drive from my parking garage on Charles Street to Shade Street in Tiverton. Number 20 was a little Cape with two dormers, cedar shingles weathered silvery, and pink rugosa roses sprawling over a split-rail fence in front. Spiky grass grew in sparse clumps in the sandy yard. A Jeep Liberty wagon—a fairly new model—was parked in the driveway. A mailbox at the end of the driveway had Thurlow and the number 20 painted on it.

These were decisive clues. I figured I'd found Aunt Faith's place.

I pulled in behind the Jeep, told Henry to sit tight, got out, and went to the front door.

There appeared to be no bell, but a brass knocker shaped like a pineapple was attached to the door. I'd heard somewhere that the pineapple was a symbol of hospitality. I lifted the pineapple and let it fall onto its brass base. It made a loud, rude bang that echoed inside the house.

After a minute the door opened.

I had to blink. Aunt Faith was a fatter, more wrinkled twin of my mother as I remembered her. It was my mother's washed-out blue eyes that peered suspiciously at me, my mother's thin mouth that was pursed in her trademark expression of disapproval, my mother's good cheekbones, aristocratic nose, generous jaw.

And when Aunt Faith spoke, it was my mother's leftover Down East accent that said, "Yes? Can I help you?"

213

"Aunt Faith," I said, "I'm Brady Coyne. Your sister Hope's boy. Your nephew."

She frowned at me, studied my face. Then she patted her chest. "Good Lord," she said. "Brady. Nephew. I haven't seen you since . . ."

"I know," I said. "It's been a long time. My mother's funeral, I think."

"Well, come in, come in." She pulled the door open wide and stepped aside.

I went in. It appeared to be a typical Cape Cod. Living room on the left, bedroom or den or something on the right, narrow staircase up the middle, kitchen and dining room along the back of the house.

Aunt Faith was shorter and plumper than my mother had been. She sort of shuffled, but she did it without a cane or a walker. She had to be in her early, or maybe even mid, eighties. She was the oldest Crandall sibling. Then came my mother, Hope. Then Moses, then Jake, then Charity, and last Mary, the baby.

In the Crandall family, the women died before the men. All except Faith.

She asked if I'd like a Coke or a beer or something. I said a Coke would be great. She went into the kitchen. I sat on the sofa. There was a brick fireplace against the side wall with an oil painting of a clipper ship hanging over the mantel. A large thin-screen television perched in the corner. A braided rug covered the floor. A large bay window looked out onto the street. It was a small, square, pleasant room that betrayed little about the people who lived in it.

Aunt Faith came back a minute later with a can of Coke for me and one for herself. She sat in an upholstered wingback chair across from me.

"What a nice suprise," she said.

"You're wondering what brings me here," I said.

"Of course I am." She smiled, and I detected a shrewd, appraising glitter in her eyes. This, I thought, was not somebody to underestimate. "It's nice to see you, of course," she said. "I still remember you as a little boy who was always climbing trees. But I've got the feeling that this isn't just a friendly visit with your old aunt, after all this time."

"Uncle Moze is in the hospital," I said. "I didn't know if you'd heard."

She shook her head. "No, I didn't know. How would I know?"

"I thought maybe Uncle Jake—"

"Jacob?" She waved the back of her hand at me, dismissing Jacob. "I ain't talked with him since . . . since I don't know when. He's so busy makin' money, he got no time for his family." She blinked at me. "So what hapened to Moses? He's somebody else who don't keep in touch with his old sister."

"He had a heart attack. He's in intensive care at Maine Medical in Portland."

"Intensive care," she said. "Is he going to be all right?"

"I don't know."

Aunt Faith took a sip from her Coke can. "Is that why you come all the way down here? To tell me about Moses?"

I shrugged. "I thought you'd want to know."

"I guess if you found my house," she said, "you probably could've found my phone number."

"I wanted to see you."

"Well," she said, "don't get me wrong. It's nice. I'm glad to see you again, too, and I don't mean to be inhospitable. But you can't blame an old lady for being a little skeptical."

I smiled at her. "I'm looking for Cassie," I said. "Moze's daughter. Cassandra. I thought maybe—"

"Cassandra was here," she said. "Surprised me one day the same way you did here today. I didn't figure she was just wanting to visit with her old aunt any more than you are."

215

"When was that?" I said.

She looked up at the ceiling for a moment. "It must've been more'n a year ago. Time goes by awful fast when you get old. I'm trying to remember what the weather was like. Chilly, I think. Cassie was wearing gloves, I recall. Expensive gloves, I remember thinking. Thin leather with fur lining. Winter before last. Or maybe it was last winter. That was a cold one, wasn't it? Cassie sat right there where you're sitting, drinkin' a Coke just like you are."

"Was that the only time you talked to her?"

"Yes. Just that once."

"What did she want?"

"Cassandra always was a clever child," said Aunt Faith. "And she thought she was being clever with me. She started reminiscing about her childhood, growing up in Moulton, Lillian being sick and then dying, growing up with Moses. And all the time she's talking, I'm thinking, So what do you want? Why don't you just get to it?"

"Did she get to it?"

"She was pretty roundabout," she said. "Finally she says something like, 'So I just started wondering if Moses and Lillian really were my parents.'"

"What did you tell her?"

"I told her the truth. I told her that Moses and Lillian were the best parents she could've had, but that it was Mary who gave birth to her and Norman Dillman who was her actual father."

"Was she surprised?"

"Nope. Not at all. She already knew it. She told me as much. She said she had recently got ahold of her birth certificate—she was getting married—and she was taken aback when she saw Mary Crandall listed as her mother and Norman Dillman as her father. Evidently Moze and Lil, they never bothered to mention that to Cassie, and if they weren't going to, it was nobody else's business. When she was growing up in Moulton, folks were too polite to say anything to her about it. Mary deserting Cassie and running off with that ballplayer, Norman gettin' himself murdered, all that was pretty scandalous.

"It's surprising Cassie never heard them stories. But evidently she didn't. Or if she did, she chose not to believe them. All along she thought Moses and Lillian were her parents. She seemed pretty upset about it."

"Upset because . . . ?"

"Upset because Moses never said nothing about it to her. Upset because there was this secret about her. Upset because everything she thought she knew about herself wasn't true." Aunt Faith looked at me. "That child has every right to be upset, if you ask me. What in the world was Moses thinking?" She shook her head. "So naturally, she wanted to know all about Mary and that no-good Norman."

"What did you tell her?"

"I told her the truth. That Norman was a good-for-nothin' bum who dealt drugs and knocked up a high-school girl and ended up in the river with a bullet in his head, and that Mary was just a child at the time, barely sixteen, and didn't want to raise a baby, so she gave it to her brother and his wife, who couldn't have kids of their own and who were wonderful, loving parents. I told her how Mary ran off with a baseball player and never came back to Moulton, and how she died of cancer, living in Iowa of all places with her second husband, a month after she turned forty." Aunt Faith shrugged. "I told Cassandra all that. She has a right to know."

"Yes," I said. "I agree."

"Well," she said, "evidently Moses don't agree, or he would've told her himself."

"Maybe he just never got around to it."

"Well," she said, "it's about time he did."

"Was that all you talked about?"

"She didn't bother to ask about my children or my husband or the rest of our family, if that's what you mean."

I shrugged. I took that as a hint. I would ask the polite questions before I left. "Anything besides that," I said.

Aunt Faith turned her head and looked at me out of the corners of her eyes. "She wanted to know about Norman," she said after a minute.

"What about him?"

"Everything. Where he came from, what he was like, if he loved Mary." She hesitated. "Who murdered him."

"What did you tell her."

"I told her the truth. That he came from Kittery, quit school at sixteen, got in with some bad people, got Mary pregnant, married her, knocked her around. I told her that nobody was sad when Moze found him in the river."

"How did Cassie respond to that?"

Faith shook her head. "I couldn't tell you. She just listened and nodded her head. She didn't say anything."

"She wanted to know who murdered Norman?"

She nodded.

"What did you tell her?"

"I told her the truth. It's an unsolved mystery. That's all."

"There must have been suspicions and rumors."

"There were. Sure. Cassie asked, but I didn't tell her about them. That's all they were. Rumors. Gossip. It was a long time ago. It's over with. Nobody cares anymore."

"It sounds like Cassie cares," I said.

"I guess so. She kept prodding and poking. I tried to explain to her that it didn't matter, that she should just forget about it. Finally I just told her it was time she started to get on with her life."

"What did she say to that?"

Faith looked at me and shook her head. "She got mad."

"Mad how?"

"She stood up and gave me this—this look, like she was looking holes into me—and she actually made a fist at me. She scared me. She said I had no right to keep secrets from her. I told her I didn't have no secrets. I just had old gossip, and I wasn't going to spread it. To her, or to anybody." She shrugged. "After a minute, Cassie calmed down. She said she was sorry she got upset. She thanked me for talking to her. And she left."

"Aunt Faith," I said, "those rumors and suspicions you mentioned, they might be important."

"Important how?"

"I don't know," I said. "The doctor thinks that Moze's heart attack was caused by somebody punching him."

"Oh, dear," she murmured. "Who'd do a thing like that?"

I shrugged.

"You don't think Cassie . . ."

"I don't know."

"And you think old stories about Norman getting a bullet in the head had something to do with what happened to Moses?"

"I don't know that, either."

"Well," she said, "I ain't going to spread gossip now, any more than I did with Cassie. You can get mad, you can threaten me, you can try to trick me. It don't matter. Norman is dead and buried, and that's that. Good riddance."

I held up both hands. "I'm not mad. Maybe you'll think about it and change your mind. If you do, will you call me? I'm a lawyer. I know the difference between gossip and fact." I took out a business card and put it on the coffee table.

"I don't intend to think about it," she said. "And even if I do, I can tell you right now, I ain't going to change my mind, lawyer or no lawyer."

I smiled. "Okay," I said. "That's fine. I understand." I sipped from my Coke can, then leaned back in the sofa and smiled at

219

her. "Catch me up on your life, Auntie. I want to hear all about it. Tell me about your new husband. Orville, right? Start at the beginning."

She smiled. "Poor old Orville," she said.

Her kids—my cousins, all four of them from her marriage to Harry—were scattered across the country, and except for Jerry, her youngest, she hardly saw any of them. After Harry died, she married Orville, a nice man from Rhode Island who owned a Ford dealership across the bay in Portsmouth. This here—Faith waved her hand around at the room where we were sitting—was Orville's old family house. He inherited it from his parents, and he'd lived here with his first wife. They were divorced. No kids.

Two years ago last March they had to move Orville to what Faith called "a retirement home." The reminiscence wing, she said, which I understood to be for Alzheimer's patients. It was quite lovely, she said. The people who worked there were very caring.

I should have been bored, hearing all those details about people I didn't know and had no particular reason to care about. But I wasn't bored. I was interested. This was my family.

I asked Aunt Faith questions. I probed her for more details. I made her write down the names and addresses of her children, my cousins. She found her Christmas-card list and was able to give me the names and addresses of a few of my other cousins, too. Aunt Charity's kids, and Uncle Jake's.

We talked until late in the afternoon. When I finally said I had to get going, Aunt Faith stood up and walked me to the door.

I turned and gave her a hug.

"Bless you," she said, and when I straightened up, I saw tears brimming in her eyes.

"Are you all right?" I said.

She nodded. "I get lonely sometimes. I miss old Orville. It was awfully nice of you to come visit. I hope you'll come back sometime."

"I will," I said. And I meant it.

Back at the car, Henry was happy to see me, and even happier to be let out so he could pee on the fence post.

As we drove north on Route 24, heading home, I told Henry about my visit with Aunt Faith.

"Cassie was there," I said. "She was asking about her parents. Faith told her about Mary and Norman, her real parents. I'm thinking that Cassie was furious at Moze for keeping that from her all those years. I'm thinking that's why she stopped talking to him. It was about the time she married Hurley, because that's when she would've needed to get a birth certificate. That's when she would've seen Mary and Norman listed as her parents. That's when she would've looked up Aunt Faith, hoping to learn the truth about herself."

I paused. Henry didn't say anything. He was sitting on the front seat beside me with his nose pressed against the cracked-open window. It was hard to tell whether he was paying attention to me or not.

"Maybe Cassie was so mad at Uncle Moze for keeping secrets from her," I said to Henry, "that she broke into his house and punched him."

Henry was ignoring me.

"Maybe that's why Moze doesn't want to talk about it," I told him. "But even if that's true, it doesn't explain her running off and leaving her husband, if that's what she did, and it wouldn't explain him—or somebody else—doing her harm. And it certainly doesn't explain who shot Grannie Webster in the head, and whacked me, and kicked you. Hey!" I gave Henry a poke. "What do you think?"

Henry turned and looked at me with those intelligent eyes of his. Then he sort of shrugged and stuck his nose back at the crack at the top of the window.

221

Nineteen

Sunday morning. Henry was licking my face. I opened my eyes. His nose was about six inches from mine, and his ears were cocked up in full-alert mode.

Evie was snoring softly beside me. I looked at the clock. Eight fifteen. I never slept that late, even on Sundays. Neither did Evie.

I slipped out of bed, went downstairs, and let Henry out. He was limping noticeably. His leg where he'd been kicked had apparently stiffened up overnight.

I made the coffee, showered, got dressed, and took a mug of coffee back up to the bedroom.

Evie was sprawled on her belly hugging her pillow. Her long auburn hair curtained the side of her face. The sheet was twisted in her legs. Both of us had gone to sleep naked.

Her skin was silky gold. I remembered how it felt on my lips, and my breath caught in my throat.

I bent over, lifted her hair, kissed the back of her neck, and whispered, "I brought you some coffee."

"Mm," she mumbled into her pillow. "Nice."

"It's on the table."

She rolled onto her back, looked up at me, smiled sleepily, and closed her eyes. She had sworn to me that today, Sunday, she would not be going to the office. She wanted to just hang around the house, she said. Dig in the garden. Read. Listen to music. Sleep late. Take a nap.

I hadn't seen her this relaxed in a couple of weeks. It was nice to see that old sexy smile.

I pulled the sheet over her chest, kissed her forehead, told her to go back to sleep, and went back downstairs.

I poured myself some coffee, picked up the portable phone, and went out to the garden. If the phone rang, I could grab it quickly before it woke up Evie.

A mourning cloak butterfly fluttered down onto an orange daylily blossom and sat there opening and closing its translucent purple wings. A nuthatch clung upside down to the sunflower feeder. A couple of song sparrows scavenged seeds that had fallen to the ground.

Henry sprawled beside me, watching all the wild things with his predatory eyes.

After a while Henry got bored with the birds. He flopped onto his side, let out a big sigh, and began snoozing in a patch of morning sunlight.

When the phone on the table beside me rang, it sounded like a gunshot.

I picked it up and said, "Yes?"

"Mr. Coyne?"

"Yes. Who's this?"

"It's Charlene Staples. Moulton PD?"

"Sure," I said. "How are you? What's up?"

"I'm here at Maine Medical in Portland," she said. "Out in the parking lot, to be exact. They won't let you use a cell inside. I've just been up to your uncle's room."

"In the ICU, right?"

"Yes," she said. "I was hoping—"

"How is he?"

"Huh? Oh. He seems okay. I heard that he had a little setback, but the nurses said he's doing better. Something about adjusting his medication. They said he was complaining about his eggs being too runny and asking for tide charts. He seemed pretty feisty to me."

"Well, good," I said. "You said you were hoping . . . ?"

"Yes," she said. "I was hoping he'd tell me who broke into his house and punched him." She paused. "He won't."

"Won't?" I said. "Or can't?"

"Well," she said, "my guess is won't. He refused to say anything one way or the other. When I walked into his room, he looked me up and down, checked out my chest pretty carefully, and gave me a big grin. I asked him how he was feeling and he said he wasn't complaining, but when I told him I was a police officer and asked him to tell me who hit him, he just turned his head away and wouldn't talk."

"As if he knew but wasn't saying."

"Yes," she said. "Exactly."

"Why wouldn't he just say he didn't know?"

"I don't know," she said. "Maybe he doesn't want to lie."

"Is he . . ." I fumbled for the right word. "Does he seem to be competent?"

"The nurses seemed to think he's plenty competent."

"I know what you're thinking," I said.

"What am I thinking?"

"You're thinking it was Cassie who broke into his house, smashed up those photographs, and punched him in the chest. You're thinking my uncle saw her and recognized her and is refusing to be a witness against his own daughter."

"That's exactly what I'm thinking," she said. "He said it was Cassie the day they brought him in. So why won't he say it now?"

"Because what he said that day was just a hallucination in the mind of a man who'd just had a heart attack and was drugged to the gills?"

"Maybe," she said. "Or maybe she really did it."

"So you're calling me because you think he'll talk to me."

"I'm calling you," she said, "because, to tell you the truth, I can't think of anything else to do. I've been investigating my ass off here, and all I'm left with is some busted-up photographs and your half-dead uncle for a witness."

"Tell you what," I said. "I was going to visit him today anyway. I'll ask him what he remembers. If he tells me, I'll ask him if he'll tell you, or if he minds if I tell you. I'll do it however he wants. Okay?"

"You're going to play lawyer?"

"I never *play* lawyer," I said. "I *am* a lawyer. I'll respect Moze's wishes, protect his privacy, that's all. I'd do that whether I was a lawyer or not."

"Well," she said, "whatever. I'm only a simple country girl, you know. I just want to catch criminals."

I laughed. "Hardly simple."

I told Charlene that I probably wouldn't get there until early afternoon. She said she wanted to be there when I was there. We agreed that I'd call her cell phone when I knew what time I'd arrive, and she'd meet me at the hospital.

I called her right after I drove across the bridge that spanned the Piscataqua River, which separated New Hampshire from Maine. It was a little after two on that Sunday afternoon. She answered her cell phone on the first ring. I told her where I was. She said she'd meet me in the hospital parking lot.

When I got there, I found her leaning against the wall outside the main entrance smoking a cigarette. She was wearing snug-fitting blue jeans and a snug-fitting T-shirt and sandals. Her toenails were painted pink. No gun, no badge.

I leaned against the wall beside her. "I remember the days when patients could smoke in their hospital rooms," I said.

She looked at me and smiled. "You must be way older than me."

"Oh," I said, "I was just a little kid in those days."

She tapped her forefinger on her forehead. "What happened to you?"

I decided not to tell her the whole complicated story. I figured Grannie Webster's murder and Uncle Moze's heart attack were connected. The link was Cassie. Horowitz knew about Uncle Moze, and I'd mentioned Charlene Staples to him, too. But it wasn't my place to open up the Webster piece of the case to Charlene. If it needed to be done, Horowitz would do it.

I touched my butterfly bandage. Under it was a lump the size of Mount Monadnock. At least that's how it felt. "This?" I said. "Nothing. Tripped on the rug, hit my head on a chair. Clumsy."

She smiled. "You don't strike me as the clumsy type." She stubbed her cigarette out in the tub of sand. "Let's go."

We took the elevator up to the ICU. When we stepped out, she said, "I'll be in the waiting room."

"Lest you inadvertently eavesdrop on a privileged conversation," I said.

She smiled. "Exactly."

"I'll come get you if he's willing to talk to you."

She nodded and headed down the corridor.

As I turned the corner to the hallway leading to the ICU, a man coming around the corner bumped into me.

"Hey," he said. "Watch where you're going."

"You, too," I said.

Then I saw who it was. Uncle Jake. His face was red, and his eyes were slitted and angry. His hands were balled into hard fists.

He pulled back and glared at me. "What the hell are you doing here?"

"Visiting my uncle."

"Yeah," he said. "Me, too."

"How is he?"

"Alive, unfortunately." And with that, he shouldered his way past me, went over to the elevator, and began jabbing at the button.

"Nice talking to you," I called to him.

He looked at me, shook his head, and turned back to watch the light over the elevator. He was clenching and unclenching his fists, as if he were disappointed that he hadn't had the chance to hit somebody.

I rang the bell to the ICU, and after a minute, a nurse opened the door. I didn't recognize her.

"I'm Moses Crandall's nephew," I said. "My name is Brady Coyne. I'm here to visit him."

She frowned for a moment, then said, "Oh, yes. We've talked on the phone." She hesitated. "He just had a visitor. You might find him a bit, um, agitated."

"His brother?" I said. "Jacob?"

She nodded.

"What happened?"

"I don't know. They were talking. Then Mr. Crandall—Jacob, that is, the brother—he started yelling, and then he come storming out of there. I went in to check on my patient. I was afraid, a man with a heart condition . . ."

"Is he all right?"

She nodded. "He was spittin' mad about something. Didn't say what. I asked if I could get him something, and he said a glass of whiskey would be nice. So I guess he's okay. Why don't you come on in and see for yourself." She held the door open for me.

I went over to Uncle Moze's cubicle and pulled up a chair

beside his bed. He was lying on his side, facing away from me. "Hey? Uncle Moze? You awake?"

He turned and looked at me. "Hey, sonnyboy." His voice was a gravelly whisper. "What in hell are you doing here?"

"I needed to see for myself that they were taking good care of you."

He lifted a hand and let it fall. "No complaints."

"The food's okay?"

"Food is food."

"Jake was here, huh?"

"Don't know why he bothered," he said. "Come to harass me, is all."

"Harass you about what?"

He shook his head. "Nothin'. It don't matter. Jake's a hostile sonofabitch, that's all. Always got some chip or other on his shoulder. I told him, I said, don't bother coming back here. Told him I didn't want to see him no more, brother or no brother. The hell with him."

"Is that why he got mad?"

"I s'pose so."

I hitched my chair closer. "Uncle Moze," I said, "I want to know who did this to you."

"Who did what?"

"Hit you."

"Somebody hit me?"

"Somebody punched you in the chest. It caused you to have a heart attack. That's why you're here."

He frowned. "I got punched, huh?"

I nodded. "Tell me what you remember."

He shook his head. "I don't remember nothing."

"It was early in the morning," I said. "You were home in your bedroom sleeping. You heard something. You got up and went

229

into the living room. Somebody was there. They punched you in the chest and you had a heart attack."

He shrugged. "If you say so. I got no memory of it."

"Something woke you up, caused you to go out into the living room. Remember?"

He shook his head. "Nope."

"Maybe you didn't see them," I said. "Maybe it was just a shadow. Maybe they said something."

"I don't remember nothing about it, sonnyboy. You can keep askin' me in as many different ways as you want, but I ain't going to suddenly remember. It's just a blank. Nothin'."

"Well," I said, "if it comes back to you, tell me, okay?"

"It don't make no difference anyways," he said. "I know what's going on. I'm a goner, that's what. I'm on my last legs."

"Oh, you're a tough old buzzard," I said. "You've got a lot of mileage left on you." I bent closer to him. "Uncle Moze, listen to me. This is important. Don't hold back on me, okay? Was it Cassie? Is she the one who hit you?"

"Why in hell would you think that?" he said.

"I don't think it. I just wondered."

He narrowed his eyes at me for a moment. "Leave Cassie out of it," he said. "I'm tired. Go away." He rolled away from me.

After a minute, his breathing became slow and regular. If he wasn't sleeping, he was pretending to sleep. Either way, he was done with me.

I stood up, gave his shoulder a squeeze, and walked out of the ICU.

Charlene Staples was standing in the little waiting room with her back to the door, looking out the window.

"Hey," I said.

She turned around and arched her eyebrows.

I shook my head.

She shrugged. "You think he really doesn't remember what happened to him?"

"I don't think it matters whether he remembers or not," I said. "If he does, he's made up his mind not to tell us. If you want to catch the bad guy, it looks like you're going to have to do it without Moze's help."

"Oh, never fear," she said, "I'll catch her."

TWENTY

I got home a little after five that afternoon. As soon as I opened the front door, I was assailed by the aroma of fresh-baked bread. I followed my nose into the kitchen. Two loaves were cooling on wire racks on the counter. So was a blueberry pie.

I peeked out the window. Evie was slouched in one of our Adirondack chairs. She was wearing shorts and T-shirt. Bare feet. Her perfect legs were splayed out and her head was tilted back to the sun and her eyes were closed. Henry was lying beside her, directly beneath Evie's hand, which dangled over the side of the chair.

I made a couple of gin and tonics and took them outside. I kissed Evie's cheek. It was warm from the sun, and soft, and smelled faintly of damp loam and crushed herbs.

Her eyes fluttered open and looked at me unfocused for a moment. Then she smiled. "Hi, sweetie."

"Smells great in there. You've been busy."

"Made the bread from scratch," she said. "Excellent therapy."

"Excellent eating, too." I sat beside her. "You feeling like you need therapy?"

She shrugged. "How's your uncle?"

I told her, and that was it for the subject of therapy.

At around seven thirty on Monday morning I was sitting out in the back garden working on my second mug of coffee when Evie came out. She was wearing a pale blue business suit—narrow knee-length skirt, matching jacket, silk blouse. Her hair was up in a bun and her sneakers were on her feet.

She bent down to kiss me. I reached up, hooked my arm around her neck, and brought her down so I could kiss her properly.

"Careful of the hair," she said.

"You're leaving early again. What's up?"

"Nothing. Work, work, work. Another damn meeting."

About twenty minutes after Evie left there was a knock on the wooden door in the brick wall that opened from our garden to the back alley.

"It's unlocked," I called.

The door opened and Roger Horowitz came in.

"Uh-oh," I said.

He came over and sat at the picnic table. "Got some coffee?"

I went into the kitchen, poured a mug of coffee, brought it out, and set it beside Horowitz's elbow. A manila file folder lay in front of him.

I sat across from him. "What's up?"

"Grantham Webster," he said. "The dead guy. How's your dog?"

"He's okay. A little lame. You gonna ask about my head?"

He shrugged. "Looks fine to me."

"So what about Webster?"

"Wednesday?" he said. "The first time you met with him in his office? I want you to go over everything that happened."

"Jesus," I said. "I already—"

"Humor me, Coyne."

So I recounted what I could remember about my visit with Grannie Webster. Horowitz was particularly interested in the phone call he'd received while I was there, and he queried me closely about Webster's reaction to it, but I couldn't remember anything more or different from what I'd told him already.

"He said it was his ex-wife?"

"Yes. Asked me to step out of the office, give him some privacy, which I did, though I could hear his voice through the door. When I went back in he said it was his ex-wife. From what I overheard, he seemed angry, annoyed, upset."

Horowitz nodded. "That's funny."

"Why?"

"Because Webster was never married. Didn't have any ex-wife."

I shrugged. "So he lied to me. So what? It was none of my business."

"If it wasn't some ex-wife," said Horowitz, "who was it?"

I nodded. "That's obviously the question. The answer is, I have no idea who it was."

"That call came on his cell phone, you said?"

I nodded.

"Now that phone's gone. Along with the CDs from his computer."

I smiled at Horowitz. "He was killed the next day. Thursday. I've got a suspicion that you didn't take the weekend off, go down to the Cape, lie around the beach."

He smiled sourly. "Not fucking hardly."

"You gonna share with me?"

"Why the hell should I?"

"Because," I said, "you wouldn't be here if you didn't want something from me. Quid pro quo, Roger. What've you found out?"

He gave me a sour grin. "Not enough. Webster was shot twice in the chest with a thirty-eight from about three feet away."

"Thirty-eight?" I said. "That's—"

"Right." He nodded. "The gun your friend Hurley reported missing was a thirty-eight. Millions of thirty-eights around. But, yeah, we're checking that angle."

I spread out my hands. "Seems pretty compelling to me."

"Compelling and evidence ain't the same thing," he said. "Near as we can figure, the shooter was probably standing on the other side of Webster's desk. Even if you're a crack shot, you can't hit a damn thing with one of those thirty-eight handguns from much farther. Forensics got some fibers and smudged prints and other shit that'll probably turn out to be useless."

"A lot of probablies there," I said.

He nodded and took a sip of his coffee. "More like maybes than probablies, actually. We'd really like to talk to your cousin.

"You think Cassie stole Hurley's gun and—?"

"I don't think nothing," he said. "I just want to talk to her."

"Well," I said, "you'd have to stand in line, except nobody seems to know where she is. She's missing. She may not be alive."

"Maybe Webster knew."

I looked at him. "I see where you're going with this."

He shook his head. "Glad you do. I don't. Nothing fits. I'm thinking she's the key, that's all. What happened to your uncle, what happened to Webster. Cassandra Crandall is the common thread."

"Her husband, the dentist, he's a common thread, too."

"Of course he is," Horowitz said. "Hurley says he was filling teeth all day."

"You can verify that?"

He shrugged. "We're working on it. We got a good idea of when Webster was shot. If the dentist took a long lunch hour that day, or left the office early . . ."

"I can't stop thinking he killed Cassie," I said. "She's missing two weeks and he doesn't report it?"

"Yeah," said Horowitz, "it's always the spouse. Except we got no body, no witness, no nothing. Far as we know, we got no crime there. No case to investigate. That's why we're talking about Grantham Webster. Him, we definitely got a crime."

I shrugged. "I wish I could help you."

"Me, too," he said. He opened the manila folder, flipped through a stack of papers, removed two of them, and put them on the table. "Forensics took that computer he had in his office, plus a laptop from his apartment. So far, they haven't found anything interesting. We got the phone records from his house and his office phones. It's gonna take a while to track down the records from his cell phone." He arched his eyebrows at me.

"What?" I arched my eyebrows right back at him.

"What did you do yesterday on a pretty Sunday in July?"

"I visited my uncle in the hospital," I said. "Had a few gin and tonics. Ate Evie's fresh-baked bread. Why?"

"Me and Marcia," said Horowitz, "we spent the day riding herd on forensics and ballistics, checking out witnesses, running down phone numbers."

"You should've been a lawyer," I said, "take Sundays off."

"Yeah," he said. "Like you."

"Any luck with witnesses?"

He shook his head. "The college is between summer sessions. No students or teachers around. Most of the administration offices were empty, too. We found a groundskeeper who was mowing the lawn that afternoon. He says he didn't see or hear anything. Those mowers are so loud, he wouldn't hear a bomb exploding, never mind a gunshot from somewhere inside a building. So far, that's it."

"What about the phone records?"

He pushed the two sheets of paper at me. "Incoming calls," he said. "Webster's office and home phone, the past month."

Each sheet had two columns of dates and phone numbers. Five of them on the sheet from Webster's home phone and six on the office-phone sheet had circles around them. They were all the same number with a 207 area code. Eleven calls, and all of them had been made during the two weeks leading up to the day that Webster was killed.

"What do you see, Coyne?"

"I see that you've drawn circles around one of these numbers that keeps coming up. It's a 207 area code, which is Maine. This number appears to interest you." I looked up at him. "You haven't seen Webster's cell-phone records?"

He shook his head. "Not yet. Cell-phone records are harder to get at." He pointed at the papers in front of me. "See anything else?"

I studied them. "I see that all these 207 calls you've circled were all made after Cassie went missing. I see that all of the calls to Webster's office phone were made on Mondays, Wednesdays, and Thursdays between two and four in the afternoon, which was when he held office hours. Whoever made these calls knew his schedule." I looked up at him. "Whose number is this?"

He shrugged. "These calls were made from a convenience store in West Canterbury called Roy's. It's not a pay phone. It's a private phone that's out on the porch for people to use. The store sells phone cards to the locals. A lot of them are too poor to have their own phone."

"I've been everywhere in Maine," I said. "Never heard of West Canterbury."

"Nobody's heard of it," said Horowitz. "Population about two hundred, not counting the goats and chickens. Mostly swamp and woods and run-down farms and dirt roads. That convenience store is about it for commerce in West Canterbury."

"You called and talked to them?"

He rolled his eyes. "That's pretty much what we mean by running down phone numbers. It's how Benetti and I spent the damn weekend."

I jabbed my finger at the sheets of paper. "So who's making these calls?"

He grinned quickly. "That's the question, huh?"

"Where in Maine did you say West Canterbury was?" I said.

"Didn't say," he said. "Turns out it's just two towns to the north and west of Moulton."

I looked at him. "No shit."

He nodded. "No shit."

"You can't go up there," I said.

"I can go up there," he said. "But I can't do business."

"Jurisdiction."

He nodded.

"You being from Massachusetts, this place being across the border in Maine."

"Yeah," he said. "That's what we're usually getting at when we talk about jurisdiction."

"I assume you got the West Canterbury cops on the case."

He smiled. "There are no cops in West Canterbury."

"The county sheriff, then."

He shrugged. "We got a call in to his office. I'm not holding my breath." Horowitz glanced at his watch, then reached over and tapped the two lists of phone numbers with his forefinger. "You done with these?"

I took another look at the 207 number, then nodded.

He picked up the lists, shoved them into his manila folder, and stood up. "Gotta go."

239

"Thanks for dropping by, sharing this with me."

He shrugged. "Courtesy call. Just filling you in. Since you found that body and took a whack on the head for your trouble, I figure you've got an interest in the case. Thanks for the coffee."

He left the way he'd come in—through the garden gate. I guessed he'd parked in the alley out back, so as not to draw my neighbors' attention to the fact that I was being visited by a state police officer.

Or maybe he just couldn't find a parking space on the street out front.

His visit wasn't a courtesy call, of course. Horowitz had no interest in courtesy.

He wanted me to check out Roy's convenience store in West Canterbury, Maine, see if I could figure out who had made all those calls to Grantham Webster.

He couldn't come out and ask me, a mere layperson, to help him. Cops didn't work that way.

Whatever I chose to do on my own, though, wasn't Roger Horowitz's responsibility.

He thought he knew me pretty well.

He was right.

As soon as he left, I wrote down that 207 number in West Canterbury before I forgot it.

TWENTY-ONE

After Horowitz left, I called Julie and told her I'd be gone for the afternoon and would be spending the morning working at home. She gave me a list of phone calls I should make and said she hoped I caught lots of fish.

I told her I wasn't going fishing, but it was pretty clear that she didn't believe me.

Next I dialed the 207 number for the convenience store in West Canterbury, Maine.

It rang five or six times, and then a man's cheerful voice said, "Hay-lo."

"Is this Roy's store?"

"Ayuh. You lookin' for Roy?"

"It's UPS," I said. "I got a delivery for Roy's in West Canterbury. I'm not sure where you're located."

"This ain't Roy," said the man. "Roy ain't here. He went bass fishin'. Dot's inside. You wanna talk to Dot?"

"I bet you can help me," I said. "I just need directions to the store."

"Where at you comin' from?"

"Kittery."

241

He laughed. "You cain't get here from there."

"That's a pretty old joke," I said.

"Pretty much true, though."

"Maybe you better put me on with Dot," I said.

"Nah," he said. "I kin tell you good as her. Comin' from Kitt'ry, you want to head west and git onto 202. Then you start looking for the West Canterbury sign. Mile or so after that, you come to a fork where 202 hooks around to the right? Take that left fork. You'll find Roy's a mile or so down there on your left. If you come to the bridge goes over the river, turn around, 'cause you went too far. You got all that, Mr. UPS man?"

"Got it," I said. "Thank you, sir."

I worked at my desk for a couple of hours, and around eleven I went upstairs and changed into my comfortable old jeans and a T-shirt and sneakers. I wanted to leave by noon so I could get there by two. I figured it wouldn't take more than an hour and a half to find Roy's, but I didn't want to be late.

I intended to stay until four. That's when the phone calls to Grannie Webster's office were made. Between two and four in the afternoon on Mondays, Wednesdays, and Thursdays.

When I came down, Henry took one look at me and ambled over to the front door. Sneakers and blue jeans meant I was going somewhere more interesting than my office. He sat there on full alert with his ears perked up expectantly.

"Sorry, pal," I said.

His ears drooped. He glared at me for a moment, and when I didn't relent, he crawled onto the sofa, curled up in the corner, tucked his nose under his paws, and pretended to go to sleep. He was sulking.

He understood the word "sorry," and he didn't like hearing it.

242

Roy's was typical of the mom-and-pop stores that serve small villages all across Maine, New Hampshire, and Vermont. It looked like an old-fashioned New England farmhouse—which it may originally have been. An open porch spanned the front. The big window beside the door was plastered with hand-printed signs—Sandwiches to Go, Crawlers and Live Bait, New Videos, Ammo, Homemade Ice Cream, Fresh Vegetables. There were two dormers on the roof with curtains in the windows, indicating an upstairs apartment where the proprietor probably lived.

I got there a little after one thirty—early as usual. I backed into a space between a newish Ford pickup truck and a battered old Toyota Corolla in the crushed-stone parking area that bordered some woods beside the store. I got out, walked over to the front, and climbed the three porch steps. On the porch were two weathered wooden rocking chairs on either side of a low plastic table. An old-fashioned black telephone with a rotary dial—the phone I was looking for, I assumed—sat on the table, along with a red plastic ashtray brimming with butts and two Diet Coke cans.

I went into the store. A plump sixtyish woman with a long gray braid and round rimless glasses was sitting on a stool behind the counter just inside the door. She was looking down at a magazine that was open on her lap.

I said hello, and she looked up and smiled at me.

I wandered the narrow aisles between the free-standing shelves that were stacked with canned goods. In the back I found a cooler and picked up a bottle of orange juice and a tuna sandwich. The sandwich was wrapped in waxed paper and secured with masking tape. I didn't know they even made waxed paper anymore.

I took my juice and sandwich up front and put them on the counter. "Nice day," I said to the woman.

"Could use some rain," she said. "That's a buck twenty-five for the juice, three ninety-five for the sandwich." She rang them up. "Five twenty."

I took out a five-dollar bill from my wallet, found two dimes in my pocket, and put the money into her hand. "Wonder if you might help me out," I said.

She shrugged. "Might. Depends."

"I have a cousin, haven't seen her in years. I seem to recall she was living in West Canterbury. Her name's Cassandra Crandall."

The woman's eyes flicked up to the ceiling, then came back. "Cassandra, huh? Nope. Don't know no Cassandra."

I'd remembered to bring the photo that Uncle Moze gave me. I took it from my pocket and put in on the counter. "This is Cassandra. Everyone calls her Cassie. That's my uncle with her. It was taken a few years ago."

The woman glanced down at the photo. "Never laid eyes on either one of 'em," she said.

I smiled. "I bet you know everybody around here."

"Just about, I guess."

"I must be remembering wrong, then," I said. "Thanks anyway." I hesitated and pretended to look around. "Say, you don't have a pay phone, do you?"

"Out there." She jutted her chin toward the porch. "It ain't exactly a pay phone. You can make a local call, no charge. Otherwise you gotta use one of them company cards, or I can sell you a phone card."

I thanked her, went out to the porch, sat in one of the rocking chairs, and used my MCI card to call Evie's cell phone. I figured, having asked about the phone, if I didn't use it the woman would be suspicious. The fewer suspicions I aroused, the better.

Evie didn't answer, so I left her a message. "Hi, honey," I said. "It's around two o'clock. I'm in Maine looking for my cousin.

I should be home for dinner. If it doesn't look like I'll make it, I'll let you know. Hope you're having a good day."

I took my sandwich and juice to my car and got in behind the wheel. From where I was sitting I could watch the front porch of the store. Although I was somewhat hidden by the truck and the Corolla on either side of me, I knew my BMW was not exactly inconspicuous, but I didn't know what to do about it.

I took my bird-watching binoculars out of the glove compartment and put them on the seat beside me.

I sat there, ate my lunch, and watched the front of the store.

Now and then a car or a truck with Maine plates pulled into the lot. Somebody got out, went inside, came out ten minutes later carrying a plastic bag or a six-pack of Coke, and drove away. None of them was Cassie, or anybody else that I recognized.

Around three a pair of teenage girls went in. A few minutes later they came out with Popsicles and sat in the rocking chairs to lick them.

While they were there, a man on a motorcycle stopped out front and used the phone.

By quarter past three the urge to urinate dominated my thoughts. Gordon Cahill, my friend the PI, once told me that he never brought anything to drink on a stakeout. I'd remembered this important piece of wisdom too late.

I slipped out of my car, ducked into the woods, and pissed against a big pine tree. When I got back, it didn't appear that I'd missed any excitement.

I kept checking my watch. The hands were moving very slowly.

At 3:52 a woman pedaled a bicycle up to the front of the store, got off, leaned the bike against the porch rail, and looked around.

I sat forward. Strands of black hair straggled out from under her blue baseball cap. Under the visor, she was wearing sunglasses.

245

She wore baggy sweatpants, a man's shirt with the tails flapping, and sneakers. From the distance between us, I might have mistaken her for a man.

But I knew I was not mistaken. She moved with the grace and sway of a woman, and even under her loose-fitting clothes, you couldn't mistake the shape of a woman's body.

Cassie. It had to be.

I picked up my binoculars, put them to my eyes, got them focused, studied her face.

I recognized her from the photo. She had the sharp Crandall nose, the high, elegant cheekbones, the slightly pointed chin, the large expressive mouth—every feature that I'd seen in every photo of her on Uncle Moze's television from the time she was a toddler.

She could have been Moze's flesh and blood, but, of course, she wasn't. She was his niece, his sister Mary's daughter.

I slouched in my seat behind the wheel of my car, though I didn't think she could see me through the glare on my windshield. I felt sneaky and vaguely unclean, spying on her.

But that didn't stop me from doing it.

She went up onto the porch and sat in one of the rockers by the telephone. A young guy—he looked like a high-school boy—came out of the store. He stopped and said something to her. She took off her sunglasses, looked up at him, smiled and shook her head. They talked for a minute, and then he shrugged and waved and headed for his car.

Cassie watched him until he drove away. Then she picked up the telephone. She dialed a number, put the receiver to her ear, looked up at the sky, and listened. Then she shook her head and replaced the receiver on its cradle.

She sat there for a minute, rocking in the chair. Then she picked up the phone again, dialed a number, listened, frowned, and hung up.

She made a fist and punched the palm of her hand. Then she puffed her cheeks, blew out a breath, put her sunglasses back on, stood up, and went into the store.

I'd found her, but I hadn't figured out what to do next. I thought about getting out of my car, walking up to the store, and saying hello to her. It was the logical, straightforward thing to do.

But Cassie's body language made me hesitate. I read alertness, apprehension, caution, maybe even fear in it. She was hiding out. She wouldn't be happy to know she'd been found. I couldn't predict what she might do when she realized it.

So I sat there and pondered my next move.

When I was a kid, I used to drive my old man nuts. He'd say, "Brady, my boy, would you prefer to mow the lawn or wash the car today?" and when I'd pause to weigh the pros and cons of those distasteful options, he'd look at me, shake his head, and say, "That's right, Mr. Hamlet. Don't just do something. Sit there."

I was still sitting there considering my choices when Cassie emerged from the store with a plastic bag dangling from her hand. She descended the front steps, put the bag into the basket on the handlebars of her bike, then hesitated. She turned around slowly, pulled the visor of her cap low, and looked directly at my car. It seemed as if she was staring straight into my eyes from behind her sunglasses. There was no expression that I could decipher on her face.

I suspected that the woman at the cash register had told her that some guy with a Boston accent had been in a few hours ago. This stranger had shown her Cassie's photo, asked if she knew her, inquired about the telephone.

The woman, of course, had denied recognizing Cassandra Crandall's name or picture. Local folks watch out for each other. They respect each other's privacy. They mistrust people they don't know.

The woman had probably noticed the car the stranger was driving—it was a noticeable vehicle, an expensive-looking green foreign job with a sunroof and Massachusetts plates—and pointed it out to Cassie.

Or maybe I was imagining all that.

Cassie got on her bike, turned it around, looked in my direction again, then pedaled away. Maybe I was wrong, but I read that look as an invitation. Or maybe it was a challenge. "Come on. Follow me. I dare you."

She was riding one of those old one-speed bikes with fat tires and a crossbar. A boy's bike. Girls' bikes didn't have those unladylike crossbars that would interfere with their skirts.

I wondered if they still made girls' bikes.

She turned left out of the parking lot and pedaled south along the side of the winding two-lane roadway until she disappeared around the bend. I gave her another few minutes, then started up my car, pulled onto the road, and turned in the direction Cassie had taken.

I drove slowly. For a mile or so the road twisted through woods and fields. Cassie had put enough distance between us that she was always out of sight around the bend or over the hill ahead of me. I kept my eye out for places where she might turn in, but there were no side roads, no old overgrown woods roads, even, so I was pretty sure she was still somewhere in front of me.

After a while the road climbed a long gentle hill, and I imagined Cassie standing on her pedals as she pumped up it. Where it crested and sloped away, she would coast down with the wind in her face.

At the bottom of the long hill I came upon a trailer park tucked into a pine grove on the left. A couple dozen small, dingy trailers were spaced out under the big pines. A few cars were parked near them.

I slowed to a crawl as I drove past, looked hard, but I didn't see Cassie, or anybody else for that matter, moving around.

248

Past the trailer park, the road flattened and straightened in front of me. I speeded up, but there was no figure on a bike in sight.

The pine woods petered out into scrub, then meadow, then a marshland. Soon I crossed a bridge that spanned what appeared to be a tidal creek. A sign indicated I'd entered the town of Amidon. Still no sign of Cassie on her bike.

A minute later the road I was on intersected a busy three-lane highway at a yellow blinking light. There was a gas station on one corner and a real estate office, a snowmobile shop, and a lumberyard on the other three. Here, suddenly, was commerce.

I stopped at the intersection. If Cassie had come this far, I'd lost her. She could've gone three different ways.

I had to assume she'd turned into the trailer park.

I turned around at the gas station, drove back to the trailer park, and pulled into the sand driveway. I stopped in what appeared to be a parking area near the road and got out of my car. The trailers were widely spaced and laid out randomly among the trees, about half and half single- and double-wides. They sat up on cinder blocks, stained with rust streaks and smudges of dirt and splotches of pine pollen and general neglect, although a few of them sported brave window boxes of marigolds and impatiens. Propane tanks leaned against their outside walls, and beat-up automobiles and muddy pickup trucks were parked in front. Kids' tricycles, plastic ride toys, and doghouses were scattered around some of the sand-and-pine-needle yards. Here and there a clothesline was strung between two trees. Flannel shirts and blue jeans and bath towels and women's underwear flapped from them. TV antennas sprouted from the roofs of several trailers.

It took me a few minutes to spot Cassie's bike. It was leaning against the side of a single-wide at the rear of the park near the bordering woods.

I still hadn't exactly planned out how I was going to approach her or what I would say. But it was time to do something, and since subterfuge and misdirection were not my strong suits, I walked directly over to Cassie's trailer. The heavy bass-line beat of rock music came thumping at me from inside. As I got closer, I recognized the tune: "Sympathy for the Devil," by the Rolling Stones. A very good oldie.

A single cinder block served as a step up to the trailer's only door. Just as I put my left foot on it, I sensed rather than heard something behind me—a quick inhalation of breath, maybe, or a moccasin stepping softly on pine needles, or just the movement of air when a body moves through it.

If the music hadn't been so loud, I might've sensed it earlier and had a chance to react.

But as it was, before I could move, something hard rammed into my kidneys. "Put both hands flat against the door where I can see 'em," came a growly woman's voice behind me.

I knew what was poking into me. It had happened before. It was the business end of a gun barrel.

I did as I was told. Now I was standing awkwardly, bent forward, with one foot on the ground and one on the step and all my weight supported by my arms.

"Cassie?" I said. I started to turn my head.

The gun barrel poked into me. "Don't fuckin' move," she said. "I got number two steel shot in here, and I can pump three loads into you before you finish blinking."

"Come on," I said. "This is uncomfortable."

"Tough," she said. "Who in hell are you, anyway, and why are you following me around, and how do you know my name?"

"Can I turn around?"

"No, damn it. I don't like being stalked."

"I wasn't stalking you," I said. "I just want to talk with you."

"Why should I want to talk to you?"

"I've got news for you," I said. "I'm your cousin. I'm Brady Coyne."

"Who?"

"Your cousin. You were just a baby last time I saw you. I have a message from your father."

"Like hell you do," she said. "I don't have any father."

"Moze," I said. "Moses Crandall."

"Moses Crandall," she said, "is not my father."

TWENTY-TWO

L ook," I said. "This is extremely uncomfortable. I'm going to straighten up and turn around now, and I'd appreciate it if you didn't shoot me. Okay?"

"Hang on," she said. "You got any ID?"

"My wallet's in my back pocket."

"Take it out. Slowly. Keep your other hand on the wall." The gun barrel stopped poking into my back.

I reached around with my left hand, slid my wallet from my hip pocket, and held it there behind me.

She took it from me. Then she said, "Okay. You can turn around."

I pushed myself away from the door of the trailer and turned to face Cassie. Creases bracketed her mouth like parentheses, and she had squint wrinkles at the corners of her eyes. She had coppery skin and coal black hair and those sharp blue Crandall eyes. She looked older than I'd expected, older than she'd appeared in the picture on Grannie Webster's desk. More timeworn.

She had stepped back. She was holding a pump-action shotgun at her hip, and it was pointing at my stomach. She looked me up and down. "So you're my cousin, huh?"

I nodded. "Please aim that thing somewhere else."

"I don't think so," she said. "Why don't you sit down. Keep your hands where I can see 'em." She handed my wallet to me.

I put the wallet back into my pocket, then sat on the cinder block with my hands on my knees. "Why the gun? What are you afraid of?"

She shook her head. "Just tell me why you were following me."

"I've been trying to track you down for a week," I said. "Your father's in the hospital."

She shook her head. "I told you. Moses Crandall is not my father."

"He's desperate to see you."

"I don't want to see him."

"Why not?"

"None of your business that I can see."

"He's in bad shape, Cassie. He had a heart attack. He's got an aortic aneurysm. He damn near died. You wouldn't recognize him. It's like he got old and frail overnight."

I watched the emotions wrestle on her face. After a few seconds she shook her head, lowered the barrel of her pump gun, and narrowed her eyes at me. "You're really my cousin?"

I nodded. "My mother was Hope Crandall. Moze's sister. He's my uncle. When I was a kid my father and I used to go out on Uncle Moze's lobster boat with him. I remember you when you were a toddler."

"I guess maybe I remember old Moze mentioning you." She gave a little shrug. "You might as well come inside. I got iced tea in the fridge."

We went in. The Rolling Stones were now singing "Gimme Shelter." The music was deafening as it thumped and ricocheted around inside the little tin trailer.

Cassie reached up to a boom box on a shelf and turned it off. The sudden silence was profound.

"I dig the Stones," I said. "Music from my youth."

"Dig." She smiled.

The trailer seemed even smaller from the inside than from the outside. There was a kitchenette you could barely turn around in, with a little pull-down table and bench seats. It was equipped with built-in miniature appliances—a two-burner stovetop, a refrigerator not much bigger than the microwave oven that sat on top of it, a square bathroom-sized sink. The adjacent living room was cramped with a faded love seat and a ragged upholstered chair and a square wooden table with a small TV on it. Beyond that a folding door closed off what I assumed was the bedroom. The whole place was finished in faded linoleum and peeling fabric wallpaper and dull aluminum and cheap wood paneling.

Cassie pointed at the living room. "Have a seat."

I went over and sat in the chair.

A minute later she came in with two glasses in her hand. The pump gun had disappeared.

She handed me one of the glasses and sat in the corner of the love seat with her legs curled under her. "Tell me about Moze," she said.

So I told her about getting that phone call from Uncle Moze after all those years and going out on his lobster boat with him. I described how he had been grief-stricken about being out of touch with Cassie and had asked me to try to track her down and how soon after that he'd had a heart attack.

I told her about visiting our aunt Faith, and how Faith had told me that Cassie had been there asking about Mary and Norman Dillman, her biological parents.

When I finished, I saw tears brimming in her eyes. "I've been terribly mad at him," she said.

"You should go see him," I said. "He's at Maine Medical in Portland. I'd be happy to drive you over there."

She shook her head. "I don't know. It's complicated."

I sipped my iced tea and said nothing.

"He never told me he wasn't my father," she said after a minute. "All these years I'm thinking I know who I am, where I came from. He lied to me. My whole life was a lie. Do you know what it's like, finding out something like that?"

I shook my head. "I can't imagine."

"It changes everything," she said. "There was no reason he couldn't tell me. I would've still loved him."

"Maybe he just thought of you as his little girl," I said. "Moze and Lillian, they raised you from the day you were born, practically. I don't think they intended to hide it from you. It wasn't really like it was a secret. After Lillian died, Moze just didn't get around to it."

"He should've told me. I have a right to know."

"It was a mistake," I said. "But a forgivable mistake."

She was shaking her head. "I don't know if it's forgivable. I don't know."

"It must've been a jolt," I said. "Finding out."

Cassie was huddled in the corner of the love seat staring down at the glass of iced tea she was holding in both hands on her lap. When she looked up at me, I saw that her eyes were red and her cheeks were wet.

"It was my birth certificate," she said. "When you get a marriage license, you have to provide a birth certificate. I'd never had any need for one before that. So I called the town clerk in Moulton and they sent me one. It said my parents were Mary Crandall and Norman Dillman. I called up the town clerk and told her it was a mistake, and she told me no, it was no mistake. So I did some research, and I learned that Norman Dillman got murdered just a couple months before I was born. He was some kind of small-time criminal, I guess. So then I tracked down Aunt Faith. I wanted to know what happened."

"Mary took back her maiden name when Norman got killed,"

I said. "I figure she wanted to be sure you were a Crandall instead of a Dillman."

"Damned considerate of her," said Cassie.

I smiled. "After you were born, she gave you to Uncle Moze and Aunt Lillian, and then she ran off with a minor-league baseball player. She died of cancer a while ago."

"Yes, right," she said. "See? That's what I mean. My father was murdered? My mother loved me so much that she gave me away? Now they're both dead? I don't know how I'm supposed to deal with that."

"Moze should've told you," I said. "But he didn't. You've got to keep in mind, you were always the main thing in his life. Still are."

She nodded. "I guess so." She looked at me. "So how do you know all this stuff?"

"I've been poking around."

She smiled quickly. "You're a nosy sonofabitch, aren't you?"

I nodded. "Moze asked me to try to find you. It's taken all the nosiness I could muster. You've got to mend fences with him."

"Is he going to be okay?"

"I saw him yesterday. He's still in ICU, but they think he's going to make it. He'll never be the same. You have a heart attack at his age, it changes you. And he's got that aneurysm. It could explode anytime."

"I had decided to just cut Moses Crandall out of my life," she said. "Forget the whole family-roots thing. My childhood, my father, everything I thought I knew. Just try to start from scratch."

"Is that what this is all about?" I waved my hand around, indicating the trailer. "Starting from scratch?"

"Huh?" she said. "This? Living here?" She laughed quickly. "Not hardly. This is, I'm hiding out, trying to figure out what to do next. That's what this is all about. Right now, this is just saving my life, not starting a new one."

257

"What do you mean?"

"That man I married?"

I nodded. "Richard Hurley. The dentist."

"Yes. Him. I found out he killed his previous wife, and I sure as hell don't intend to wait around for him to kill me."

"What did you say?" I leaned forward. "He killed his wife? Do you know that?"

She nodded. "I overheard him talking with his daughter. Rebecca. Arguing, I mean. What I heard, it was clear what happened. Ellen—his wife—she had an asthma attack, fell down and hurt herself, couldn't breathe, couldn't really move, and he . . . Richard . . . he refused to get her inhaler. He just stood there and . . . and watched her gasp for air and suffocate and die. That's murder, isn't it?"

"Yes," I said. "That would certainly be murder. Are you sure of this?"

She shrugged. "What I heard, it was jumbled, both of 'em talking at once, mostly, but you couldn't mistake the gist of it. I've been playing that scenario in my head over and over ever since I heard it, picturing this man I married standing there watching his wife die."

"His first wife," I said, "Becca and James's mother, she committed suicide. Do you know anything about that?"

Cassie shook her head. "Only that Becca came home from school and found her mother in her car in the garage with the motor running. Richard was at work all day. He couldn't have had anything to do with that."

I was thinking about the legal case against Richard Hurley for the murder of his second wife. Based on what Cassie had said, without Hurley's confession, unless Becca or James had witnessed it, there was no case whatsoever.

I looked up at her. "So," I said, "here you are. Do you have a plan?"

"Do I intend to live here forever, do you mean?" She smiled quickly. "Not hardly. I got a friend who's helping me. He's the one who found this place for me, brought me here."

"Grantham Webster? Is that who you mean?"

She nodded, then arched her eyebrows. "How do you know about Grannie?"

"I talked to him. I told you I've been looking for you. He said he didn't know where you were. He—"

"Grannie wouldn't tell you anything," she said quickly. "He'd lie for me, no matter what. I know that much. I guess he's pretty mad at me, though. I sort of dumped him when I decided to get married. But he came through for me when I had to get away from Richard. Except now he doesn't want to speak to me anymore."

"Is that who you were trying to call today?"

"When you were spying on me at Roy's, you mean?"

"You knew I was there?"

She smiled. "I hope you're not a private investigator or something."

"Actually, I'm a lawyer."

"Well, good," she said. "Because you'd make a crummy detective. Dot told me you'd been asking about me, showing my picture around, and that you were still out there in the parking lot in the green BMW with Massachusetts plates."

"Oh, well," I said. "So you were trying to call Grannie?"

She nodded. "He knows it's me, and he won't even answer anymore. I guess I don't blame him. I didn't treat him very well. I made a huge mistake. I still love him. He's a great guy." She shrugged. "That's it. That's what I want to tell him. That I really do love him. That I blew it."

"Did you try his cell phone?"

"Cell phone, office phone. He was supposed to be having office hours this afternoon."

259

I reached over to touch her hand. She flinched, and then relaxed.

"Cassie," I said, "I've got some bad news for you."

"I don't need any more bad news."

"I'm sorry." I hesitated. "Grannie was killed on Friday."

She looked at me. "Killed?"

"He was shot twice in the chest," I said. "He was in his office."

"Murdered?" She blinked. "You saying somebody murdered him?"

I nodded.

She hunched her shoulders and put her hands together as if she were praying and covered her mouth and nose with them. Her eyes darted wildly around the inside of the trailer. Then they stopped on my face. "It was him, wasn't it?"

"Who?"

"Richard. He found out that Grannie helped me get away. He's after me. He figured out that I know what he did to Ellen, and he's going to find me and kill me, too."

I squeezed her hand. "No he's not."

"You don't know Richard Hurley," she said. "He always gets what he wants."

"Well," I said, "the first thing to do is get the hell out of here. If I was able to track you down, I guess anybody could. We'll go talk to the police. Then we'll head up to Portland and visit Moze. Okay?"

She let out a long breath. "Whatever you say. I'm tired of making decisions. I'll do whatever you think I should do."

I stood up and held my hands out to her. She looked up at me, gave me a sad half smile, took my hands, and pulled herself to her feet. She was nearly my height, and she looked intently into my eyes as if they might tell her that she could trust me.

Then she smiled, put her arms around my neck, and hugged me. "Good to see you again, Cousin," she whispered.

I put my arms around her. "You, too."

"I'm awfully sad about Grannie," she murmured into my shoulder. "It was because of me. What happened to him. I treated him terribly, and he was still always there for me. He was the only one I had. The only one I could depend on. Even after I dumped him. He'd get awfully mad sometimes, but he was still there for me. Grannie was like my only real family."

I patted her back. I couldn't think of anything to say.

She leaned back and looked at me. "Well, I guess I do still have some family, even if old Moze isn't my father."

"He's at least your uncle," I said. "And you and I, we're cousins either way."

"So you think we should talk to the police? I mean, would it do any good?"

"We've got two murders," I said. "Hurley's wife and Grannie. And . . . there's one other thing, too."

Cassie frowned. "What?"

"When they brought Moze in with his heart attack, the doctor noticed a bruise on his chest. It looked like the mark a fist would make."

She shook her head, pulled away from me, and sat down heavily on the love seat. "You're saying somebody punched him?"

"Evidently." I hesitated. "The police think he knows who did it, but he won't tell them."

"Why wouldn't he tell them?"

I shrugged.

She looked up at me for a minute. Then she said, "Oh, shit. I get it. They think it was me? They think I punched old Moze, and he's protecting me?"

I nodded. "There's something else."

"What?"

"Moze had a collection of framed photos lined up on top of his TV. Photos of you, fifteen or twenty of them, from when you were a baby. And—"

"Those photos are still there?"

I nodded.

Cassie smiled. "He's always been so . . . so reserved. Dour, almost. About his feelings, I mean. He expects you to know he loves you. He doesn't think you need to hear it."

"You might find that he's changed," I said.

She shrugged. "So what about the photos?"

"They were all smashed and broken."

"What do you mean?"

"It looked like somebody threw them against the wall."

"Threw them?"

I nodded. "As if in a rage."

"They think I did that?"

"They think whoever punched him did it."

"But why? I don't—" She stopped and narrowed her eyes. "It was Richard, wasn't it? Just like he killed Grannie. The bastard."

"Well," I said, "it makes sense, but we don't know any of this. I think we should go to the police and tell them everything. They'll sort it out. We can start in Moulton. I've been in contact with the officer there who's on Moze's case. Let's go talk to her."

"You mean right now?"

"Why wait?"

Cassie was shaking her head. "He killed Grannie and he hit Moze because of me. He knows that I know all about him. I'm so dumb."

"Forget it," I said. "We've got to go to the police."

"And I married him." She shook her head. "I knew it was stupid, and I did it anyway."

"Come on, Cassie. It's done. Forget it."

She stood up. "Okay. Let's get going. Let's do it."

She stood up and started for the door.

"Don't you want to brush your hair or touch up your lipstick or change your shoes or wash your face or put on some earrings or something?"

She turned and frowned at me. "Huh? Don't I look all right?"

I smiled. "You look terrific. I just thought . . . I mean, in my experience, no woman just stands up and goes anywhere. They always have to do something first."

"Well," she said, "not me. I'm ready. Let's go."

"Actually," I said, "I've got to use your bathroom."

She laughed. "It's right there." She pointed at a door next to the kitchen. "You've got to hold the handle down or it won't flush right."

I squeezed in. The doorway was so narrow that I had to turn my shoulders to get through it. Cassie's bathroom was about the size of the kind you find on an airplane except it had a coffin-sized shower stall.

As I was holding the handle down and the water was sloshing around noisily in the toilet, I thought I heard Cassie say something.

When I opened the door and stepped out, I said, "Were you talking to me? The toilet was—"

I stopped. The front door of the trailer was open and Cassie was standing in front of it. She was holding up her hands in a gesture of surrender.

As I watched, she took a step backward into the kitchen, and then a hand holding a gun appeared in the doorway. The gun was a stainless-steel snub-nosed revolver. A Smith & Wesson Chief's Special .38, if I wasn't mistaken.

TWENTY-THREE

The gun was followed by an arm, and the arm was followed by Rebecca Hurley.

Cassie backed up until she was stopped by the wall opposite the door. Her eyes were wide and confused.

Becca stepped into the tiny kitchen, reached back, and pulled the door shut behind her. The handgun held steady on Cassie's chest.

"Over there." Becca gestured with the revolver at the living-room area, then aimed it at Cassie again. She looked at me as if she wasn't the least bit surprised to find me standing in the bathroom doorway. "You, too. Both of you. Sit on that sofa. Keep your hands on your knees."

Cassie went over and sat down. I sat beside her.

Becca perched on the edge of the chair across from us. She held the stainless-steel revolver on her lap with both hands. It pointed unwaveringly at Cassie.

Cassie was staring at her. "Becca, what—?"

"Shut up," said Becca. She looked at me. "I should've killed you the first time." She smiled. "Oh, well. Here's a second chance." She flicked the gun at me for a moment, then returned it to

Cassie. The chair she was sitting in on the other side of the tiny living room was no more than six feet from us. From that distance, even an inexperienced marksman with a notoriously inaccurate short-barreled revolver would have trouble missing some vital part of a human torso.

"How did you find me?" said Cassie.

"I've got your boyfriend's cell phone," said Becca. "You've been trying to call him from that store. The number comes up when it rings. I called it, found out where it was. Then your cousin here, he was considerate enough to leave his car right out front for me." She looked at me. "Thank you. Saved me some time."

I shrugged.

"Why are you doing this?" said Cassie.

"You tell me. Why did you run away?"

Cassie shook her head and said nothing.

"You heard us that night, didn't you?" said Becca. "You figured it out."

"It was impossible not to hear you," said Cassie. "The two of you were yelling."

"Well," said Becca, "it doesn't matter. Sooner or later, I was going to have to kill you anyway."

"Because I know what Richard did to Ellen? That he watched her die and did nothing? That he murdered her?"

Becca smiled. "Is that what you think?"

"It's what I heard you two arguing about."

"You didn't hear so good, then, sweetie. Daddy never killed anybody."

"She had an asthma attack," said Cassie. "She fell off a stepladder. She couldn't breathe. Richard was there, and he refused to get her inhaler. He just stood there and watched her gasp for air and suffocate. That's what you two were yelling about."

266

Becca was smiling and shaking her head. "You've got it a little confused, dear stepmother."

"It was Becca," I said to Cassie. "Richard didn't refuse to get Ellen's inhaler and stand there and watch her die. She did." I looked at Becca. "Right?"

She shrugged. "It was long overdue."

"But why?" said Cassie.

Becca shrugged as if it were obvious. "She wasn't the one he loved." She smiled. "My daddy had a lover. The love of his life. Poor Ellen was up there on her stepladder washing the windows. Such a dedicated housewife. She tried so hard. I stood beside her, and I looked up at her on her stepladder, and I told her. I explained the truth to her. I said, 'Daddy doesn't love you, you know. All these years, he's only loved one woman. And it's not you.'"

Becca turned and smiled at me as if she and I shared a secret, and when she did, her Chief's Special turned in her lap and pointed at me.

She returned her gaze to Cassie. "When I told her who it was, the poor thing, her face got red and she started gasping and her hands went to her throat, and the next thing I knew, she just toppled backward right off her ladder. Stress would always bring on one of her attacks. That's why she kept those inhalers all over the house. It was kind of sickening, how hard she landed. I thought sure she'd broken her back or something." She shrugged. "She couldn't breathe. Turned blue. It didn't take her very long to die."

Beside me, Cassie was shaking her head. "I still don't get it. What did you have against Ellen?"

"She's saying she's Richard's lover," I said to Cassie.

"Who—?" Cassie's mouth opened and closed. She turned to me. "Her? Becca?"

"Yes." I looked at Becca. "And your baby?"

She smiled and nodded.

Cassie turned to me and frowned.

267

"She's saying that little Danny's father is also his grandfather," I said.

"Jesus," mumbled Cassie.

"What about Moses Crandall?" I said to Becca. "What was that all about?"

She shrugged. "I was trying to track down Miss Cassie here. Figured he might have a letter or a phone record or something. I was poking around in his house with my flashlight and he came out of his bedroom. He kind of squinted at me there in the darkness and said, 'Cassie? That you, honey?' Like that."

"So you hit him," I said.

"Made me mad," said Becca with a shrug, as if anybody would understand that. "He went down like a big tree falling. I thought he died right there."

"And you smashed all those photos," I said.

"Like I said. Made me mad. Miss Cassie here, she makes me mad. My daddy thinks he loves her."

Beside me, Cassie let out a groan. "I think I'm gonna be sick," she mumbled. "I gotta go to the bathroom." She started to push herself to her feet.

Becca waved her gun at Cassie. "Don't you move."

"Let her go into the bathroom," I said to Becca. "You want her to throw up right here?"

"I could just kill her now," she said. "Put her out of her misery."

Cassie leaned forward with her head between her knees. She was taking long deep ragged breaths. I slid off the sofa, squatted beside her, put my arm around her shoulders, and bent my head close to her ear. "Be ready," I whispered.

Cassie hesitated, then gave me a tiny nod.

I darted my eyes at Becca.

Under my hand I could feel Cassie's shoulder muscles tighten.

"Move away from her," said Becca.

"She's really feeling sick," I said. "I'm going to help her to the bathroom."

I started to stand up.

"Sit down," said Becca. "Just don't move, either of you, or I'll shoot you, I promise."

She had shifted the business end of her revolver so that it was pointing at me now. She had it braced on her lap with both hands wrapped around the butt. Her right thumb rested on the hammer. I couldn't be sure, but from my angle it looked like she hadn't cocked it.

If not, I had a second or two.

If it was already cocked, I had no time at all.

Rebecca Hurley knew how to shoot the gun, and she was willing to do it. I'd seen the evidence. She'd centered Grantham Webster's chest.

There was no reason to think she wasn't equally willing and able to shoot Cassie and me. We could wait around and talk about it for a while until she decided it was time. We could hope that maybe she wouldn't, that we could talk her out of it, that she'd see the error of her ways, that she'd listen to reason, that she'd come to her senses, repent of her sins, throw down her gun, surrender to the authorities.

Sure. Clichés happened.

Or maybe the cavalry would come galloping over the hill in the nick of time and rescue us. Or a god might descend in a machine to straighten out our sad little Greek tragedy. Maybe just as Becca was about to pull the trigger, lightning would strike the utility poles and the lights would go out. Or an earthquake would shake her arm and spoil her aim. Or the cat would leap at her and sink its claws into her face.

In the movies, maybe.

I was looking into Rebecca Hurley's eyes. Her commitment

was unwavering. She was calm. She'd killed people before, and it had worked out just fine. She could do it again.

She wanted to do it again.

She had her mind made up, and there would be no cavalry, no deus ex machina, no serendipitous intervention.

Cassie didn't even have a cat.

We could sit there and wait for Becca to decide it was time to shoot us.

Or we could try to do something.

All these thoughts whizzed through my brain as I crouched there beside Cassie, gauging distances and reaction times and my own quickness and agility and middle-aged reflexes and dubious courage.

Don't do something, my old man used to say. Just sit there.

Becca's gun was pointed at me. I watched her, and when her eyes slid over to Cassie, I figured that was as much of an edge as we'd have.

I yelled, "Now!" as loud as I could, shoved Cassie away from me as I sprang up from my crouch, and leaped wildly at Becca. I did all those things in one sudden movement, hoping it was startling and loud and scary and swift, but it played out in my head in slow stupid motion, like one of those dreams where your legs are pumping but you aren't going anywhere.

The gun exploded near my face. There was a great flash of white light and the booming echo of a bomb bursting inside that little aluminum trailer.

I crashed blindly against Becca Hurley, plowing into her and the chair she was in with my shoulder. She twisted away from me. She was quicker and stronger than I'd expected. I grappled for the arm that held the gun. We slammed onto the floor. She was scissoring her legs, twisting and writhing under me. . . .

Then the gun exploded again, and instantly my left hand—the hand that was clawing and grabbing at the wrist that held the

270

gun—went numb. I felt Becca squirming under me, and I sensed rather than saw her revolver turn slowly toward my chest, and I had no strength in my arm to stop it.

Then Becca said, "Oh . . ." It was a long, quiet, wet sound, more of an exhalation of breath than an articulated word, and I felt her go limp under me.

I rolled off her and lay there on my back, panting for breath. White lights were exploding behind my eyes. A loud whistle rang persistently in my ears.

I looked up. Cassie was standing over me. Her mouth was moving, but all I could hear was that high-pitched screeching in my ears.

I noticed she was gripping the barrel of her shotgun in both hands.

She knelt beside me. Her mouth moved again. This time her voice filtered through the ringing inside my head.

"Are you okay?" she said.

"Why wouldn't I be okay?"

She touched my arm, then showed me her finger. It was red and wet.

About then the burn began to register in my brain. It felt as if someone were aiming a blowtorch at my left biceps.

"How does it feel?" said Cassie.

"It hurts," I said. I pointed at my ear. "Sorry. I'm kind of deaf right now."

I used my good arm to push myself into a sitting position, and I hitched backward until I was leaning against the sofa.

Becca Hurley was sprawled on her belly. One arm was outstretched. The other was twisted awkwardly beneath her.

I looked at Cassie. "Did you shoot her?"

She shook her head and patted the butt of her shotgun. "Gave her a good whack on the head," she said.

The silver revolver lay on the floor beside Becca. I pointed at

271

it. "Kick that away from her," I said to Cassie. "Don't touch it with your hand."

She stood up and kicked the gun to the other side of the room. "Now what?" she said.

"Call the police."

"I don't have a phone."

"My cell's in my car," I said. I tried to stand up, but a wave of dizziness made me sit back down.

"I'll get it," said Cassie. "Here. You better take this." She handed the shotgun to me.

I held the shotgun in my functional right hand with the barrel resting on my knees, aimed more or less at Becca, who was groaning and twitching on the floor.

"You okay?" said Cassie.

"I'm good," I said.

Cassie went out. I sat there watching Rebecca Hurley. After a minute her eyes flickered and she lifted her head. She turned and looked at me. Then she kind of shrugged, and she laid her head back down and let her eyes close.

Cassie came back and handed me my cell phone. She was shaking her head. "There's twenty-two trailers here in this little village," she said. "Most of 'em, two or three people are living there. I know everybody. We say hello every day. I just walked to where your car was parked and back, and not one single person came out. No one saying, 'Is everything all right?' Or, 'Anybody get hurt?' Or, 'What was that explosion I heard?' I know they're here. Some people never leave this place. They just watch TV all day and wait for their welfare checks to come. Those gunshots must've sounded like hand grenades going off, but nobody had the curiosity, or the interest, or . . . or the kindness to even take a look." She smiled. "We could've gotten murdered, and Becca would've just strolled out of here and driven away and nobody would know the difference."

"It's the way of the world," I said.

TWENTY-FOUR

I called Roger Horowitz's cell phone. He'd know what to do. When he answered, I told him what had happened.

He listened without interrupting, and when I finished, he said, "It would've been a helluva lot more convenient if you could've arranged for all this to happen in Massachusetts, you know."

"Sorry," I said. "Inconsiderate of me."

"Yeah, apology accepted. Don't worry about it. Anybody need an ambulance or something?"

I looked over at Becca. She was now sitting with her back against the wall watching us. Her face registered bemusement and mild curiosity.

Cassie was sitting beside me on the sofa with the shotgun leveled at Becca.

"We're good," I said. "I just want to turn our prisoner over to somebody and get the hell out of here."

"Okay," he said. "Sit tight." And he hung up.

No good-bye. No thank-you. No "Good work, Coyne." No "How are you feeling?"

That was Horowitz.

I clicked off the phone and looked at Becca. "Tell me something," I said.

"Sure," she said.

"Why didn't you kill me when you had the chance?"

"In Webster's office, you mean?"

I nodded. "You put your gun against my head and cocked the hammer. But you didn't pull the trigger."

She smiled. "I remembered how you gave Danny a Cheerio. That was sweet. I didn't want to kill you."

"Sweet," I said. I shoved the cell phone into my pants pocket, and the movement sent a dart of hot pain up my arm and made me wince.

"Lemme have a look at that," said Cassie.

"It's okay," I said.

I watched her touch the area around my left biceps with her fingertips. It was pretty bloody. I couldn't feel her fingers.

"Looks like the bullet just scratched you," she said. "It's all red and black and blistery. Pretty nasty."

"Powder burn," I said. "Could've been worse."

"A lot worse," she said.

By the time the troops arrived at Cassie's trailer, she had cleaned my wound and doused it with antiseptic and wrapped a bandage around it. Becca was holding a bag of frozen peas from Cassie's freezer against the side of her head where Cassie had smashed her with the butt of the shotgun.

There were four or five Maine state troopers plus the county sheriff and a couple of his deputies, and I sensed that a little local turf war was building already.

They hadn't seen anything yet. Rebecca Hurley had committed two murders in Massachusetts, most recently Grantham

274

Webster. This was Horowitz's case and Becca was—or would soon become—his prisoner.

All they had here were a few firearms violations, maybe an assault with a deadly weapon, and a superficial gunshot wound.

They handcuffed Rebecca Hurley and whisked her away in a state-police squad car. They bagged her Chief's Special for evidence, and the sheriff and one of the police officers took statements from both me and Cassie and made sure they knew how to reach us. The whole thing took a couple of hours. I had the sense they were going through the motions. They'd figured out that Becca would quickly be extradited to Massachusetts. Horowitz had already made that clear.

After everybody left and Cassie and I were alone, I turned to her and said, "Now what?"

"I want to go see him. We've got a lot to talk about."

"Moze?"

She nodded.

"Now?"

She shook her head. "I need to do some thinking first. Work up some courage. Tomorrow, I think."

"What about your . . . Hurley."

"My husband?" she said. "I'll divorce him as soon as possible. His own daughter?" She shook her head. "I don't want to ever lay eyes on that . . . that monster again." She looked at me. "You're a lawyer . . ."

"It would be my pleasure," I said. "We'll get you a tidy settlement."

She shook her head. "I don't want anything from that man. I should never have married him in the first place. I did it for all the wrong reasons. I just want it over."

I shrugged. "We can do it any way you want."

"It's weird," she said, "you know? I kind of feel sorry for Becca."

"Speaking of monsters."

"I know," she said. "But how did she get that way?"

"How does anybody?"

She nodded. It was a rhetorical—and an unanswerable—question.

We sat there for a few minutes, saying nothing. Then Cassie turned to me. "Hey, Cousin. Will you do me a favor?"

"Sure," I said. "What?"

"Take me home?"

"Home?"

"I've only had one home in my life."

Uncle Moze's house, she meant.

"I'll be happy to," I said. "Your bedroom is waiting for you."

"Huh?"

I smiled. "You'll see."

She stood up. "It'll only take me a minute to get my stuff together," she said. "What I took from—from that man's house—it's in a trunk. I haven't even unpacked it."

The same trunk, I thought, that Howard Litchfield watched Cassie and Grantham Webster carry out of Hurley's house on Church Street in Madison that Saturday night just a few weeks ago.

While Cassie packed her trunk, I went outside and called Evie. She answered on the second ring.

"Honey," I said, "it's me. I'm up here in Maine, but I'll be heading home pretty soon."

"Is everything all right?"

"Everything's fine," I said. "I just got tied up with a few things."

"Tied up." She laughed. "Sounds like fun."

"It wasn't," I said. "I'll tell you all about it."

276

Fifteen minutes later I pulled into the sandy driveway in front of Uncle Moze's little house in Moulton. I turned off the ignition and opened the car door.

Beside me, Cassie remained sitting.

"Coming?" I said.

"Yup."

I glanced at her. Tears were streaming down her cheeks.

"Take your time," I said.

She turned and smiled at me. "No, I'm good."

We got out, slid her steamer trunk from the back of my car, lugged it to the front door, and put it down.

Cassie turned the knob, and the door pushed open.

"He never locks up," she said. "It's a stupid point of pride with the old coot."

"Let's get the trunk inside," I said.

"Just leave it here." She turned to me. "I want to do this by myself. Is that okay?"

"Sure."

"You can go," she said. "I know you want to get home. Go ahead. I'm fine."

"I'll be happy to stay with you for a while if you want."

She shook her head. "No. Thank you. I'd like to be alone."

"Want me to pick you up in the morning," I said, "take you to the hospital?"

She looked at me for a minute. Then she nodded. "I should be able to do it myself. To—to see him again. To get reacquainted. To apologize. But . . . yes. That would be nice. It would be really nice."

"I'll be here around ten, then?" I said.

She put her arms around me and hugged me close. "That's perfect. Thanks, Cuz. Thanks for everything."

By the time I left my car in the parking garage and started walking home, the streetlights on Charles Street had come on. I was thinking I should've called Evie again, given her a better idea of what time I'd be home.

She'd turned on the porch light for me. I went in and called hello, but Evie didn't answer, and Henry didn't come bounding at me with his tail wagging.

I walked through the house and looked out through the back-door window to the garden.

Evie was sitting in an Adirondack chair. She was wearing a flowery summer-weight dress with a scoop neck. High heels. Her hair done up in a complicated bun. A string of pearls—inherited from her mother—hung around her graceful neck.

I tried to remember. I was pretty sure this was not the outfit she'd worn to work, which meant she'd changed into it when she got home. Which raised the obvious question, since Evie loved to "get out of her school clothes," as she put it, first thing upon getting home from work. She loved sweatpants, T-shirts, cut-off jeans, no bras.

She'd hitched her dress halfway up her thighs, and her long bronze legs were stretched out in front of her. Her head was tilted back. I couldn't tell if her eyes were closed or she was staring up at the sky.

Then I noticed that our silver ice bucket was sitting on the picnic table. The neck of a bottle was sticking out of it, and two tall stemmed glasses sat beside it. Champagne, I assumed.

Huh? Champagne?

I stepped out on the porch. Henry, who'd been lying beside Evie, lifted his head, blinked at me, then pushed himself to his feet and came limping over.

I scootched down, gave his muzzle a scratch, then went over to Evie.

She looked up at me, smiled, and lifted her hand to my face.

I bent down and kissed her cheek.

She steered my mouth to hers, then hooked her arm around my neck to hold it there.

It was a long kiss.

When she finally let me up for air, I waved my hand around the garden and said, "What's the occasion?"

"Does there need to be an occasion?"

"Certainly not," I said. "But I've got the feeling that there is one."

She looked at me for a minute, then smiled and said, "I got it."

"Got what?"

"The promotion. The raise."

"Wait a minute—"

"Brady," she said, "sit down, okay?"

I sat down.

Evie reached over and grabbed my hand in both of hers. "I've been such a bitch lately."

"That's okay," I said. "You're entitled to be a bitch sometimes. I just wish I'd known what was going on, that's all. I could've been there for you better."

"I didn't want you to be there for me," she said. "I was—I was so afraid I wasn't going to get it. That's why I never told you. I didn't want your pity if I didn't get it. I don't know why I wanted the stupid job so bad, but I did. I kept getting mixed signals. I almost pulled out about a dozen times. Wanted to tell them, fuck it. Fuck you. I don't need this. Except I did. I felt like I needed it. It's a great job. A big step up. Huge raise. More responsibility. More fun, too." She paused. "I guess, mainly, I just wanted to know that they appreciated me."

"I could never pity you," I said.

She smiled. "I know."

I picked Cassie up at Moze's house at ten the next morning, and the nurse let us into the ICU around eleven.

Moze was lying on his side facing away from us.

I went over to his bed. Cassie stayed behind me. When I turned to look at her, I saw that her cheeks were wet.

I touched Moze's hip. "Hey, Uncle," I said. "Come on. Wake up. You got company."

He twitched and groaned, then slowly rolled onto his back. He blinked at me. "Sonnyboy," he said.

I turned around, reached for Cassie's hand, and tugged her beside me.

Moze stared at her.

"Hi, Moze," said Cassie.

"Cassandra," he said. "Jesus Christ."

"It's me," she said.

"You are a sight for old eyes," he said. He hitched himself into a sitting position. "I was thinking I'd never see you again."

"I'm here," she said. "I'm sorry."

Moze blinked. His eyes were glittering.

"I've been awfully mad at you," Cassie said.

I found a chair in the corner of the room and dragged it over beside the bed.

Cassie looked at me, smiled quickly, and sat in it. She reached for Moze's hand and held it in both of hers. "How are you feeling?"

"Cooped up," he said.

"I found out about Mary and Norman," said Cassie. "My real parents. You lied to me all that time. It was hard to understand."

280

"Me and Lillian was your real parents," he said. "We raised you."

"You know what I mean," she said.

"You're right," he said. "I should've told you. I meant to. I knew it was the right thing. You deserved to know. It just—I never found the right time to do it."

"Well," she said, "it's okay. I've got my head around it now."

Moze smiled. "Grudges are no good."

"You gonna forgive me?"

He nodded. "Sure. Forget about it." He cleared his throat. "It's awful good to see you, you know."

She squeezed his hand. "You, too."

He was quiet for a minute. Then he said, "Something I got to get off my chest, honey. Ever since I found out about my—that goddamn aneurysm—I been needing desperately to talk to you. I kept thinking, I can't die before I clear the air with Cassie."

"Well," she said, "now I know. You weren't my real father. You and Mum—you weren't my real parents. It's okay. You were the best parents in the world."

"That ain't all of it." Moze looked at me. "Come over here, sonnyboy. I want you to hear this, too."

I found another chair, pulled it over, and sat beside Cassie.

Moze was looking at me. "You remember Norman?"

I remembered a white, bloated body floating in the Piscataqua River. I remembered how the flesh had flaked away when my old man stuck a boat hook into his leg.

I nodded. "I'll never forget it."

He looked at Cassie, then back at me. "It was me and Jake," he said. "We—"

"Wait a minute," I said. "Don't say anything. I'm going to leave the room."

"No," he said. "I want you to hear it, too."

"Then you've got to hire me," I said.

"Huh? Hire you for what?"

"I'm a lawyer."

"Why the hell would I need a lawyer?"

"Moze," I said, "just ask me if I'll be your lawyer, okay?"

"It's bullshit, ain't it?"

"No. If you're going to say what I think you're going to say, and if you want me to hear it, it's best if you're my client."

He shrugged. "Okay. Will you be my lawyer?"

"Yes," I said. "Now, what were you going to say?"

He closed his eyes for a minute. Then he opened them, looked at Cassie, and smiled. "Okay," he said. "Here it is." He cleared his throat. "One night, it was back thirty-odd years ago, my baby sister Mary shows up at your grandmother's house all beat up and crying. She's pregnant out to here, and she's sayin' how her husband, Norman Dillman, punched her and busted her arm and kicked her out and called her a whore so all the neighbors could hear. So me and Jake, we went to Norman's trailer to have a little talk with the sonofabitch about the way a man is supposed to take care of his wife." He looked at Cassie. "I'm sorry. I know he was your father. But he was a sonofabitch."

Cassie nodded. Her eyes were wet.

"Talkin' to Norman didn't turn out to be all that satisfactory," said Moze, "so me and Jake, we drug him outside and took him around back, and we talked to him some more, and then Jake said the hell with it and plugged him in the head with his old army forty-five. Then I backed up my truck and we loaded Norman in back. He was a big bastard. We drove down to the river, piled some rocks in my dinghy along with Norman's body, and rowed out to my boat. We piled everything—Norman and them rocks—into the boat, started up the engine, and drove out to that deep hole near the bridge, where the currents swirl around?"

He made it a question for Cassie. She knew the river as well as he did.

She nodded.

"So then," he said, "me and Jake, we filled a lobster pot with them rocks, and Jake trussed Norman to the pot with the buoy line, and we dumped him in the river. I made Jake toss his pistol over, too. He didn't want to do it. He brought that thing home from Korea." Moze shook his head. "Jake always did tie poor knots. Otherwise Norman would've stayed down there, been lobster food, done somebody some good for a change. I shoulda tied them damn knots myself."

"You guys murdered Norman?" I said.

"Guess we did. Don't know what else you'd call it. I never regretted doin' it, I don't mind telling you. Not even for a minute. Oh, I worried about gettin' caught, and I worried about Mary and my mother learnin' about it. Worried plenty on them subjects. Otherwise . . ." He looked at Cassie and shrugged.

She was staring at him. I couldn't read her expression.

"Who else knows about this?" I said.

He shrugged. "Just me and Jake. I think Faith might've figured it out, the way she looked at me sometimes. She never said nothing, though, and maybe it was just my guilty conscience. I never regretted it, exactly, but it still weighed me down sometimes."

"What about your wives?" I said. "You and Jake. Did they know?"

He smiled. "Tell a woman something like that? You know better."

"What about neighbors, people who knew Norman, knew what he did to Mary, knew how you and Jake felt about it?"

"Folks had their suspicions, all right," he said. "But as far as I know, nobody liked that sonofabitch except Mary, and she stopped liking him about the time he started hitting her. I reckon just about everybody figured the world was a better place without

283

Norman Dillman in it." He looked at Cassie. "Sorry, honey. But that's how it was. I never felt bad, you thinking I was your daddy. Because I knew your real daddy got what was coming to him."

"I guess you did the right thing," she said.

He looked at her. "You mean that?"

She shrugged. "I guess."

"Moze," I said, "Jake was in here the other day. I ran into him when he was leaving. He seemed awful mad."

"Oh, he was." Moze smiled. "Me and Jake, we made a pact that night after we shoved Norman and his lobster pot over the transom of my boat. We promised each other we'd never say a word about it to anybody. Police or relatives or anybody. I never trusted Jake, though. He talks too goddamn much. Always shooting off his mouth. And I suppose Jake never trusted me. Hard to blame him. Brother or not, that's a damn big secret to be sharing. So after that night, me and Jake, we pretty much avoided each other. We lived in the same town, couldn't help running into each other now and then. But we pretty much decided we didn't like each other very much." Moze paused and looked from Cassie to me, then back at Cassie.

She nodded.

"Anyway," said Moze, "the other day when Jake come in here, I told him that if I caught up with Cassie, I was going to tell her about it, because sonofabitch or no sonofabitch, Norman was Cassie's real father. And I also told Jake that if it looked like I was gonna croak before I saw Cassie, I was gonna tell you, sonnyboy, give you the job of finding Cassie and telling her." He looked at Cassie. "That's why I been so damned desperate to see you, honey. That's why I asked Brady here to help me out. You had the right to know this, and I knew Jake'd never tell you."

Cassie bent over and kissed his leathery cheek. "I'm glad you told me," she whispered.

"So you gonna forgive me?"

"Anybody would've done the same thing," she said.

"That don't make it right."

"You made it right today," said Cassie. "Now your job is to get better."

EPILOGUE

U ncle Moze was sitting on the old lobster pot that Cassie and I had wrestled aboard *Miss Lil* for him. He was wearing his long-billed fisherman's cap, a blue denim shirt rolled up over his elbows, a pair of worn and faded blue jeans, and black hip boots folded down to his knees. A half-smoked unfiltered Camel stuck out of the corner of his mouth, and he was squinting into the midday September sunlight that blazed down from a cloudless sky and ricocheted off the riffled surface of the Piscataqua River. He kept one hand on top of his head so that the salty breeze from the moving boat wouldn't catch under the bill of his cap and lift it off. His alert pale eyes kept scanning the horizon. He was looking for a flock of diving gulls and wheeling terns that would signal feeding striped bass.

The boat rods were lined up in their holders, all rigged with trolling plugs and ready to be grabbed the instant we spotted fish. The stripers, Cassie said, had been swarming into the river on the incoming tide, hungry, aggressive gangs of them. The big predators, responding to the changing angle of the sun and falling water temperatures and other signals beyond our understanding, had started their southward migration from the Atlantic waters off the coasts of northern Maine and Nova Scotia. They chased the thick schools of peanut bunker that in places darkened the water. They corraled them against the bank and slashed and swirled at them, vicious and mindless and lethal.

Pretty soon they'd be gone. Then it would be winter.

I'd promised Evie that if we landed a keeper striped bass, we'd actually keep it, and I'd bake it with lemon slices and Ritz cracker crumbs and fresh-ground pepper the way Gram Crandall used to cook them. The fillets from a twenty-eight-inch striper would feed four people amply.

I generally put back the fish I caught, regardless of what the regulations allowed. I didn't disapprove of people who killed a fish or two for the table. It was a personal thing with me. I just liked the idea of giving big fish another chance to pass on whatever gene they had that enabled them to grow big.

But today was an exception, a special occasion. If the doctors were right, Uncle Moze's aneurysm would kill him before the fish returned to the Piscataqua River in the spring on their northerly migration. That was if his heart didn't get him first. Today might turn out to be his last voyage on *Miss Lil.*

Moze had left his aluminum walker back at the marina. A thick black cane rested against the side of his leg.

Evie was sitting on the lobster pot beside him. She was wearing cutoff jeans shorts and a skimpy white tank top. Today, she figured, would be her last chance of the year to catch some serious rays.

She was ragging on Moze about smoking. He was saying that he already knew what was going to kill him, and anyway, he'd be damned if he was going to give up the last pleasure he had left. Been doin' it since he was eleven, he was saying, and for emphasis, he worked a speck of tobacco onto the tip of his tongue, turned his head, and spat it out.

Moze liked looking at Evie. It was hard to blame him. She looked awfully good. She flirted with him and laughed at his

Down East colloquialisms and tried to imitate him, and that made him laugh.

It was pretty clear that there was at least one thing that still gave Uncle Moze pleasure besides unfiltered cigarettes.

His skin was white. It hung in wattles under his chin. Deep creases crisscrossed his face, and his forearms looked skinny and soft.

But enthusiasm and humor still glittered in those sharp blue eyes.

Cassie was at the wheel. She wore the same lobsterman's outfit as Moze, from the long-billed cap to the folded-down hip boots, and she hunched forward and squinted out through *Miss Lil's* salt-spattered windshield just the way I remembered Moze doing it back when I was a kid.

We'd hauled his string of pots. I'd used the boat hook to grab the line and loop it over the power winch and guide the heavy pots onto the platform on the gunwale. Cassie opened the trapdoor, plucked the lobsters from the pots, and measured them quickly with the steel ruler. She tossed the two-clawed keepers into one tub and the one-claws into the other. The shorts went overboard.

Evie had taken charge of rebaiting the pots. She seemed to get a kick out of handling the salted herring and jabbing them through their eye sockets onto the steel hook.

I learned new things about Evelyn Banyon every day.

I'd glanced at Moze a few times while the rest of us were tending his string of lobster pots. It was hard to miss the wistful smile that played on his lips. It was one thing to have your grown daughter living with you and cooking for you and helping you move from your chair to your walker to your bed. But having other people—even family—tend your lobster pots for you, well, that was damned near unacceptable.

Now Cassie was chugging slowly around the bay. Her curving route might have looked aimless, but Cassie knew the water and the tides and the way migrating striped bass behaved in the middle of September. She hadn't done it for many years, but some things you just don't forget.

I'd been sitting on the transom with the breeze in my face, looking for fish signs, watching Evie flirt with Moze, and thinking bittersweet thoughts about old age and mortality and the turning of the seasons.

I wasn't seeing any signs of fish. If there were signs to be seen, Moze would spot them before I did anyway.

I moved up front and stood beside Cassie.

She glanced sideways at me. "So how's it goin', Cuz?"

"I'm fine," I said. "How 'bout you?"

"Oh," she said, "it's good. Hard but good. I want to do more than I can, you know?"

"Moze seems pretty content."

She shrugged. "He's taking his days as they come, and he seems to be able to find something to enjoy in every one of them. He likes having me around, I know that."

"That must make you feel good."

"Oh, I've got my regrets."

I'd visited Uncle Moze a couple of times when he was in rehab, and Cassie and I had talked on the phone several times in the days after Rebecca Hurley came to kill us at the trailer in West Canterbury. But except for the Tuesday afternoon in mid-August when Cassie dropped in at my law office to sign her divorce papers, I hadn't seen either of them since they'd let Moze go home.

We watched the horizon for a few minutes. Then Cassie said, "Evie's a cool lady. You gonna keep her?"

"Gonna try."

"So what are you hearing about the case?"

"Rebecca Hurley, you mean?"

Cassie nodded. She kept her eyes on the water.

"I'm hearing nothing," I said. "Nobody'll say anything to me. I'll have to be a witness if it goes to trial. They don't talk to potential witnesses."

"Why wouldn't it go to trial? I mean, there's no question she killed Grannie, is there?"

"No question about that, as far as I know," I said. "But Becca is a seriously disturbed woman. If she's really been having an incestuous relationship with her father all these years—"

Cassie's head snapped around. "Whaddya mean, if?"

I shrugged. "It could all be in her head. A delusion."

"You think she just made all that up?"

"I don't know what to think," I said. "I doubt that she's lying, in the sense that it's her perception of the truth and she surely believes it. But that doesn't make it true. She was the one who found her mother's suicide. That kind of thing can have profound psychological effects on a person. Like post-traumatic stress disorder. Either way, Becca's a mess, and it wouldn't surprise me if they didn't find her fit to stand trial."

Cassie was shaking her head. "I've been thinking about Becca. I mean, I was friends with her. I liked her. She seemed . . . ordinary, you know? Normal. Normal and nice."

"Well," I said, "she was pretty intent on killing you."

"To get rid of her . . . her lover's wife? Or her imaginary lover's wife? Like she did to Ellen?"

I nodded. "So it seems."

"She hated me that much," said Cassie softly. "And dumb me, I didn't have a clue."

Cassie and I watched the water through *Miss Lil*'s windshield. There didn't seem to be anything else to say.

Suddenly she leaned forward. "O-*kay*," she said. "Here we go."

She pointed at the smooth water close to the shore.

I didn't see anything. "What is it?" I had the weird thought that she might've spotted a dead body.

"Nervous water," she said. "Look."

I squinted where Cassie was pointing, and after a minute I saw it—the subtle agitation of calm water made by a large school of fish traveling just under the surface. It's no more than a quiet shimmering. The water seems to be twitching and quivering. Nervous water is barely noticeable, but it signifies that under the seemingly calm, quiet surface something serious and important is happening. Unless you're trained to look for nervous water, and to recognize it, and to understand what it means, you'd never even notice it.

As I watched, a swarm of seabirds materialized over the ripply surface. At first, there were just a couple of terns, but in a minute there were dozens of birds, a mixture of gulls and terns, squawking and diving and wheeling low over the water. Underneath the birds I began to see the spurts and swirls and splashes of dozens of big fish crashing and slashing at frantic schools of baitfish.

Cassie goosed the throttle, and the clunky old boat cut a turn and surged forward. She looked back over her shoulder and grinned at Moze, and above the roar of the big diesel engine she yelled, "Hey, Daddy. What're you waitin' for? Grab yourself a rod and git a plug into the water. It's time to go fishin'."